FLY THE STORM

by

James Stevenson

Magna Large Print Books
Long Preston, North Yorkshire,
BD23 4ND, England.

British Library Cataloguing in Publication Data.

Stevenson, James
    Fly the storm.

    A catalogue record of this book is
    available from the British Library

    ISBN   978-0-7505-3611-0

First published in Great Britain in 2010 by Friars Goose Press

Cover illustration by arrangement with James Stevenson

Published in Large Print 2012 by arrangement with
Friars Goose Press

Magna Large Print is an imprint of Library Magna Books Ltd.

Printed and bound in Great Britain by
T.J. (International) Ltd., Cornwall, PL28 8RW

FLY THE STORM

Blanche Longhurst is a pilot with the Air Transport Auxiliary, delivering Spitfires from factories to air bases around the country during WW2. She believes herself to be safe from the direct conflict but during one routine trip, bad weather causes her to lose her bearings and projects her into activities that go against her sense of morality. She finds herself in another war, in another country where the anti-Nazi offensive is filled with subterfuge and personal betrayal. Eleven years later and now with a 10 year-old son, Blanche still suffers from memories of the war.

FLY THE STORM

PROLOGUE

Wiltshire, Friday 5th of June 1953

I'm rubbing cleanser into my cracked skin and Blanche Longhurst who lives on the other side of the mirror is raising her non-existent eyebrows at me. She looks a lot older than thirty-five with her frizzled hair brushed forward over the bald patch and face permanently scarred by fire. Her conscience has also been damaged because she is responsible for the deaths of a number of innocent men.

The bed is cold. I pull the sheets to my chin and close my eyes. Over the past eleven years I've learnt how to ward off some of my flashbacks by concentrating on happier things, so tonight I'll think about something that happened before the war. Peter is undoing his straps and climbing out of the Gypsy Moth. He says he doesn't want to fly with me any more because I'm too dangerous, funny man, what a way to tell a girl she's ready to fly solo for the first time. Alone at last I take off, climb away from the field and look down on the hangar. Is that Peter standing outside the clubroom? I won't look at him. I'll pre-

7

tend he's not there. Turn crosswind, keep the altimeter steady at one-thousand-feet on the downwind leg and close the throttle for the gliding turn. Have I misjudged it? I know what Peter is thinking – *overshoot, Blanche, don't risk it, go round again.* That's Peter all over – too cautious. But look at me now – *bounce, bounce, bounce.* I'm down safely. Three hops across the airfield – *thump, thump, thump...*

Thump, thump, thump – it's only a motorbike on the road outside.

I close my eyes again because I want to feel the hug that Peter gave me, and I want to hear him say that he always knew I could do it...

I'm drifting off when...

What's that?

A creaking floorboard. The door handle is turning. There's a man in my room.

I jump out of bed. He advances towards me. The wall is against my back, garlic in my face. I dodge past him and dash for the open door. His boots are behind me on the spiral staircase as I hurl myself down to the kitchen. I wrench open a drawer. It falls. I stoop, grope, my fingers close around a horn handle. The light clicks on. The man rushes at me through the dazzle. I don't want to fight but I raise the knife, drop it, stumble back, reach for the fuse box and... *Phut...* Darkness.

He bumps against me. I smell his sweat. His fingers tighten around my throat and I try to bend them back with both hands. Headlights sweep the room, a car door slams. I can't breathe.

Before the darkness comes I hear the crash of a falling chair.

I'm falling too...

PART ONE

CHAPTER ONE

The Arrival,
Monday 16th of March 1942

Long hair, smooth skin, lips a little too red – Blanche looked at her reflection in the train window and listened to the dull beat of steel wheels over the rail joints. Dear God keep him alive – she hardly dared think it, tempting fate – but she whispered the words aloud and hoped that somebody up there was listening.

An hour later she was still thinking about Peter as the train slowed with brakes squealing and drab buildings sliding past the window. A soldier picked up her parachute bag and Blanche held his rifle while he opened the carriage door for her. On the platform she dumped her bag outside the telephone kiosk, dropped two pennies in the slot, dialled the number from memory and pressed button A.

'Second Officer Longhurst here, is that the factory?'

'Hello Blanche. We're expecting you. Wally's on his way.'

In the ladies' convenience Blanche unzipped her parachute bag, pulled out a pair of flying overalls, wrapped her skirt around her legs, stepped in, zipped up, took off her shoes and put on her favourite flying boots. Sepia-tinted photographs in the waiting room reminded her of what life had been like before the war – children building sandcastles, a Punch and Judy show, a string of donkeys on the sand. She leaned back. People who called themselves statesmen were sitting at their Whitehall desks forcing sons and brothers and husbands and lovers to kill men and women in foreign countries – and it didn't seem right, even though it was done in the name of Freedom. The decision had been difficult but although Blanche Longhurst was a dedicated pacifist she was already part of a war that she totally despised. But she was in it up to her neck even though she was, unofficially, a conscientious objector.

A familiar sound coming through the open door of the waiting room made everything seem right again. She went out to the car park. The chief engineer was on his motorcycle, engine still running. She walked over to him and gave him a thumbs-up. 'How's life at the factory, Wally?'

He pushed up his goggles. 'Can't complain.'

Dropping her parachute bag into his sidecar she said, 'Why the long face?'

'You'd have a long face if you'd been here

14

yesterday. I'm lucky to be alive and no mistake.'

'Go on.'

'It gave me such a fright I nearly spilled my tea – low-level job in broad-bloody daylight.'

'And?'

'A Dornier 17E hit one of our balloon wires and lost a wing. Four of them inside, three fried beyond recognition and one with a bashed-in head, not a day over eighteen by the look of him. Other than that everything's apple pie and hunky-dory apart from my bike. Will some kind person inform me where I can find new exhaust valves?' He flipped out the footrests and Blanche swung her leg over.

Putting her arms around his waist she said, 'Valves or no valves, if you can get this heap up to fifty-five between the pub and the post office I'll give you a smacker right on the lips.'

'You're a teaser and no mistake, anyway the Speedo's kaput. Tell me where I can find an S6 cable and I'll marry you.'

When the guard saw them coming he raised the barrier and at the crew room Wally stopped for Blanche to hop off. 'Your aircraft is all ready for you, love, I'll see you later.'

She walked along the perimeter track with her dark curls under fierce attack from the wind. Camouflaged hangars looked like ancient burial mounds merging into the backdrop under a sky that sapped colour from the surrounding farmland. She glanced at the windsock, pushed in through the spring doors of the control tower and picked up the weather report. It wasn't brilliant but still flyable. Unzipping the chest pocket of her overalls she took out a dog-eared map and spread it on the sloping board to make her flight plan with the help of a protractor marked Air Ministry Property. After inserting a sheet of carbon paper she made her entry in the Operations Book. Date: 16 March 1942. Type of Aircraft: Spitfire Mark Five. Registration mark: W3297. Take off: 09.30 hours. Destination: RAF Exeter. Course: 240 degrees. Track: 232 degrees. Estimated Ground Speed: 222 mph. Estimated time of arrival: 10.24 hours.

Clumping up the metal steps she handed the torn-off sheet to the Despatch Officer. 'There you are John – Henley to Exeter in fifty-four minutes.'

He took the paper and peered at her over the top of his specs. 'Good grief woman. I know there's a bit of a flap on at the moment but have you see the weather report? Wind's all over the shop and so is your hair.'

'It's been in rollers – don't know why I bother.'

He hunched his shoulders and lowered an eyebrow onto the black patch that covered his left eye. 'Far be it from me to question your judgement, Blanche, but I'd hate to see my favourite ATA pilot break her pretty neck. We both know the rules – if a pilot isn't happy with the weather he doesn't fly, *she* in your case.'

Dear old John – shot down over France during the last lot so fly by the book and die of old age was his motto thee days. He persisted: 'Nobody will think any the worse of you if...'

Blanche cut his short. 'Pilot's decision is final, is that what you're trying to say?' She watched him turn away, suddenly conscious that she might have overdone the beetroot juice on her lips. Surely he knew how many times she'd done the Henley to Exeter trip? Dead easy, with a railway line by courtesy of the Great Western Railway along the entire route. In no time she'd be standing on the edge of the Exeter tarmac, waiting for her Squadron Leader to come in over the boundary fence after one of his routine 'stooges around' over the Channel.

'Don't you remember what you said to me last Thursday, John?'

The eyebrow went up again.

'You said the only way to stop the RAF making rude jokes about the Air Transport Auxiliary was to keep on supplying their replacements in ever increasing numbers, day in, day out – and at night if need be. If pilots sit on their bottoms, you said, and read magazines every time a cloud appears on the horizon, aircraft pile up in the factories, Adolf wins the war and sits in the Royal box at Ascot. Exeter, here I come – and this time I'm spending the night down there.'

She pushed out into blustery air, walked across the field to the dispersal and saw Spitfire W3297 looking sleek and ready to fly in its livery of brown-and-green paint. Blanche touched a wing and spoke to it aloud: 'Soon be there. Exeter tarmac is one heck of a lot easier to land on than this soggy grass.'

'And let's hope she has plenty of them – safe landings.'

Blanche turned. 'Hello again Wally – come to kiss your new baby goodbye? What do you reckon? Are those clouds going to keep off my back all the way to Exeter? Met guarantees a cloud base of 4000 feet minimum across all counties west of here – and they reckon the wind won't pick up for at least another hour.'

'Here's your parachute love. Let's hope you never have to use it.'

She wasn't expecting Wally to comment on the weather because it wasn't his job to know about winds and clouds and drift but, while doing up her parachute, Blanche couldn't help noticing that the top blade of the propeller looked like a warning finger pointing at the sky. The mechanic cupped his hands for the leg-up and Blanche climbed in.

Once settled he leaned over to place harness straps over her shoulders and she slotted the metal ends into the buckle, tightening them over fireproof overalls that hid the dress that Peter had brought back from France when his squadron was recalled two years ago – it was meant for Peter's sister but she was killed by falling masonry before she'd had a chance to open the parcel.

Today the Spitfire cockpit seemed smaller than usual, narrower too and smelling of what they all smelled of – lubricating oil, petrol and new-paint. After adjusting the throttle for starting she watched six barrage balloons, wires aslant in the wind, winching down to give an unobstructed path for take off. She began the drill, saying it out loud like she always did. 'Fuel cocks on…'

Wally produced cotton waste from the pocket of his overalls, wiped the already spotless windscreen and leaned in with some crack about pre-war perfume smelling a heck of a lot better than high-octane fuel.

'Propeller pitch fine. Radiator shutters open…'

The mechanic jumped down, pulled up the accumulator trolley, plugged in the wire and gave the traditional gesture with an oilstained thumb. Blanche shouted, 'Switches on,' and pressed the starter. The engine coughed, the propeller made two jerky turns and brand-new Spitfire W3297 burst into life like a breaking storm. How often had Wally said it? Every time I hear a new Merlin engine starting up I imagine half-a-million molecules of high-grade steel farting out with the exhaust. She knew what he was thinking too: *keep your eye on that needle and let her tick over until you've got forty-five pounds of oil pressure.* Happy man he may be, Blanche thought, but wetter than a mother duck with his cotton-wool Rolls-Royce engines.

She applied brake to the starboard wheel and swung the Spitfire to face the wind. She was thinking about Peter again, barely fifty minutes away and she raised her lucky ring for a quick kiss before running through the final checks on engine temperature and oil pressure. But watching the dials somehow triggered thoughts of death and the fact that she may never see ... *no, not that.* Half of Europe may be under the jackboot and looking to the English-speaking world to sort things out but dear God how will it end? Will it *ever* end? And let's hope I don't have to kill anyone in the name of Freedom, Patriotism, Defence or any other so-called worthy cause.

She slid the throttle forward until it touched the safety gate and the power of a thousand impatient horses shook the aircraft like windows in a gale. 'Brakes off.' Accelerating across the grass she asked herself how Peter could go on throwing dice week after week and score sixes every time. Luck, that's what mattered these days, that's what kept Squadron Leader Mason alive. And now *she* was on her way, doing *her* bit for the umpteenth time with spray spiralling out of the turf behind her. She eased the stick forward to raise the tail and lifted into the air between the balloon cables, skidding in the crosswind. 'Wheels up. Boost plus nine.' The powerful music dropped a quarter-octave as the aircraft settled into the climb. She took her left hand off the throttle and slid the cockpit cover forward to shut out the clamour and – from somewhere – Peter's hand was covering hers, arms around her shoulders, stubble on her cheek. She continued to think about him while the Spitfire made the climb – and what she had said to him when she first took this job. A to B, that's what they told us, dead easy, climb aboard, strap in, start up, fly unarmed aeroplanes from places marked A to other places marked B all over the British Isles, piece of cake, nothing to it, doing one's bit for the war – and safe, that's what they told us when we first joined – but terribly sorry girls, we don't give you radios because we don't want you cluttering the airwaves with chit chat about knitting and sewing. Oh and by the way, if you lose sight of the ground consider yourself lost.

She turned the aircraft onto the bearing for Exeter and saw the reliable brickwork of Reading sprawling under her left wing, but above her head the cloud base appeared to have lowered considerably. 'Bloody Met will they never get it right?'

At two thousand feet the Spitfire was pushing against a ceiling that appeared solid and drooping and sagging on three sides to obliterate the horizon, hiding barrage balloons lying in wait for the unwary. While changing course in an attempt to escape the trap she had visions of old John sitting in his control tower, sadly shaking his head.

Suddenly there was no way back – no alternative but to press on. Forget the flight plan but keep within sight of the ground at all costs, head west and get down safely at Exeter. She saw a crossroads and a curved lake, a large house next to a ruined barn and a ploughed-up tennis court growing vegetables – unfamiliar landmarks in a valley she'd never seen before while clouds pressed down on her, forcing her to fly lower and lower. Mist-shrouded trees raced under her wings. Wisps of condensation spiralled back from the propeller. Fear-induced pins and needles tingled the backs of her hands. How far away is the steep edge of Salisbury Plain?

She knew the rules backwards. *Air Transport Auxiliary pilots are prohibited from flying in bad weather. No flight shall be commenced unless the cloud base is at least 800 feet and horizontal visibility 2000 yards. No flight shall be continued in conditions less favourable than the aforesaid. Flying in or above cloud, mist, fog or out of sight of ground is forbidden.* At the start of this flight all those conditions had been met – but now…? As if trying to prove the rules a tall chimney appeared out of the swirl and whizzed past her port wing. 'Wadworth's Brewery – how many times have I used that landmark?' Upturned faces in Devizes market place and glimpse of the Bear Hotel's windows made her wonder, for a stupid moment, how long it would take for the creases to fall out of her dress once safely down at Exeter.

'That's enough. Break the rules. Go over the top.' She opened the throttle far too quickly and a faltering cough from the engine produced shirt-wetting sweat in her armpits.

But the Spitfire recovered quickly and clawed upwards into the soup, flying blindly, shaken by unseen forces with Peter's voice telling her, in a put-on voice, to use the instruments rather than trust sensations emanating from the seat of her knickers. Artificial horizon, turn-and-bank indicator, altimeter, rate-of-climb – the blind flying instruments were all there in front of her and she knew how to use them in spite of the fact that *bad weather flying for ferry pilots is strictly prohibited.*

In steadier air the aircraft rose like a lift in an all-embracing cocoon of cloud. She spoke to herself against the din with a voice that made soundless vibrations inside her head. 'Make a climbing turn onto the Exeter heading, get above cloud and everything will turn out fine.' She watched the clockwise rotation of a luminous needle marking her upward progress: 7,000 feet – 8,000 – 9,000 – 10,000... After a long twenty minutes she was thankful to see the cloud's gloom turn to a yellowy-grey, a lighter grey, five seconds of increasingly brilliant white followed by dazzling sunlight as he burst out of the cloud top at a height of eighteen thousand in a glare strong enough to hurt her eyes. *Flying above an altitude of ten thousand feet without oxygen equipment is strictly prohibited.* Somebody had said it was like driving a car after a night on the beer, but having never driven a car Blanche hadn't the faintest idea if that were true.

Now she was in a white and blue world of gravity-defying mountains, shadowy valleys and hills that rose from a never-ending, froth-covered plain that rolled away as far as her screwed-up eyes could see – and she was unaware that a lack of oxygen was affecting her brain. Those roads, railways, buildings, rivers, towns – all so clearly marked on the clipboard strapped to her knee – where the hell were they now? ATA also meant *Anywhere to Anywhere* but where was she? In a snowy landscape that stretched unbroken in every direction – might as well throw away the map.

Maximum endurance, that's what was needed now but the drill wasn't coming easily. Beginning to swear at herself, Blanche unbuttoned the breast pocket of her flying overalls and pulled out her Pilot's Notes. She managed to find the right page but sunlight shining through the Perspex canopy was making the print illegible and she couldn't remember if the information was there at all. Then slowly it came to her – *mixture weak – boost two pounds – propeller speed 1800 rpm.* What would Peter advise now? *Stick to the Exeter heading, Blanche, find the gap and stay calm.*

What difference can a lucky ring make? It would look better alongside a band of gold. Marriage? Not just yet. Sex, yes – sex mattered but she never thought she'd hear herself say it. Is this really me – this strange woman with insatiable hunger in her guts? She closed the fingers of her right hand around the safety ring on the spade handle in front of her, turned it to fire and depressed the button. Silence, because there were no machine-guns or cannons to bang and clatter above the roar of the engine. *Don't you know there's a war on? If you girls have any desire to stay alive then keep yourselves out of harm's way. It's a tough world these days. Air Transport Auxiliary pilots will fly unarmed at all times.* It was a big surprise to meet Peter again on that famous day when Blanche delivered her first

Spitfire to Exeter – seeing him in RAF uniform for the first time instead of the tweed jacket he always wore while teaching his students to fly at Cramlington. She drank beer with him in the Duke of Cumberland and heard what it was like to use the Spitfire for its intended purpose. It wasn't pleasant but nonetheless exciting to hear him describe what it felt like to kill a complete stranger in a dogfight. All RAF aircrew were talking about the Focke-Wulf 190 these days and Peter was no exception. Unlike some, however, he seemed totally disdainful of Germany's latest fighter aircraft and even refused to refer to it by its nickname of Butcher Bird because he was the one who was quite good at butchering them, sometimes during bad weather after ordering the rest of his squadron to stay on the ground.

It was lovely up there, like summer with a puff or two of drifting cloud – but deceptive because this high-altitude world was a deadly place for pilots who had no oxygen and no communication with the ground. 'Landmarks – please God show me a railway line, perhaps the Trowbridge to Frome loop, maybe the Great Western snaking across the Vale of Pewsey or the long straight that passes below the big White Horse carved into chalky hills near Westbury – or even Connie's cottage with its oblong garden and the big tree where the swing used to hang. Show me a coastline that I can recognise like Chesil Beach or the Isle of Wight.'

But after seventy-three minutes of flight she could see no gap, no safe way down, and there was no way of telling if these clouds, though white at the top, might be black and stormy at the bottom hiding hills and balloon cables and trees and buildings and... But Blanche had always been lucky. In a crazy moment she remembered an afternoon before the war when she won fifty-three shillings on a horse called Hopeful Friar at Redcar races and then flirted with the jockey while sharing his champagne. Continuing to search for that elusive hole in the cloud she remembered her first uniform, made by a gentlemen's bespoke tailor who was too shy to snug his tape into the warm divide of a female crotch. Oh those sad trousers! And then she had a more sinister thought, something she'd been trying to ignore ever since breaking through the top of these clouds. Amy Johnson, daughter of a Hull fish merchant and world-famous aviatrix, had joined the ATA a few weeks after Blanche with 2,300 hours already flown and a commercial 'B' licence held since 1930. May 24th 1931 – everyone who had the flying bug knew that date by heart, even though it was eleven years ago. On that day Amy landed her tiny biplane in Australia after taking off from Croydon nineteen days before. She had hopped her way across the world to Darwin enduring sandstorms, electric storms, two crash landings and endless hours of trying to stay awake.

The first icy fingers of panic touched Blanche as she pictured her fiancé vainly waiting for her at RAF Exeter. Taking her hand off the throttle she again pressed the *DEAR* ring to her lips, kissing each stone in turn – the Diamond, the Emerald, the Amethyst and the Ruby – but far below the white carpet stretched unbroken and the sickening realisation that she must have flown at least 350 miles since leaving Henley weighed like lead in her stomach. She could be well past the toe of Cornwall by now and heading out over the Atlantic. Turn into the reciprocal heading. Keep searching.

What's this? As Blanche banked into the turn, she noticed how the sun appeared to move in an unexpected direction relative to the aircraft. Crosswind – it had to be – coming from the north. Must be blowing like hell up here four miles above the earth. Then suddenly there it was – the life-saving gap, acres of it, clearly visible far away to the south on the edge of a stationary whirlpool of frothy cloud.

She turned towards it, closed the throttle and let down towards the dazzling cloud floor. Down and down she sank towards it. She could almost feel the movement inside her wristwatch counting away the final minutes of powered flight. The altimeter unwound slowly. Damned turbulence again. Aircraft bobbing around like a cork at sea. Sea? Oh God, give me a few feet of clear air above the waves, that's all I need. A light on the dashboard flashed and flashed again. I'll never make it – and then, inevitably, she heard the dreaded series of irregular bangs, the dying cough followed by the faint *whick-whick-whick* of a windmilling propeller.

'Flaps DOWN'. But it was no use, she was falling short of the gap, sinking into intensifying darkness and it seemed as if the ghost of Amy Johnson was with her in the cockpit. Ghost, yes, because fourteen months ago Amy had drowned in the Thames Estuary after what should have been an incident-free flight from Blackpool to Kidlington. Pride had induced Amy to attempt that flight in bad weather but she had been forced to climb above cloud to get lost and overshoot her destination by more than a hundred miles. Amy ran out of fuel, crashed in the sea and drowned – as did the naval officer who dived off his ship in a vain attempt to save her life. The comparisons were chilling. Blanche was an experienced pilot and so was Amy. Both pilots had survived forced landings, both had taken off in marginal conditions to become trapped above cloud. If a long-distance specialist like Amy could get lost and crash and die, so could Blanche Longhurst. Same old problem – no radio. The trap was closing.

In cloud Blanche felt little sensation of movement but knew that the aircraft was arcing down towards the ground like a spent arrow. The darkness intensified and so did the inevitable question – land or jump? She could see the Birdman – feel his final hand-shake at the 1937 Cramlington Air Pageant and smell the whisky on his breath. She remembered watching the Birdman falling onto a screaming crowd with a half-open parachute streaming behind him like an empty shroud.

Don't jump, Blanche told herself. Stick with the aircraft. Make a gliding descent on a southerly heading. Get under cloud and, if over the sea, turn for the coast and find a field. The fear was real – lost at sea, or dashed to pieces on the side of a hill, maybe buried at the bottom of a crater dug in an English field by four tons of hurtling aluminium.

The Spitfire continued to glide blindly down with needles circling – 5,000 feet – 4,000 – 3,000 – 2,000. Blanche peered forward and pulled down her goggles to protect her eyes in the crash. Where is the sea? Or will it be a hill, a cliff, a house, a balloon-cable, a tree? At 200 feet a curving line quickly resolved into an unmade road that flashed under her speeding wing – a barn – a hedge – and a grassy field smooth enough for... 'Wheels DOWN. Hell, no hydraulic pressure. Harness TIGHT. Airspeed NINETY. Hold off. Stick BACK. Nose up to kill the speed – belly-landing...'

The tail-wheel exploded on impact. Harness straps cut into her shoulders and in a confused state of terror and relief she heard metal crumpling like tissue paper during a seemingly endless slide.

Silence.

Stunned and shaken, Blanche sat back, leaned against the bulletproof shield behind her head and let go a gigantic sigh of relief. This was her second crash and she had survived it, this time on smooth grass not a turnip field. She flicked off both magneto switches and slid back the hood.

Before leaving the cockpit she forced herself to breathe deeply, willing her body to relax but when she closed her eyes she could see the Exeter Duty Officer with his ear clamped to the telephone.

She undid her harness, struggled to open the entry flap and stepped down onto firm turf – and knew at once that if she'd managed to get the wheels down she would probably have got away with it.

Clean air swayed the tops of tall trees at the far edge of the field but her knees were buckling as she walked to the front of the aircraft.

Variable-pitch propellers were rumoured to be worth half-a-year's salary and this one had been reduced to a stump – and the engine? Wally's voice was almost real inside her head. *Crankshaft's buggered more than likely.*

How do I do it, what do I say to whoever answers the Exeter telephone – *Mark Five Spitfire W3297 is badly bent and lying in a field somewhere in the south of England* – will that do? And the Station Commander – she could hear him now – *Wait until I get my hands on the cretin who entrusted my valuable replacement to a woman.*

She sat on damp grass, leaned back against what was left of the Spitfire and wished she were somewhere else. She knew the drill because every good Air Transport Auxiliary pilot knew the Accident Procedure by heart – *Note the time – pinpoint the position on your map – get a responsible person to guard the aircraft and ask him to make a list of eyewitnesses – telephone the destination aerodrome...*

A cluster of farm buildings on the far side of a sloping pasture looked reassuring and a light breeze was cooling the sweat and helping her to become calmer, more relaxed and rational. She spotted a ploughman standing by his horse and looking in her direction from a sloping field half hidden in the mist. Across another field, a massive barn dwarfed the white cottage beside it – maybe they had a telephone but Blanche was in no hurry to confess her sins after the fuss they kicked up last year when she accidentally put a wheel into the sergeants' vegetable patch at RAF Digby while taxiing on the perimeter track.

Massaging a bruised wrist she looked at her Rolex – it was still working. She'd been airborne for almost two hours so the Spitfire must have travelled at least four hundred miles since taking off from Henley. Dear old John, if only she'd listened to his warning – *if only* – how many pilots had uttered that despairing phrase after a crash? She closed her eyes again and cursed herself for not staying on the ground at Henley to read old copies of *Picture Post* for as long as it took – and spending the night there if necessary.

Distant shouts…

Blanche opened her eyes. Two men were running across the field towards her. Why so frantic? Why are they waving their arms like that, can't they see…?

'*Hé vous!*'

She jumped to her feet.

'*Attendez-vous là!*'

What the–?

'*Hé! Hé vous!*'

CHAPTER TWO

The Test

Blanche ran, tripped, fell, got up, glanced back, put her head down and sprinted for the trees while the men kept yelling at her in French. 'Stop, don't run, stop, stop, we want to speak to you.'

She reached the edge of the field and hurled herself into thick undergrowth, sucking in pine needles with every breath as she wormed her way under the tangle. Lying still, heart pumping, not daring to raise her head, she heard twigs snapping as somebody came so close that she could almost smell the hard-worked leather of his boots. She waited for several seconds then raised her chin by a fraction. Through a screen of leaves she could see a man leaning against a tree. She could hear his panting breath and saw his lips move when he broke the silence.

'*Où êtes-vous?*' The question came softly as if he already knew where she was.

Blanche remained motionless except for her eyes that continued to watch him, rat-like, small, unshaven. After a pause the man spoke again, telling her to show herself, each

French word spoken with menacing soft-ness. He fumbled for a cigarette and lit it. He finished his cigarette and lit another.

My only option now is to … she stood up with the thought unfinished. He whirled to face her, snatched a pistol from his belt and stared, eyes wide with surprise. The cigar-ette fell from his mouth.

Blanche faced him squarely. Wiping a damp leaf from her chin she said, 'I have come from England. I am a friend of France.'

He came closer, jabbing the pistol into her chest, shrugging his shoulders and shaking his head, evidently unable to understand what she had said. Stepping back, Blanche vainly tried to brush the gun aside then, drawing on a fluency known since child-hood, spoke to him in his own language. 'I was trying to deliver a Spitfire to an airfield in England – and will you kindly stop point-ing your gun at me.'

He lowered the pistol. 'Women do not fly Spitfires.'

'In England they do.'

He looked her up and down. The curve of his lip made it clear that he didn't believe what she was saying. Waving his gun in the direction of the buildings he said, 'Follow me.'

Blanche wanted to run, hide, escape, find a friend – but the dice had rolled and she knew she would have to do exactly what he said or else risk violent death. They skirted the edge of the wood. While crossing another field she saw the barn that had appeared so suddenly under the wing of the gliding Spitfire.

They entered a cottage with the pistol jabbing painfully between her shoulder blades. A cluttered table occupied the centre of the main room. The smell of cooking under the low ceiling and the cry of a hungry baby, coming from another room, reminded Blanche that a slice of bread and a cup of tea was all she had been able to grab before catching the early train to Henley.

A woman descended the stairs, snatched a hand to her mouth and with wide eyes took in Blanche's bulky overalls and flying boots. 'Who is this girl, Gilbert, where has she come from?'

The man poked the pistol back into his belt. 'Claims she's English.'

The woman said, 'I heard an aeroplane come down – surely she didn't...'

'It crashed in the bottom meadow.'

'Then you'll have to go and deal with it, Gilbert. I'll look after the girl.' She tugged at Blanche's sleeve with one hand and pointed to the stairs with the other. On a narrow landing on the first floor she pushed Blanche into a small room and stepped back. The dry-hinged door swung shut, a key turned, and she heard the woman's feet clumping noisily down the stairs.

Blanche pushed fingers through her hair and looked around. A small table and two chairs stood randomly in the centre of the room under an unlined roof that showed chinks of daylight between the tiles. A portable lavatory and a made-up bed reminded Blanche of her desperate need of both. After testing the lavatory she crossed the room and knelt by a low window under the eaves. The Spitfire was squatting on the grass like a legless bird, men had gathered around it waving their arms and shouting at each other. Kneeling there by the window Blanche thought of England – her man, his laugh – but would he be laughing now? By now Peter would know that the replacement Spitfire had gone missing and she could imagine him hoping, and going on hoping and then go cold and silent like he always did when one of his men failed to return from a mission. The only way to stay sane was to keep laughing, Peter used to say that, but days would turn to weeks and the Air Accident people would come to the conclusion that Second Officer Blanche Longhurst had ditched in the sea because no wreckage was found. *Pilot presumed dead* – that's what they'd think – another dead colleague for Peter to mourn while other ATA pilots delivered more aeroplanes so that endless streams of wide-eyed boys fresh from basic training in well-pressed uniforms would be able to crash them and burn them like Barry Young and David Gibson did. Oh yes, Blanche Longhurst would become yet another pilot who failed to make a happy landing.

She watched a pair of horses cropping the grass while frantic Frenchmen threw ropes over the Spitfire. Soon the horses were harnessed and the wheel-less aircraft was inching its way across the field, but they would have to cut off the wings if they intended to hide it in the barn.

Blanche turned away from the windows, unzipped the front of her overalls and it was only after she had thrown herself onto the bed that she realised how tired she was. Tired but anxious – I'll get out of here once I've convinced them who I am and where I've come from. It isn't only Peter who'll worry about me, what about Father? She could picture him standing on the doorstep of the big house in Northumberland, opening the telegram. He'd keep the news to himself because he lived by himself and there was no one else to tell – apart from Sampson, but Dad would get little comfort from telling a dog that his daughter had been reported as missing. What about Connie – old school friend – who would tell her? Connie would take it on the chin because she was that kind of person. She'd go on filling shells in the munitions factory as if nothing had happened and hide her feelings like she used to whenever those terrible nuns punished her in the convent school.

But it was Peter who kept invading Blanche's thoughts. She remembered her first flight to Exeter, drinking beer with him in the Duke of Cumberland, knowing that he would always mean more to her than pre-war flying lessons or drinks around the piano. Meeting him again had brought a new awareness of the danger he was in – life and death – living for the moment and wondering if each meeting might be their last. She willed him to stay alive for one more day, then another precious day, and another after that, and another day until at last the day they had both been waiting for would come. But the idea of getting married on Peter's birthday no longer made any sense because he might be killed long before July the first. She could see his two-fingered salute to Hitler, hear his voice and the laugh that wobbled her knees and had long ago dissolved her girlhood ambition never to sleep with a man until she was married to him.

In the upstairs room of the French farm-house Blanche fell asleep at last. In a confused dream she saw herself as a child playing with her French aunt on a beach near Lille. Peter was there too but in the dream he was her overbearing father telling her to swim towards a distant horizon where a yellow sun raised steam from a freezing sea at the end of a catastrophic day.

The sound of squealing hinges woke her. Although it was dark she could see the woman crossing the room to place a lamp on the table and make a rapid sign of the cross. Blanche got off the bed but the woman retreated into the darkness and clumped down the stairs. There was somebody else in the room. A floorboard squeaked behind the glare of the lamp and the outline of a man was moving in the shadows. A chair creaked, clasped hands rested on the table and a bald scalp leaned forward into the light, scarred with a deep furrow that ran the length of the man's head from front to back.

He spoke softly in French. 'Please sit down.'

Blanche scraped the other chair to the table.

'What is your name?'

'Blanche Longhurst.' She could hear rustling of paper and the scratch of a nib as he wrote.

'Why have you come here?' Unprepared for the question she hesitated, staring at the scar and unsure of what to say. One hell of a wind, that's what it must have been – she knew it now – a high-level wind from the north that must have drifted her southward. But would he understand?

The top of his head was almost motionless

in the glare. 'Answer me, why did you land here?'

'I took off from the Vickers factory in bad weather.' She watched the flame through smoke-blackened glass, knowing she would have to tell the truth. 'I was on a delivery flight to RAF Exeter – didn't realise how bad conditions were until it was too late. Low cloud was the problem. I had to climb through it. I was lost. I had no radio, couldn't see the ground. I was trapped and spent two hours trying to find a hole through which I could safely descend and here I am, in France.'

'It's a most unusual story. If you were trapped above cloud why didn't you parachute from the aircraft while you were still over England?'

Blanche kept her eyes on the lamp. 'I didn't jump because I'm...'

The man sighed audibly. 'Go on – afraid – is that what you were going to say?'

She nodded.

'An experienced pilot afraid to jump, do you really expect me to believe that?' He paused and in the silence Blanche could hear her heart thumping. 'If you tell lies you will die and I can guarantee that your body will never be found.' A gust of wind rattled the window and a sudden draught wobbled the flame. 'The farmer says you are British, shall we see if that is true?' He continued in

41

heavily accented English: 'How long have you been a pilot?'

The smell of lamp oil was strong in the room, 'Since 1935.'

He stroked his chin. 'The world was a happier place seven years ago but unfortunately the long awaited storm has broken and soldiers are at war. And let's not forget the humble spy who works alone and is hated by everyone. I am a spy so I know what I'm talking about – and I suspect that you are also a spy. We spies – you and I – we wear no uniform.'

Blanche snatched a protective hand to the open neck of her flying suit. 'I'm not a spy and I *do* have a uniform but I wear this dress under my overalls whenever I fly to Exeter, my fiancé bought it in Paris.'

'A foreign woman fluent in French wears a dress made in Paris and crashes into our midst and says she's been brought here by the weather.' He leaned back out of the light. 'I never imagined that I would be obliged to…' He cleared his throat. 'The problem is that we find ourselves living in a violent world and the age of chivalry is long past. Severn years ago I would never in my wildest dreams have considered killing a beautiful young woman with black hair.' He wiped his forehead with the back of his hand. 'The problem is that I already know how you people operate and the lengths you go to. An enemy spy lands a captured Spitfire in a farmer's field and then waits to see who comes to her aid. Very clever, most ingenious, but we have to be absolutely certain who you are – and if we are not certain then I'm afraid we are left with no alternative.' He shrugged his shoulders, opened his hands and flexed his fingers.

'I'm English. I'm able to speak French because I have a French aunt. I spent summer holidays with her in Lille when I was a child. I've been fluent since…'

'Name the principal church in Lille.'

'Notre Dame de la Treille.'

'What are you doing here in France?'

'I've told you. I landed here by mistake.'

'Tell me where it is possible to see fine paintings by Dutch and Flemish artists – or should I say where *was* it possible to see such things in Lille before the German looters and rapists came to occupy the town.'

Blanche focused on his half-lit face, fat jowls, unshaven chin and sharp eyes under heavy eyebrows. She wished she were in Lille now, walking free in cool spaces under the great vaulted ceilings of the Palais des Beaux Arts. She could hear Aunt Francoise and see her winkled smile as she pointed at the paintings and spoke about the artists. Blanche wanted to tell this man all about it – but something inside made her want to challenge him, put him down a little in spite of his threats – and the denial was out before she could stop herself. 'I don't remember.'

After a long pause he said, 'I'm beginning to think that you have never been to Lille. Why should I believe otherwise if you can't answer simple questions about the place? Tell me this – in the Grande Place in Lille there is a monument, describe it to me.'

Blanche closed her eyes, trying to recapture something she had seen only twice as a child. 'A stone column, a tall one – it has a statue on the top.'

'What does it commemorate?'

'A victory of some sort, that's all I know.'

'A victory indeed – a brave defence against the Austrians in 1792.'

'I'm hopeless with dates. I don't know any more. Please believe me.'

'Why should I believe you when I already know that the Royal Air Force does not employ female pilots?'

'I'm nothing to do with the RAF, apart from the fact that I'm engaged to a Squadron Leader called Peter Mason. I deliver their aircraft that's all. I'm a First Officer in the ATA.'

'How old are you?'

'Twenty-four.'

'Where did you qualify as a pilot?'

'At the Newcastle Aero Club.'

'When?'

'I obtained my Private Pilot's Licence in 1935 when I was seventeen. After that I

44

worked for a travelling air circus.'

The chair creaked again. 'Tell me about the flying club.'

'Our president was Sir Joseph Reed. Our motto was By Your Own Efforts Shall Ye Rise.' *Cramlington, God help me to remember something that will convince him.* 'This may sound stupid to you but one of our members drew up a list of rules entitled Misdemeanours to be Witnessed by a Scrutineer – for a joke he pinned it up on the notice board. First on the list was a Rumble, that's using your engine to extend a glide when approaching an airfield – the fine for doing it was one penny. A Bounce was threepence. A Humble, meaning a Rumble followed by a Bounce cost fourpence. The penalty for a Bengal Bounce was sixpence. Highland Taggles were graded by degrees staring at one shilling. The fine for getting stuck in the...'

'What do the letters ATA stand for?'

Perhaps it was the sight of his hand sliding forward to turn up the lamp that distracted her. 'Ancient and Tattered Airwomen.'

He stood up so suddenly that his chair fell backwards with a crash. She rose too keeping her face level with his. 'I'm telling you the truth. Refusing to believe me does neither of us any good.'

He retrieved his chair and sat down again. 'But you are a woman.'

She remained standing, forcing him to look up at her. 'If I were a man I'd be fighting for my country but where I come from women aren't allowed to do that so for my many and varied sins I deliver aeroplanes. I'm doing my incompetent best to kick Hitler's bottom so hard that he'll realise once and for always that he's not required or welcomed in countries where he doesn't belong.' She sat down so abruptly that she almost missed the chair.

He leaned forward again. 'When did you first fly an RAF fighter aircraft?'

'That's easy, July the nineteenth last year. I was one of the first five women to pass the test. After we'd each done two circuits in a Hawker Hurricane we took the train to London and celebrated at the Écu de France – can't think why we chose a French restaurant.'

'What other aeroplanes have you flown?'

'Most of the single engine types – Defiant, Lysander, Battle, Proctor, Tomahawk, Swordfish, Fulmar. I fly twin-engine aircraft too like the Beaufighter and the Mosquito and the Wellington. I was due to start training on four-engined bombers until this happened.'

He stroked his chin with stubby fingers. 'Tell me more about the air circus.'

'I joined it when I was eighteen. We travelled to air shows all over England. My

46

first job was to give joyrides in a three-seater Spartan, five shillings for a circuit of the local town. One day my plugs oiled up and we came down in a turnip field. After that I flew with the Birdman then I specialised in skywriting. Local firms sponsored me to write their names across the sky in red smoke – all quite new at the time. I was just beginning to earn a name for myself when my father put his foot down, said he preferred me with my neck unbroken and made me train to be a nurse. When war came I joined the ATA in spite of my father.'

He studied his fingernails in the lamplight. 'I'm not convinced.'

Thinking wildly, trying to keep calm but at the same time realising that her life could be in danger, Blanche unzipped the breast pocket of her flying suit. 'Take a look at that.'

He took the ring-bound booklet from her, held it close to the lamp and read aloud from the cover. 'Ferry Pilots' Notes for Official Use Only.' He opened the first page and produced a pair of wire-rimmed glasses from his pocket. *The ferry pilot should always carry this book open at the page referring to the aircraft in which he is flying.* 'He looked into her eyes. 'It says *he*.'

'He, him, she, what different does it make? The ATA has male pilots too you know, one with an eye missing another without a hand and most of the others too old for combat.

47

We get a new page to insert every time a new aircraft comes into service. One day that book will be thick enough to stop a bullet, might even save my life.'

He slipped the book into his pocket.

'Just a minute, that's an official document subject to the provisions and penalties of the Official Secrets Act. I'll be shot at dawn if I lose...' *Shot at dawn* – but biting her tongue on the words failed to curb the feeling of indignation that made her continue. 'You don't know who I am and I don't know who you are but now it's my turn to say something. I am not a spy. I'm British. My country is trying to liberate you people from Hitler so the least you can do is help me get home.'

He picked up the lamp, crossed the room and opened the door. 'I'm afraid that won't be possible. Please come with me.' She followed him to the bottom of the stairs where he called softly to the woman who, when he whispered something into her ear, crossed herself for the second time.

With a firm grip on Blanche's elbow the man led her outside. Moonlight shone on the barn roof and high above it the air was clear as far as the stars. She pulled her arm free. 'Are you afraid I'll run away or something?'

'If your story is true you have nothing to fear.' He opened the back door of a small van and told her to climb inside. Blanche sat on folded sacking in a suffocating atmosphere of stale fish. She had to push her feet against the opposite wheel arch and brace her back against cold metal as the van jolted and bounced over rough ground. Half a dozen words from England, she thought that's all it needs to prove who I really am – but maybe these people have no means of communicating with England.

After a long ride the van stopped. The man helped her to her feet and applied a blind-fold. Taking her by the arm they walked together over rough ground until he made her stop while he knocked on a door. Urgent whispers followed and then a softer arm and a smaller hand guided Blanche along a corridor so narrow that her shoulders brushed the walls on either side. She heard a key turn and another door open. The woman who had led her removed the blindfold and steered Blanche down steps into a bare-bricked room. The door banged shut behind her.

Standing motionless in the middle of the room, Blanche watched the moon shining through the bars of a high window casting patterns on the opposite wall. She could see a bed with folded blankets and a small table with a china bowl and jug. A bucket covered with a cloth stood in the corner. Blanche arranged three flat cushions to form a mattress, unfolded the blankets and lay down without undressing.

Fear, real fear at last – she could picture the

bald man, his scarred scalp, disbelief on his brow – a man who would probably never believe for one moment that an experienced pilot could land a Spitfire one hundred miles from its destination, and in the wrong country. Hunger. Hell when did I last eat? Do I scream? Do I beat on the door with my fists? Blanche got off the bed but a strong desire to sleep was already quenching her anger and numbing her indignation and worry, damping her fear. From some long forgotten school lesson a quotation surfaced. *Come sleep, oh sleep, the certain knot of peace the balm of woe, the poor man's wealth, the prisoner's release...*

Blanche woke suddenly but her dream was still running – she was flying, wind in her hair, parked cars and charabancs catching glints of sunlight below. She looked back and saw Mr Thornton diving the Arrow Active to gain speed for the final dash to the finishing line. Photographers under black cloths in the competitors' enclosure jostled for position because the ignorant had pointed fingers and had laughed at Blanche before the start of the London to Newcastle Air Race, but soon *she* was laughing and drinking champagne from the victor's cup with smooth silver cooling her bottom lip.

She turned over and saw dawn light shining through the barred window. In the present world I'm a loser, she thought, a loser lying

50

on a lumpy mattress looking at a distorted rectangle of light on a concrete floor. A cock crowed in the distance, and crowed again, and a third time from some ordinary place in a normal world. In her normal world there had been happier moments. *Blanche Longhurst by courtesy of Major Savage's Air Circus.* She remembered taking off in the SE5A, depressing the lever to test the equipment, glancing back at the long squirt of red smoke as she tipped the aircraft into steep turns and loops and dives with the engine surging loud and soft while her own special brand of art flowed out behind and suspended itself across the sky in bold signatures. *Swan-Hunter – Cramlington – Fenwicks – Shields Gazette.* She could imagine the cheers from the upturned faces of her audience as each word took shape before smudging in the wind and thinning and fading to the colour of rust before drifting out over the North Sea.

These and other memories stayed with her during the days that followed, helping to kill the boredom and the fear during intervals between meals that came regularly on a tray carried by a silent youth. But this wasn't prison food. Tender chicken cooked in wine, delicious mackerel dressed with toasted breadcrumbs, poached sausage with horseradish sauce. Perhaps they already knew who she was – and that hope kept her going as four days passed, giving time to reflect on the series of events that had brought her to this place.

The release, the escape from the family home, started one Sunday in December 1939 during a previous day off from the hospital and with the war less than a hundred days old. Blanche remembered it as a perfectly ordinary day – the bike ride from Tarvin Hall to the village took the usual seventeen minutes and Dad's usual newspaper was ready for collection. The shopkeeper's smile was the same as ever and his cat was on its usual shelf behind the counter. Everything was normal except Blanche's sudden impulse to buy a *Sunday Pictorial*. Page four was to change her life.

PAULINE GOWER TO LEAD BRITAIN'S NEW AIR SQUADRON

The Women Pilots' Section of the Air Transport Auxiliary will make history. For the first time in the great story of British Aviation women will pilot RAF planes from the manufacturers to the flying schools and reserve centres. They will pilot light machines at first, but later may be called upon to handle bombers and 350 mph fighters. Britain's 'Eves of the RAF' are chosen from seasoned women pilots. They will have to face 'sticky' flying. There will be no wireless in their planes, they will have to fly in all weathers. Miss

52

Gower is now recruiting women who will be the first to take off.

Boarding the southbound train to London without telling her father had been an easy decision and her letter to him had been brutally short.

Dear Dad,
I have arrived safely at the all-female ATA Ferry Pool Number Five at Hatfield. It is close to one of the De Havilland factories just north of London. I shall start by flying Tiger Moths to RAF training stations, which are mainly in Scotland. Please don't worry.
All my love,
Blanche.

CHAPTER THREE

The Release,
Saturday 21st of March 1942

The cock started to crow well before dawn and after breakfast the small woman who had shut Blanche in the cell five days ago unlocked the door and handed her a dressing gown. 'The bathroom is at the far end of the corridor.'

Hot water, soap and a proper lavatory at last – but was the simple act of taking a bath the last luxury, the final request granted to a condemned woman? She immersed herself and soaped herself and allowed the heat to penetrate her body. Behind closed eyes the nightmare was back. In the silence of the bathroom she could hear a crackling loudspeaker. *Mr Matthew Clement, the man who glides like a vulture, the man who holds the laws of gravity in contempt, a man shunned by Insurance Companies throughout the world, the Birdman, our hero, who has travelled a thousand miles to be with us today...* She could see him at his jumping place on the wing of the Avro, leather-clad with black mask and folded batwings rippling in the slipstream. Through steam rising from the bath came another spectre, the thin figure of the Birdman's widow – black coat, white face, bedraggled hair – glaring at her across an open grave in a rain-soaked country churchyard while the wind hit the vicar's cassock and billowed it like a sail. *I am the resurrection and the life, saith the Lord. He that believeth in me, though he were dead, yet shall he live.* The Birdman had been drinking. He pulled the ripcord a fraction too late. *Thou knowest, Lord, the secrets of our hearts; shut not thy merciful ears to our prayer.* The rain ran cold on Blanche's cheek. She saw small rivers twisting like tears down a heap of newly dug earth by the open trench.

The days of man are but as grass: for he flourisheth as a flower of the field. Dark-coated men leaned back to lower the coffin on its supporting straps – shining wood, brass handles...

Blanche got out of the bath, dried herself and put on the dressing gown. Returning to the cell she found a new set of clothes neatly arranged on the bed – silk stockings and underwear, two dresses and a linen overcoat, all the right size. When she had finished dressing the woman appeared again. 'I've taken away the dress you were wearing. It has a French label so I'll return it to you as soon as it's been washed and ironed. Please follow me.'

Outside the sky was clear and the air smelled clean. The woman pointed to the man with the scarred scalp who was waiting for her by a ragged hedge on the far side of an orchard. She walked towards him and as she got closer could see that he was smiling. He held out both arms, embraced and kissed her and spoke to her in French.

'I am truly sorry to have caused you all this trouble, Miss Longhurst, but in my job I can't afford to take risks.' They walked together under the trees with morning sun filtering through a high layer of cloud. The stiff formality shown during their last meeting had gone and it was with some relief and curiosity that she undid the top button of her new coat, felt the sun on her throat and waited to hear what he had to say.

His hand was under her elbow as they walked. 'I've met a number of aviators from your country but never a female member of the ATA. You'd be surprised at the people I meet who speak perfect English and wear RAF uniforms and who claim to have been shot down by the Germans. Some of them are impostors who are working for the Luftwaffe or, even worse, the Gestapo. Happily they nearly always fail the test.'

'What test?'

'The identity check.'

'Is that what you subjected me to at the farm, an identity check?'

He shrugged. 'Mere formality, I like to know who I'm dealing with before checking them out with London. The Air Ministry is delighted to hear that you are safe and well but understandably disappointed about the Spitfire. I'm disappointed too because you told me a lie.'

'That's ridiculous. I told you the truth.'

His cough failed to disguise the look of amusement in his eyes. 'I am reliably informed that the fine for a Bengal Bounce at the Newcastle Flying Club was never less than one shilling, but I'm prepared to let that pass as a simple lapse of memory on your part.'

'Suppose I had failed your identity check,

what then?'

'You are a very curious young lady, Miss Longhurst. Please take my advice, as long as you are here in my country it is wise not to ask too many questions.'

'That's one-sided, and anyway, how do I know who *you* are?'

'My real name is of no importance but you may call me Dadan, everyone else in our organisation knows me by that name.' He took her arm and they walked together under the apple trees. 'I'm aware that you have an important job to do in England but I have something else in mind.'

'What do you mean? I have to return to England at once.'

'I'm afraid that won't be possible.' They walked on together. 'One of these days, maybe soon or maybe not, the Allies will cross the Channel. They will come ashore along our entire coastline and sweep inland to liberate my country and go on to capture the capital city of the Third Reich. When this happens the war will be over and our two countries will be free from danger. For the time being, however, we have work to do here in order to prepare the way.'

Blanche said simply, 'I understand what you're saying and I want to help, but if I stay in France I won't be able to help win the fight.'

'That's where you are wrong. If you stay

57

here with us you can help resist the occupiers of my country.' He stopped, turned to her and passed a weary hand over his eyes. 'I was in the last war. I still have Boche steel in my leg. War is a cruel business and it makes people do cruel things. I am a Jew so believe me I know what I'm talking about.' He took a handkerchief from his pocket and blew his nose violently. 'You will be told what to do when the time is right. Your identity papers will be ready tomorrow morning and I also have people working on your cover story. In the meantime you will be quite safe with us provided you do as you're told.'

'What cover story?'

'London confirms that you are a qualified nurse so let's pretend you were born in Lille and that you were trained at the Hospital Saint Michelle. Let's also pretend that you enjoyed your work there except for some differences of opinion you had with the hospital matron, a lady by the name of Chantal Viarouge who had dark hair rather like yours but was nowhere near as pretty. She was too much of a disciplinarian for your liking so you resented her. When German troops burst into the hospital and shot her to death your resentment changed to admiration. Remembering details like that will help to make your story more convincing.'

'But I don't need a story. I don't want to be somebody else. I've told you already I have work to do in England.' Her ankles were wet from the dewy grass. She glanced at her ring wondering if they'd told Peter where she was.

'What do you know about the Hospital Saint Michelle.'

'I've seen it once but only from the outside. Anyway what difference does it make?'

Dadan turned to face her. 'Difference? The difference between life and death.'

'But I don't...' The sudden appearance of low-flying aircraft from behind a tall stand of trees – three of them with German markings – cut her short. Dadan looked up and waved at them with both arms but, above the din, she could hear him swearing and saw his hands fold into fists as the aircraft disappeared behind buildings. He turned to her. 'You were saying?'

Blanche felt herself shaking. How many times had she seen those distinctive shapes on curly-edged aircraft recognition posters in crew rooms and control towers all over Britain? *Butcher Birds* with black crosses on their wings and swastikas on their tail fins. She said, 'I can't remember what I was going to say.'

He touched her arm and the smile was back. 'Until I can find a way to get you home you will be a valuable member of our team. Up until now you have been English. Now you are French so you must be able to recall exactly what it was like to be living in Lille when war broke out. You heard the BBC's French language service reporting Nazi activity in Danzig but, like everybody else, you thought the British Expeditionary Force would be able to defeat the invaders. You were proved wrong when, a few months later, you heard the squeal of tank tracks outside your window, exploding shells, the screams of wounded men, orphaned children crying for their mothers. You were one of the countless refugees who fled the city. Broken vehicles jammed the roads. You were ragged, you were hungry. You pushed your belongings in a wheelbarrow and you scrambled into ditches to save yourself from attacking aircraft while German tanks crushed and scattered everything in their path as they raced to encircle the British.'

Dadan's eyes caught a watery reflection as he continued. 'My country is split. To the south we have the Vichy Regime under Marshal Pétain who collaborates with the enemy and accepts the Germans as his friends. He believes the allies will make peace and that France will soon be part of Germany. But in the north things are different. Here in the north we have Paris and we have the Channel coastline.'

'Why are you telling me this?'

'For your protection. As you are now one of us I want you to feel the pain of occupation as acutely as we all do. Remember that in the north many of us secretly resist the occupiers.' He took a handkerchief from his pocket and blew his nose.

Blanche shook her head. 'Secrecy, danger, new identities – it all seems so…'

'Identity, I'm coming to that. For your own safety and for the safety of everyone within our organisation you must never reveal your true name, not even to those whom you may come to love and trust while you are here in France.'

'Why?'

'Because if you are arrested you will be forced to reveal everything you know and then they will shoot you or, if you're unlucky you will be sent to Ravensbruck.'

'What happens there?'

'Ravensbruck is a concentration camp for women. We have reliable information that some of the inmates are assigned to a brothel where they must open their legs for the enjoyment of the savages who think they already own my country. All other women in that place are worked to death with barely enough food to keep them alive. Regular inspections decide who is fit to work and death is the reward for those who are not. The female guards are cruel and we hear rumours of medical experiments.'

He looked up at the sky as if half expecting to see another flight of Butcher Birds. 'Only you and I know who you really are, try to remember that. Nobody, literally nobody else must ever be allowed to discover your true identity while you remain with us here in France.'

He paused, shifting his weight and kicking at a stone in the grass. 'I have some other news from London, something that concerns you directly. I'm afraid your fiancé is dead. He was killed in action.'

'*What?*'

'Squadron Leader Peter Mason was shot down over England.' Dadan's voice seemed to be coming from far away. 'It has been confirmed. His Spitfire crashed into a field in Somerset and burst into flames.'

'I don't believe it. I can't believe it. How do you know– Oh God.'

Dadan embraced her. 'You must be strong.' Kissing her on both cheeks, he whispered, 'Take courage, you are now a friend of the French Resistance.'

She felt tears on her cheek – and they were his.

CHAPTER FOUR

The Chateau,
Saturday 21st of March 1942

Blanche was still numb with grief when she caught her first glimpse of Chateau Chatelain through a gap in overhanging branches as Dadan drove his van slowly along a tree-lined drive. He parked in a yard bordered on two sides by stable buildings.

She opened the door on her side and found the rounded cobblestones strangely reassuring through the thin leather of her shoes. While Dadan walked across the yard and entered the first stable, Blanche looked up at mullioned windows, louvered shutters, round corner turrets and dormer windows set high in a steep roof. Dadan had said something about a cookery school – could it be?

He walked back briskly pushing a wheelbarrow. Refusing Blanche's offer of help he took a large wooden box from the van, loaded it into the barrow and put her borrowed suitcase on top. Gesturing for her to follow he led her towards the chateau through an impressive stone portal past neatly tended rows of vines with the silence broken only by the iron wheel bumping over uneven joints in the paving.

At the foot of five shallow steps he put down the barrow, straightened his back, took Blanche by the arm and climbed up to the main door – but before his hand touched the ram's head knocker the door was opened by a thin woman in her early forties, straight-backed and elegantly dressed, proffering her cheek for Dadan's kiss.

He indicted Blanche with a quick movement of his head. 'This is the girl I told you about.'

A gold tooth flashed. 'Good morning, my dear. Dadan, will you please introduce me?'

'Her name is Lucette Moreaux.' Turning to Blanche he said, 'And this is Madame Henriette Cazalet who has agreed to let you stay here in her house.'

Madam Cazalet shook her head. 'I'm afraid there has been some misunderstanding. Dadan tells me you have been homeless ever since your escape from Lille, but you must realise that I am desperately short of...'

Dadan cut in. 'Just remember one thing, Henriette, the price of fish is rocketing and supplies are scarce. Make the most of what I've brought you today because it might be the last you'll see for some time.'

She took a sideways step and glanced down at the wheelbarrow. 'I appreciate what you do for us, Dadan, and I confess I don't know how you do it but…'

He shrugged. 'We help each other, it's the only act of charity left to us these days. You need fish and this girl needs a safe place to live. Trust me. Call me mad if you like but I wouldn't have brought her here if I didn't think she'd fit in. Oh and by the way, did I mention that she's a qualified nurse?'

Madame Cazalet narrowed her eyes. 'A nurse, is that so?' She turned to Blanche. 'Where did you qualify, my dear.'

'At the Hospital Saint Michelle in Lille.'

The gold tooth flashed again. 'Sometimes Dadan brings trouble to my house but this time – yes, perhaps he was right to bring you here after all.'

Dadan took an envelope from his pocket, turned his back on Blanche and lowered his voice. 'This came through last night, let me have it back when you've read it.' He handed over the envelope, kissed both women and descended the steps.

Blanche watched him walk back towards his van. Could it be true? Was Peter really dead? Was it grief that was making her feel like this or was it hatred for the anonymous enemy who had killed him?

The woman standing next to her, aged about forty, thin and alert, watched over her new protégé like a vulture. A new protégé – that's what she had become, Blanche Long-hurst had disappeared and someone else

65

had emerged in her place, a French nurse from Lille, a displaced person with forged papers who didn't understand the politics of war – a woman feigning acceptance of foreign occupiers, a friend of the French Resistance who would never be able to revel her true identity until the day she set foot in England again.

Madam Cazalet said, 'Pick up your suitcase my dear and come with me.' She gripped Blanche's arm with bony fingers and led her down a long corridor lined with rows of stags' heads and almost pushed her into a small sitting room where an attractive girl in her twenties put down the book she was reading and stood up.

Madame Cazalet touched the girl's wrist, 'Hélène, we have a new arrival. Meet Lucette Moreaux, she's been having a hard time ever since her escape from Lille three years ago and she'll be living with us for a few days. Kindly show her to one of the empty rooms on the top floor and help to make up the bed.' She turned to Blanche. 'When you've unpacked your things, my dear, I'd like to see you in my study.'

Blanche followed Hélène up the stirs and on the first landing asked, 'Are you a student here?'

'Student? Oh yes, I suppose we're all students – in a way.'

'I was told that this is a cookery school.'

66

Hélène laughed and continued up the next flight, pausing on the top landing to take bedclothes from a cupboard. 'This is where the servants used to sleep before the war. The bathroom is at the end of the corridor – lavatory, bidet, hot and cold, everything works but the pressure's a bit feeble. This is your room. I'll help you make up the bed.'

Blanche put down her suitcase on bare boards. There were no curtains on the arched windows. An ornate iron bedstead, painted white, dominated the small room.

Unfolding the bedclothes Blanche said, 'What brought you here?'

The girl shrugged. 'Like you I had nowhere else to go – my parents were killed when our house was bombed.' She spread a sheet on the bed without looking up. 'I never expected I'd get involved in work like this but as long as there's a war I have no choice.'

'But what do you do here?'

'Hasn't Madame told you yet? Don't worry, she will.'

When the girl had gone Blanche turned to the window and looked down on neat rows of vines in freshly cultivated earth. Beyond them she could see stable roofs and the long avenue of trees that led to the gate. Taking the identity card from her pocket, the one that Dadan had given her, she looked at the entries she'd made along the dotted lines. Surname: Moreaux. First name: Lucette. Date of Birth: March 9th 1918. Height: 1m 67cm. Eyes: Brown. Face: Oval. Hair: Black. All true of course but the thumbprint on the bottom made her feel like a criminal and in a way that's what she had become, an impostor in a forbidden country and acting under a false name.

At the end of the corridor the bathroom was like a museum dedicated to man's earliest achievements in plumbing – huge pipes, massive taps and a decorated lavatory pan that gushed rusty water but only in response to repeated tugs on an iron chain mended with wire. She tried the basin and washed herself by courtesy of a series of unproductive coughs from a tap marked 'C'. After pecking at her hair in front of a cracked mirror she descended the long staircase where a different girl came forward, kissed Blanche on both cheeks and led her to the study.

Madam Cazalet stood in front of net curtains drawn across the window. 'Ah, Lucette – thank you, Armande, you may leave us now and please close the door behind you.' She turned to Blanche. 'I trust you have found somewhere comfortable to sleep and that you don't suffer from nightmares.'

'Nightmares, why do you ask?'

Madame Cazalet looked her up and down

with narrowed eyes. 'Never mind. Tell me about the German occupation of Lille, it must hold some sad memories for you.'

'I'd rather not talk about it if you don't mind.'

'Very well, if that is your wish.' She perched on a narrow sofa and patted the place beside her. 'Can you swim?'

Blanche sat down. 'Swim? Yes, quite well. My father taught me how to do the crawl in the public baths in Lille when I was a child.'

'Tell me about your father. Where is he now?'

'Still in Lille, he refused to leave.'

'And where is your mother?'

'One day she went in search for food and I never saw her again.'

Madame Cazalet seemed to be either considering the truth of this or else trying to picture the scene. 'You have had a difficult time, my dear but I must warn you that life here can be difficult too. We have some rather interesting neighbours that I will introduce you to once you have settled in. For now I want you to close your eyes and imagine yourself on a beach in the company of a young German officer – can you do that for me? As a nurse you will know that sea water has a wonderful effect on feminine skin and you are a pretty girl, albeit in a rather pastoral way.'

Blanche kept her eyes open. 'I don't know what you're talking about, Madame. Surely the Germans are our enemies.'

'We try not to use the word enemy, it has a rather sinister ring don't you think?' She opened a silver box by her elbow and fitted a miniature cigar into an ebony holder. 'When a pretty girl flirts with a German officer she can sometimes learn things that might be of interest to our allies. It's a sad fact that the beaches of Normandy are seldom used for swimming these days – indeed the Germans have put our shoreline out of bounds to all civilians. However, when in the company of a German officer we are sometimes able to break the rules. Dadan is a man of few words but no doubt he has already told you that the Luftwaffe has taken over our airfield at Maupertus and their officers like to make friends with us.'

'What do you mean?'

'Just friends, you understand. Of course we never allow ourselves to fall in love with them.' Madame Cazalet narrowed her eyes as if sharing a conspiracy. 'I'll give you an example. I was recently enjoying a drink in Cherbourg with Oberst Wilhelm Schieder, the newly appointed commander of our local aerodrome. Wilhelm has a good heart and I admire men who believe in God. This one however is a little too stern and serious for me. I've been working on him for some

70

time and he has mellowed enough to enjoy snatched liaisons with me in a cottage formerly owned by a Jewish gentleman. Coming from Lille I don't suppose you're familiar with our local apple brandy but take it from me it's the ideal fluid to lubricate the tongue of a gentleman. Last week Wilhelm told me about Directive Forty.'

'What is Directive Forty.'

'Perhaps one day I will tell you – when we have got to know each other a little better.' After a pause she continued. 'You are not unattractive, my dear, I think we will find that German officers will be wanting to entertain you, buy you drinks, take you out to dinner maybe. An officer might even offer to drive you back to the chateau after a pleasant evening, but you will have to make sure that you kiss your man goodnight in the stable yard where there is space to turn a car. This is my strictest rule – never let your German friend approach my house.'

Madame Cazalet screwed her half-smoked cigar into a crystal dish. 'What else do you like to do apart from swimming?'

'I play the piano.'

'But that's wonderful. My wooden-framed upright hasn't been tuned since the occupation but I'd like you to play it whenever you feel inclined. We must never ignore life's simple pleasures just because the world has been turned upside-down – and piano players never have any difficulty in making friends.'

Blanche looked away. Is this woman completely mad, liaisons with the enemy, kissing them goodnight in the stable yard, playing the piano for them? She remembered a day when she was grounded by fog and stuck without a train to take her back to White Waltham. Hearing somebody trying to play the piano she soon found herself at the keyboard with a French-Canadian pilot standing on top of the piano leading an unruly ensemble in a raucous rendering of Allouette to words that made her blush. Was she expected to behave like that with the Luftwaffe?

A different girl brought a tray and unloaded cutlery and a small casserole onto a round table by the window. Madame Cazalet waited until the girl had left the room before lifting the lid to survey the contents. 'Forgive the simple meal, Lucette. I teach my girls to do what they can with dried codfish but we don't only rely on preserved ingredients in spite of the fact that nearly everything fresh goes down the throats of the Luftwaffe. They strip every shelf in the village – butcher, fishmonger and patisserie – and our Friday Market is a battleground. But all is not lost, my gardener is still here and he grows vegetables. We also have a small flock of hens and two cows.' She paused for breath. 'Dadan says that I must trust you so I might as well tell you that cookery classes are just part of what we do here.' She put down her knife and fork. 'All will become clear after I've asked my little nurse from Lille to do something for me, something rather important and something that she is well qualified to do.'

They left the study and entered a large drawing room where Madame Cazalet pointed to a glass-fronted cabinet and said, 'I'm very proud of my Meissen figurines – plain white is far subtler than gaudy colours, don't you agree? Just look at the detail on the toes of my Art Deco Nude. But this one over here is my favourite – the Dying Gaul. Can you feel his agony? And what about my animals, like this little frog who dares to fight a crayfish twice his size. I've never been a boastful person but I believe that my collection ranks with the finest in the country.' She pointed to a massive wall tapestry of huntsmen and a deer chased by hounds. 'Think of the work that has gone into that, such detailed foliage and the fear of God in the eyes of an animal about to die. And my paintings – I believe Winslow Homer was trying to tell us a story when he painted those dark faces, contrasting so nicely with the cotton that they are picking. But out of all of them George Weatherill is my favourite artist. Just look at that sea, can you smell it? Do you want to pick those flowers? Such a sensitive style and that is something quite unusual for an Englishman. Oh and that reminds me. Dadan tells me you speak a few words of that language.'

'I was top of my class at the Lycée. I also gained a certificate in German.'

Madam Cazalet looked across the room to check her wristwatch against an ornate clock that dominated the mantelpiece. 'This is another of my treasures, it's a family heirloom. The eagle on top of the dial is the American national symbol and the Egyptian sphinxes on either side of the pendulum remind us of our glorious French Empire, now so sadly depleted. This clock has a curious history. In 1789 Emperor Napoleon commissioned it as gift for George Washington but privateers captured the ship and sold all its cargo in Newfoundland. Luckily for me an ancestor of mine happened to be at the sale.' She fitted a brass key into the face of the clock and wound, counting the turns out loud.

Sliding the key under the clock she said, 'If you were top of your English class you must be almost fluent. Very soon you'll have an opportunity to practise that language with somebody who lives in my cellar – shall we go and find him?' She took an attaché case from a cupboard and handed it to Blanche. 'You'll need this.'

74

They left the room and walked through a large kitchen where saucepans of every size and shape hung from a rack suspended from the ceiling. In a dark corridor leading off the kitchen, Blanche dislodged flakes of plaster with her shoulders as she followed Madame Cazalet who walked ahead along a narrow passage. After pushing through a half-open door at the end of the passage they paused at a place where cracks of light outlined a trapdoor in the floor. Madame Cazalet bent down, lifted the cover and laid it back. 'Be careful, my dear, the steps are worn and rather slippery.'

Light from a long line of barred windows revealed a double line of pillars supporting a low ceiling. Wooden wine racks, back-to-back in a long row down the centre of the cellar seemed to stretch along its entire length Madame Cazalet said, 'I don't mind if my boys help themselves to wine as long as they keep quiet and don't get drunk.'

English voices became increasingly distinct as they walked towards the far end and, when they reached it, Madame Cazalet stepped into an open doorway where half a dozen men dressed in blue jackets and collarless shirts got up from chairs and mattresses on the floor. The smell of sweat blended with the cellar's damp decay. Madame Cazalet spoke to them slowly in faltering English. 'Today I bring to you one nurse. Her name is Lucette.

Bernard how is your arm today?'

One of the men stepped forward. 'I'm sad to say it's not much better.'

Somebody said, 'You'll have to parlez if you want a smile from this one.'

Madame Cazalet pushed Blanche forward. 'Bernard has an infected wound, see what you can do for him.'

The man held out his arm and Blanche peeled back a crudely applied bandage to reveal a cut in his arm that stretched from wrist to elbow. Trying not to gag on the smell she spoke English in a put-on accent. 'How long has it been like this?'

'Five days, maybe more.'

She cleaned the wound with cotton wool soaked in alcohol and applied a fresh bandage. 'You should be in hospital.'

Madame Cazalet said, 'If all goes well he'll be in England tomorrow, will it keep till then?'

'If he gets to a hospital as soon as he lands he should be fine.'

So this was it. Returning allied airmen to England was another of Madame Cazalet's secret duties, but how? And then another thought crowded in. Could Lucette Moreaux be returned to England by the same route?

Madame Cazalet put her hand on Blanche's shoulder. 'Are you all done now?' Turning to the men she said, 'Tonight you

will be eating the mackerel, all fresh. Maque-
reaux à la Façon de Quimper – fresh, very
fresh.'

Making their way back to the kitchen Madame Cazalet said, 'I have six sets of civilian
clothes with caps and everything, but if
Dadan can't find a pair of shoes to fit Flight
Sergeant Bernard Simpson by four o'clock
tomorrow morning he'll miss his chance,
wound or no wound.'

Blanche looked on while Madame Cazalet
gave her instructions. 'Nicole, go and see if
the hens have obliged us with half a dozen
eggs. I trust they have because I'd like you to
stir them with mustard and pepper with a
generous splash of vinegar. Dadan's fish will
be wasted if the sauce is too bland. Armande,
bring me some parsley from the garden.'
Rolling up her sleeves Madame Cazalet
counted out ten mackerel from the box while
Blanche stood by feeling helpless until...
'Lucette dear, fetch me a large tray and five
plates, Marie will show you where we keep
them. After last night's potato and dried peas
I think our boys are in for a pleasant surprise.
When the meal is ready I want you to take it
to them, but don't break your leg on those
steps.'

When all was ready Blanche retraced her
way down the corridor. She put down the
tray in semi-darkness and lifted the trapdoor. Madame Cazalet might have accepted

77

her as a genuine refugee from Lille but was it necessary to maintain the lie while talking to a group of hungry compatriots about to return to England?

She trod carefully down the steps. At the far end of the cellar the men crowded around her. One of them said, 'We like French girls don't we lads? When this lot's over we'll come back to France, mark my words, and we'll throw a party for all those who risked their ruddy necks to get us back to Blighty.'

'How will you get back to England? Who will take you?'

'Don't know love. Nobody tells us anything.'

'But you are going aren't you?'

'That's what the lady said. Back to dear old England so that Jerry can have another go at frying us.'

Oh God. Blanche could see a blazing aircraft and Peter's cheeks melting in the inferno. She looked away, trying to imagine herself wearing a white dress and clutching a bouquet – but what was the vicar saying? The wedding has been cancelled. The bridegroom has been burnt to death.

These men – how many of them would survive this war? She watched them eat, listened to their banter and quickly realised that they were all members of bomber crews shot down over France. All had been helped and

78

sheltered by people like Madame Cazalet, brave people prepared to risk their lives and prepared to stop at nothing to hinder the German invaders and one day kick them out of France. These were the kind of people who were prepared to risk death and torture to get simple appreciators of fresh mackerel back to the place where they belong.

Maintaining her French accent Blanche said, 'Could a civilian woman find her way back to England in the same way?'

A voice said, 'Hang on a minute, are you English?'

'I only asked.'

'Your accent, it had me fooled at first – not any more.'

It was no use. She already knew the answer so why ask? She loaded the tray with empty plates. 'I have to go now. I hope you enjoyed your meal.'

Later that night, lying awake, Blanche finally allowed herself to release a pent up flood of tears. Light flooded the bedroom from a moon that had been hurtling around the earth in endless orbits ever since the Creation, and would go on doing so into a never-ending future while generations of boys and girls grew up to get caught up in wars that would never alter a single thing. Peter was a warrior. Blanche is a pacifist. But is there a place for such a person in a world where freedom is at stake? How can the oppressor be subdued if men and women are unable to fight because of their high-flown beliefs? And yet what kind of world is it now where children are conceived and born and reared by loving parents only to be cut down by political conflicts that are none of their making? These questions stayed with Blanche throughout the night, jumbled with horrific visions of her own special warrior burned to death in the wreckage of his aeroplane.

When she opened her eyes and looked up, early morning light from the window had outlined a damp stain on the ceiling shaped like a map of Africa – and Madame Cazalet's borrowed nightdress was sticking to her like glue. Peter was dead but Lucette Moreaux was about to embark on her second day in the chateau. What am I getting myself into? And how will those airmen get back to England?

She remembered one of Peter's friends describing how he had returned safely to England after being shot down over France. He had walked by night until hunger forced him to seek help. Frightened farmers had shouted at him to move on but Toby took a railway journey to the foothills of the Pyrenees, walked through woods and meadows and climbed a mountain where eagles spiralled over valleys in the Massif de Couserans before crossing into Spain. After that he followed a railway line, stowed away on a train bound for Portugal, walked into the British Embassy in Lisbon who arranged his flight to England in a DC3 operated by KLM – the only airline still flying from that staunchly neutral country.

Blanche turned onto her side. From the far end of the vineyard a pigeon cooed as if trying to imitate the laughter of those who refused to believe Toby's story. The Pyrenees Mountains were five hundred miles away. Would Madame Cazalet's men be going by the same route?

She got out of bed and stood at the window watching raindrops zigzagging down the glass. Dad had been as lonely as hell ever since the terrible bereavement, immersing himself in work after Mother's death and continuing to run his publishing business in spite of the grief. He'd be equally depressed now since his daughter had gone missing. She could picture him in the morning room with an unread newspaper on his lap and his coffee going cold.

Was it raining in England? Was Peter strapping himself into the cockpit of his Spitfire for another sortie against his enemies? Could he *really* be dead?

CHAPTER FIVE

The Task, Friday 3rd of April 1942

'Come with me, Lucette, I have something to say to you.'

They left the kitchen and entered the study. Madame Cazalet closed the door and they sat together on the sofa.

'You may not have realised it but I've been watching you closely during the fortnight you've been with us. I have to tell you that it's not only Dadan who thinks it's time you were told a bit more about some of the things we do here – apart from acting as travel agents for Allied airmen that is.'

Madame Cazalet fiddled with the brooch pinned to the front of her dress. 'Do you remember me mentioning Directive Forty?' She lit one of her miniature cigars and leaned back on an embroidered cushion. 'The British are an impatient race and they expect us to do extraordinary things at the click of a finger. They constantly ask us to obtain information that they claim will shorten the war. Sometimes I think they've forgotten what conditions are like over here and that France is no longer a free country.'

'But what is Directive Forty?'

'It is Hitler's name for something that interests an important man in England, and it has taken on a new urgency now that the sleeping giant has heard our bugle call.'

'The sleeping giant, what do you mean?'

'The United States of America has heard our call to arms and about time too. We've been blowing it for two long years. Directive Forty is a line of defence, a big building project, and it's our duty to watch its progress. Directive Forty has another name – the *Atlantikwall,* a barrier that will stretch from Denmark to our own coast here in Normandy. A second Great Wall of China is how some Germans describe it, designed to protect the whole of Europe against invasion from the sea. If you think that's impossible just think what the Boche have achieved already. They built the Siegfried Line on the Franco-German border, over six hundred kilometres of it, with fortresses along the entire length from Holland to Switzerland. I don't think this one will be an actual wall, rather a line of fortifications and wire entanglements. My friend Wilhelm Schieder talks of heavily defended tidal rivers and beaches protected by gun batteries. He describes army patrols and, yes, some walls too. Allied soldiers will need to know the nature and strength of these defences if they are to successfully invade our shores. So we must watch and we must listen to every rumour however far-fetched it may seem. This will be your job in the coming months.'

Blanche tried not to show her dismay. *Months, how many months? How long does she expect me to stay in France?*

'When making direct contact with the enemy you must try to prevent them speaking to you in German. They don't belong here so the least they can do is to speak to us in our own language.'

She inhaled a luxurious lungful of smoke. 'So you see, there are many ways in which women can help our country to regain its freedom apart from killing the enemy. We listen to the Germans, we remember what they say and then we put all our information together so that Dadan can transmit it to London by radio. That is how we work – in a team. Together we will help the Allies to win the war.'

Madam Cazalet paused, and once again Blanche could see a glint of conspiracy in her eyes. 'So much for the *Atlantikwall*. Lately we've been asked to concentrate on something almost as important, perhaps even more so and certainly more urgent. The Luftwaffe has a secret weapon – a new aeroplane of revolutionary design and it's already in service.'

Blanche remembered something that

Dadan had said about never revealing her identity and wondered why this woman had suddenly switched the subject to aircraft? Did she know something? Was it possible that she already knew the true identity of Lucette Moreaux?

Madame Cazalet blew out a perfect O of smoke that enlarged and drifted towards the ceiling. 'You have settled in well and I must say that having a trained nurse in our team brings me enormous peace of mind – but it's not every day that our airmen need medical help so you will have plenty of time to make friend with Luftwaffe officers.'

'But I know nothing about aeroplanes.'

Madame Cazalet paused long enough for Blanche to wonder if the *Nurse from Lille* had been compromised. 'Of course you don't, none of know about aeroplanes but that won't deter us. We will learn about their aeroplanes, especially their new pride and joy – the Wurger – that's their name for it. Rather apt don't you think. A Wurger is the German word for a cruel bird that kills little songbirds and impales their bodies on thorn bushes like butchers displaying meat outside their shops, like they used to do before the Boche took over our country. The official name of this aircraft is the Focke-Wulf 190, it's a powerful fighter than can carry a five hundred kilogram bomb. That's all we know so far, apart from the fact that all five units at Maupertus were equipped with this new type two months ago. The British call it *Butcher Bird,* and they went to know its secret.'

Blanche leaned back and wondered how Lucette Moreaux, who knew nothing about aircraft, could be expected to infiltrate the social life of the local aerodrome and discover what makes the Butcher Bird such a deadly weapon.

Madame Cazalet continued. 'RAF aircrews are suffering heavy losses because of the Wurger. They need engineers' drawings and handbooks but above all they want to know what pilots and mechanics say about it – its strengths and weaknesses. If the Butcher Bird remains unchallenged then I'm afraid the great Allied invasions might never happen.'

Blanche got up. Through the window she could see an endless tangle of unclipped hedges that might have been a garden maze in happier times. France is a maze, she thought, a maze with forty-two million civilians trying to find a way out.

'You have already proved to me that you are a valuable member of our group, Lucette. You are pretty enough to turn the head of the dullest of men, but beauty alone is not enough.' She got up and stood beside Blanche. 'The German male is really quite a pleasant creature when you get to know him – perhaps a little less romantic than our boys, maybe a little rough at times, but very relaxed on the subject of sex when the moment comes. You will soon discover that undoing the buttons of a Luftwaffe uniform is no more difficult than opening an oyster or garnishing a Daurade aux Moules.'

She went to the corner of the room and picked up a framed photograph. 'I took this one myself, badly focused I admit but it's of a lovely man. Emile was my husband, he's dead now. He was one of thousands who fought against the Kaiser in 1914.' She kissed the glass and replaced the photograph. 'Perhaps it is just as well that I never re-married because now I have many lovers, but I am not *in love* with any of them.'

'Tell me more about the German aeroplane.'

'What more can I tell you? Not much I fear. We know that German pilots are not allowed to fly it over England, at least not yet. The Reischsmarschall is afraid one of them might fall into Allied hands.'

'The Reischsmarschall?'

'Hermann Goering, he's Hitler's most faithful companion, always jovial and a man who knows how to flatter women. Perhaps I shouldn't say this but I find him attractive even though he's fighting on the wrong side. You should see his medals – Knight's cross, Blue Max and a lot more.'

'You've met him?'

'Of course I have. He's chief of the Luft-waffe. When he visited Maupertus three months ago he invited my girls and me to a wonderful party. That's how I found out about the ban on flying Butcher Birds over England. I have to admit I was quite carried away by him and was tempted to return his hospitality here at the chateau. Perhaps it is fortunate that my cellars were overflowing with Allied airmen at the time.'

She tilted her head. 'I've kept back six dozen bottles of my best vintage for the day when Allied ships cross the Channel and land the biggest army the world has ever seen, right here on our beaches.'

Blanche was thinking that if optimism could win a war then the Germans might as well surrender now. She smiled. 'I'm ready to help in any way I can.' There, she had said it. There could be no going back now.

'My darling girl what can I say, but let me explain that we do things by stages and we try not to get nervous about it. We stay calm, and most important of all we learn to enjoy the company of German officers. The first stage for you will be the introduction. Tomorrow you will accompany me to the Café de Paris in Cherbourg where I will introduce you to some of my friends. If we are lucky one of them will be attracted to you. If you are charming and responsive towards your new friend he will invite you to dances and parties. At first you will talk to him about things of no importance but gradually, when you get to know him better, you will talk about the Wurger and the Atlantic wall.' She raised a warning finger. 'But if you ever feel yourself falling in love with your German officer you must come and talk to me.'

CHAPTER SIX

The Introduction,
Saturday 4th of April 1942

As the bus slowed, Madame Cazalet rubbed the window with her sleeve. 'There, can you see it?'

Blanche looked to where she was pointing and saw gilt lettering on a glass panel, Café de Paris, shining dimly out of a long row of blacked out buildings.

Blanche stepped off the bus. Madam Cazalet took her arm and they teetered across the cobbled road. 'Just be yourself, Lucette, and remember why I've brought you here. Whatever you don't fall in love with any of them.'

Under the luminous sign Madame Cazalet pressed a coin into the hand of a one-legged man who opened the door for them. A wave of hot air laced with sweat and alcohol wafted into Blanche's face as they entered. Uniformed men packed the extensive room. Some sat quietly on leather-covered benches while others leaned on the bar, played cards, arm-wrestled and spilled beer. A coffee machine bubbled behind the bar and Blanche felt a smoke-laden breeze spiralling down from an overhead fan as Madame Cazalet steered her purposefully towards a small table in the far corner.

A greying man with rows of ribbons on his chest got to his feet, kissed Madame Cazalet on the lips and pulled out two chairs.

She patted his cheek and picked a speck of dust from his lapel. 'Wilhelm darling, this is my new friend, Lucette Moreaux.' Turning to Blanche she said, 'Wilhelm Schieder is my dearest friend and a very important man, he is also the commanding officer of Maupertus aerodrome.'

Shieder clicked his heels and took Blanche's hand. 'So you are the nurse who escaped from Lille. Henriette has been telling me about you. I trust that in spite of your unhappy experiences you harbour no bitterness towards the liberating forces that now protect your country.'

Blanche answered with a brief shake of the head and sat down. A waiter brought glasses and filled them from a bottle already on the

90

table. Blanche took a sip and the liquor burnt her tongue like fire. The whole idea of meeting the enemy had filled her with dread and now it was happening. Madame Cazalet was sitting next to the boss of Maupertus aerodrome, her chosen German officer, and putting her teaching into practice by staying calm and enjoying his company. But Blanche was far from calm. She was terrified, barely able to think or speak and gripped by fear like never before in spite of Madame Cazalet's eyes transmitting messages of encouragement from her side of the table.

Schieder leaned forward and touched Blanche's wrist. 'What's the matter Mademoiselle? Would you prefer something different to drink, some white wine perhaps? You seem afraid. Are you afraid?'

'Just a little.'

Schieder spread his hands. 'But we are friends, and I don't mean only here in our favourite watering hole where the lads like to relax and enjoy themselves. Our friendship extends throughout your country which means that French civilians are no longer in danger. Believe me, there is no possible reason why you should feel the slightest bit afraid.'

Blanche took a deep breath and tried to remember that if she was going to act her role convincingly she would have to show this man that Lucette Moreaux had come through hell to get to this congenial table.

She put a handkerchief to her eyes. 'But I am afraid. I'm afraid of what will happen to my country. I witnessed war at close hand when your forces entered Lille two years ago and I am afraid what the Allies will do to our women and children should they ever set foot on our beaches.'

Schieder put his arm around Madame Cazalet's shoulders and laughed. 'This new friend of yours is not only pretty she has a vivid imagination.' He drained his glass and refilled it from the bottle. 'The Allies are done for. They are already defeated. They are dying by the thousand as we speak. You must have seen those devils trying to gain a foothold in France two years ago but we all know what happened. They scurried home like a bunch of fleeing rats. If we ever see their armies on French soil I'll publicly expose my genitalia on the town hall steps of Cherbourg for all to see.'

Madame Cazalet dug him in the ribs, 'Just you watch your language, Wilhelm. We are not in the barrack room now.'

A dozen airmen, shouting and laughing in the far corner of the room, were dragging an unwilling performer to a piano and slapping him so hard on the back that he was spilling his beer.

The man began to play, his companions

sang raucously and Blanche knew enough German to follow the words...

Wir Flieger, zum Kämpfen geboren,
Wir feurn mit sicherer Hand.
Wir haben dem Führer geschworen,
Entschlossen zu schuetzen das Land.

Madame Cazalet lifted her eyes to the ceiling and blocked her ears. Planting a kiss on Schieder's cheek she said, 'Am I expected to believe this stuff? When their mothers gave birth to them did they know their sons were born to fight? And as for shooting their weapons with steady hands, I don't think any of them would be capable of doing such a thing when tomorrow's hangover blots the sun from their sad little souls. Blind allegiance to the Führer is all very well, but don't forget that you people occupy my country against the will of its people.'

Unaware of the smudge of lipstick on his cheek, Schieder said, 'If you really loved me you wouldn't use that word. We don't *occupy* your country. France and Germany are united in friendship and God willing will always be so.'

Madame Cazalet inclined her head towards a group of tightly laced whores seated at the bar. 'Perhaps we should be taking a leaf from their book. I'll wager that most of those ladies will be united in friendship before the night is done but let's hope they never tout for business in the ballroom of Hotel de Fleuve.'

Blanche took another sip of Calvados and found it less fiery, almost smooth. A German officer was standing at the bar, tall and straight-backed. She watched him fill an ashtray from a jug on the bar and lower it to the floor; an English Fox Terrier put its head between his boots and lapped greedily at the water. When the officer straightened up he caught Blanche's eyes and came over to the table with the dog at his heels. He put his glass on the table, took Madame Cazalet's proffered hand and brushed it with his lips. 'Good evening, Madame. Good evening Herr Kommandeur.'

Schieder put up his fists in a playful challenge. 'Hands off Otto, these women are mine. Pull up a chair. Help me convince them that life is too short for arguments.' To Blanche he said, 'Allow me to present my comrade in arms Major Otto Stoeckl, a man who enjoys danger in its purest form.'

Stoeckl bowed, clicked his heels and sat down. The dog disappeared under the table.

Schieder leaned over. 'This is our new friend, her name is Mademoiselle Lucette. She is a nurse. Perhaps the nurse from Lille would like to work in our hospital if she is not too busy at the chateau.'

Madame Cazalet came to the rescue. 'I

94

don't see nearly enough of you these days, Otto. Where do you hide yourself? I'm sure you will like Lucette. Her home was destroyed by you people in this bloody war that you're so keen about so now she lives with me. I teach her Cordon Bleu cookery but the only ingredients we rely on these days are tap water and fresh air – good for soufflés but not very nourishing.'

Schieder's fist came down with an almighty thump and narrowly missed the bottle. 'One minute you're happy, the next you're finding fault with everything we Germans try to do for your country. When will that pretty head of yours understand that France and Germany are...' He broke off and leaned across the table. 'Otto, you're forever lecturing us on the politics of Europe, see if you can explain it to them.'

Otto downed his drink in one swallow. 'When this war is over every country in the world will be friends apart from Britain. That country will always stand aloof. I was a student at Oxford before the war. I know what I'm talking about.'

Stoeckl hit the table again. 'That's enough. Why are we talking about English pigs?' He winked at Blanche. 'Otto talks of Friendship but don't allow him to become too friendly with you unless you want to get yourself into trouble.'

With the hot breath of the dog on her

ankle, Blanche took a sideways glance at Otto. Pale blue eyes, thirty-five or thereabouts and hair slanting down his forehead like a boy.

Madam Cazalet took a cigar from Schieder's and skilfully cut off the end with her fingernail. Otto leaned over and rolling the flint of his lighter said, 'This is an American Zippo, it always lights first time.'

Schieder laughed. 'The gallant major owns the finest cigarette lighter in the whole world but he's the only fighter pilot in the Luftwaffe who doesn't smoke. He only uses it to light the cigarettes of beautiful women.'

He snapped down the lid. 'Spoils of war – I took this lighter from the body of an American fighter pilot shot down over France during our attacks on English airfields in the summer of 1940. He was a member of one of their Eagle squadrons. It's rather decorative don't you think.' He showed it to Blanche. 'Look at the engraving, that's a Red Indian headdress under an English monarch's crown. I wouldn't be surprised if every pilot in our Group has one of these before the summer's over, now that the Yankees are at war with the Third Reich.'

Madame Cazalet blew out a plume of smoke. 'Take no notice, Lucette dear. His brave exterior hides a sensitive soul – and he's something of a virtuoso on the violin.

There, you see? You two have something in common already.'

Otto smiled at Blanche. 'Does she play the violin?'

'No, Lucette is a pianist. She plays my old piano so well that sometimes I forget that the wretched instrument hasn't been tuned since Hitler ravaged my country.'

Schieder gave a grunt and straightened his sleeve. 'I think I can help you there, Henriette.'

'In what way?'

'Your piano, I'll have it seen to by the man who tunes our Steinway.'

'I wouldn't hear of it. You may have every imaginable facility at your disposal, Wilhelm dear, but I wouldn't dream of asking you to worry yourself over my piano. Half the keys are missing and it's quite beyond repair – isn't that right, Lucette?'

The commanding officer persisted. 'But if Mademoiselle Lucette plays it so well, it can't be that bad. I'll arrange for it to be seen to immediately, a complete overhaul if necessary. I'll get one of my truck drivers to…'

Madame Cazalet dismissed the idea with a wave of her cigar. 'You have a far better instrument in that hotel ballroom of yours. Now if Lucette could get her hands on the Steinway she'd really show you something.'

Schieder shrugged. 'Let's have no more

talk of pianos except to say that Otto is not only bad news for the enemy, he's also our Entertainments Officer, and a worried one at that. It seems we lack a reliable pianist for the forthcoming concert, am I right Stoeckl?'

Otto nodded. 'I was counting on Milch, all the men liked him.'

'Hazards of war, Otto, you'll have to find somebody else, somebody who isn't going to...' Schieder glanced at Blanche and then put down his glass. 'Why don't you ask Mademoiselle Lucette? It will be good for morale. She is young, she has a pretty face and she's a French civilian. What more do you want?'

Otto pinched his lower lip and brightened visibly. 'That's an interesting idea, Herr Kommandeur.' He turned to Blanche. 'I'd be most grateful if you could help us, Mademoiselle.'

A sudden burst of steam from the coffee machine almost drowned the singing. 'I'd rather not. I don't know any German songs.'

'The men will teach you. They can sing almost anything when they are drunk, and the concert isn't until the seventh of June, which gives us plenty of time to rehearse.' He playfully blocked his ears against another surge from the far corner. 'Let's join them and see if we can raise the standard a little?' As Blanche got up, Madame Cazalet gave her arm a reassuring squeeze.

She followed Otto across the room. The singers fell silent and the ladies at the bar pouted in surprise. Otto thumped the top of the piano and held up his hands. 'Gentlemen, I want you to meet Mademoiselle Lucette Moreaux, she is an accomplished pianist.' Blanche kept her head down in spite of the cheers and heartily wished she were somewhere else. Otto continued: 'This is Lutz, he cooks three hundred meals every day but I'm afraid he'll never make a pianist. Get off that stool and make way for the lady.'

The man shrugged, retrieved his beer and stepped back. Otto gripped the shoulder of another man and turned to wink at Blanche. 'Here's another musician, the ever-smiling Helmut Voss. I keep him so busy servicing my aircraft that he complains he has no time to practise on that spittle-filled harmonica of his.'

Helmut blew a quick scale.

Blanche hesitated. 'I prefer to play from written music but I might manage Gentille Allouette if that's all right by everyone.'

Otto's arm tightened around her waist. 'They know that one already, sung it so many times they've become heartily sick of plucking feathers from the body parts of French skylarks, gentle or otherwise. We like new songs, isn't that right lads?'

Blanche straddled the stool, her feet found the pedals, she spread her fingers on the keys and the men closed in around her. The sharp edge of a metal button pressed against her naked shoulder. Somebody's hand ruffled her hair and she had to swallow against something sour rising in her throat. Trying to smile she said, 'Let's start with this one. None of you will know the words so I'll say each line before I play it.'

An overhead light drew coloured sparks from her ring as she played. The men began to sing in a ragged unison of basses, baritones and tenors. The bar girls watched in mute surprise.

> 'Roll out ze barrel, we'll haff a barrel of fun,
> Roll out ze barrel, we got ze blues on ze run.
> Zing! Boom! Tararel! Ring out a song of good cheer,
> Now's ze time to roll ze barrel, for ze gang's all here.'

On the other side of the room the Commanding Officer's face had drained to the colour of cheese. Otto had collapsed onto a chair and the dog was jumping up, trying to lick his face.

Blanche played faster. The men sang louder inventing their own words and suddenly it was like an evening in the Old White Hart in England with servicemen and civilians crowding around the piano trying to forget that they might not be here the next time she played, not around any more, killed or missing, *missing, missing.*

Blanche got up off the stool, Otto steered her back to the table and pulled out her chair.

Schieder's face was white. His eyes were narrow slits and he failed to smile when Blanche sat down. 'I won't tolerate traitorous rubbish like that. For God's sake, woman, where did you learn to sing such excrement?'

'My father taught me, and soldiers taught him, British soldiers, his comrades in arms during the last war.'

Otto broke in quickly. 'I had no idea that Mademoiselle Lucette was going to play an English song, Herr Komandeur, but I was impressed. The men enjoyed it and I didn't have the heart to stop her.'

Schieder swallowed a full glass of calvados in one gulp. 'It's treason, Stoeckl.' His chin was wet. 'Treason I say – perhaps you are unfamiliar with the word.'

Madame Cazalet said, 'There's no need to get cross about it, Wilhelm dear. Music has nothing to do with politics. I'm sure Otto appreciates that fact even if you don't. You seem to have forgotten something. France and Germany are friends now, how many times do I have to remind you?'

Otto got to his feet and raised both his arms like a referee. 'Please, Mademoiselle Lucette, please will you perform for us at the concert?'

'If the Kommandeur allows it, I'd be happy to help in any way I can.'

Schieder crushed his cigar into the ashtray with a fierce twist. 'You are the entertainments officer, Stoeckl, but for heaven's sake try to remember that we are fighting a war in this God-forsaken...'

Madame Cazalet's wagging finger cut him short. 'Don't you dare lose your temper Wilhelm. Lucette is only trying to be friendly. I've listened to your Steinway more times than I care to remember – before the war I mean – at musical soirées in Hotel de Fleuve long before you people started using the place as an officers' mess. The Steinway is a fine instrument. She will do it justice.'

'All right, the young lady is free to come to our hotel to practise for the concert but only if accompanied by Otto at all times – and she must leave the moment she's finished and never play English songs.'

Madame Cazalet pinched his cheek. 'Who is a grumpy boy tonight? What you need is a nice day on the beach. The weather will improve soon, you'll see.'

'How many times do I have to tell you...?'

'That the beach is out of bounds, I know,

102

I know.' She turned to Otto. 'Why don't you take Lucette to the hotel this evening and show her the Steinway, let her get the feel of it. I can already see you two playing together. Duets are so friendly don't you agree?'

Otto shot a glance at his commanding officer before replying. 'Violin and piano, that's a nice idea for a more serious number. If you'd like to accompany me, Mademoiselle, my car is outside.'

Blanche got to her feet. *Christ, help me.* The rain was little more than thin mist blowing in from the sea. Chinks in the blackout curtain threw shining spears across the street. With high heels wobbling on the uneven cobbles, Blanche reached involuntarily for Otto's steadying arm as they walked together with the rain in their faces. The tang of salt was on her lips – and in her heart the fear of death was somehow beginning to relax its grip. Otto opened his car door on the passenger side and Blanche felt a brush of wet fur against her leg as the dog scrambled onto the back seat.

They drove through deserted streets. Was Otto 'her' man now? Was she about to become his property? Had she become another cog in Madame Cazalet's plan to mesh with all the other cogs in a secret plan to speed the downfall of Germany?

Stoeckl broke the silence. 'Thank God

we're out of that awful place, just in time if you ask me.'

'What do you mean by that?'

'You don't know Oberst Schieder. He can be volatile like a volcano, Mademoiselle. When the Commanding Officer loses his temper the party is over believe me.'

'My name is Lucette.' She spoke without turning her head.

'You are right. Let's forget formality, it has no place in a dangerous world.'

She watched the wipers on the windscreen. 'Are you in danger, Otto?'

'How serious you are. Yes I am in danger. Danger is my job but that doesn't mean I'm ready to die for some marvellous cause that I don't agree with. I want to live. I want to see the end of this business and die of old age many years from now with twenty grandchildren gathered around my bed.' Blanche glanced at his face, saw his smile and the way he nodded his head with suppressed laughter. 'You were wonderful, Lucette. You were wonderful and daring and to hell with old Stoeckl and all his boring talk about treason. How does that song go – *kiss me goodnight sergeant Major?* I liked it, never heard it before but you gave us a treat. This may sound strange but I have some happy memories of England. I was a student at Magdalen College in Oxford but perhaps it's different now. My happiest memory was the river, punting down the river Cherwell with the pole slipping through my hands and water running down the sleeve of my white shirt while a girl called Maggie Ellis laughed at me and made eddies in the water with her hand.'

Blanche looked into his eyes. 'And now you want to kill these people, all those friends you made at Oxford.'

He pushed hair off his brow. 'It's what I have to do, Lucette. I have sworn a solemn oath to the Fuhrer. He has my sacred promise and to a soldier that means everything.'

'Do you think Hitler is right?'

'You be careful. You can get yourself into trouble asking questions like that. As for me, I adore the Fuhrer but sometimes I wake up in the night – Oh God...'

'Go on.'

'It's nothing.' He continued to drive with the wipers making a half-circle on the glass. 'Damn Schieder and damn everything. I didn't like the way he spoke to you. He makes a great show of being my friend, comrade in arms and all that, but I have no time for a man who deliberately tries to upset a perfectly innocent girl who has offered to help us. As for the rain, it has its compensations. Bad weather keeps our aircraft on the ground and allows pilots to think of pleasanter things.'

'It gives you a rest from the job of killing the enemy.'

'Yes, and if you want to know why I kill the enemy I'll tell you. The British tried to annihilate us during the last war and I'm supposed to hate them for it. For your own safety I hope your love of English songs doesn't mean that you have sympathies in that direction.'

'One English song, is that a crime? Is it the duty of the occupying forces to dictate our taste in music?'

He took one hand off the steering wheel and wiped the inside of the windscreen with a cloth. 'Of course not, but you heard what Schieder said. France and Germany are friends – that's about the only thing he and I agree on. In fact we are more than friends. We are allies. Our two countries have been taking turns to fight the British for generations and here we are in 1942 continuing that long tradition.'

The car crunched over gravel and stopped under a tree. The blacked-out hotel was barely discernible. Otto made no move to get out of the car and they sat together in a silence interrupted only by the sound of the dog licking its paws.

He turned towards her. The curve of his cheek caught a glimmer of light and she could see his lips. 'Russia, Egypt, Africa – if things go on like this the whole world will be part of Hitler's Fatherland. The British are something else. Have you ever been to England?'

Blanche's heart was beating high in her throat. 'No, and I have no wish to even when this terrible business is over and Britain has been crushed to death. I could never bring myself to go anywhere near the place. I've never been abroad apart from Belgium. Everyone who comes from Lille has been to Belgium. But England, never – but you must know all about the place if you were a student there.'

He put his arm across her shoulders and she felt the touch of his finger against her ear. 'Oxford, must we go there again, back to my Student days?'

He opened the car door for her and his hand felt warm in hers. He told the dog to stay in the car and they entered the hotel through revolving doors.

Otto spoke to a man at the reception desk. 'When you've finished looking at that magazine, Gustav, perhaps you'd enter Mademoiselle Lucette Moreaux's name in the visitors' book.'

Together they walked down a passage and into a ballroom where men sat reading newspapers and playing cards. A white-coated waiter steered them to a quiet corner and Otto pointed to a raised platform at the far end of the room. 'There's the Steinway. Play it now if you want to, but maybe we've had enough music for one night.'

Blanche looked up at the ceiling's elaborate plasterwork. Heavy chandeliers cast bright reflections across the polished floor. She closed her eyes for a moment and raised a hand to her mouth, secretly kissing Peter's engagement ring. I will never allow a member of Hitler's gang to seduce me however attractive I find him.

The waiter brought a bottle and two glasses. Otto proposed a toast. 'To the salvation of Europe.'

She touched her glass to his. 'Salvation?'

Otto looked around and lowered his voice. 'Hitler is our saviour and I'll tell you why. Did you know that staple foods like bread were almost impossible to buy when I was a teenager? The price of a loaf rose from two hundred marks to two hundred thousand million marks in a matter of weeks. We had to resort to barter until Hitler came to our rescue. Imagine a world where money has no value.'

Blanche took a sip. 'Here's to a swift victory.'

Lowering his voice he said, 'Victory means the extermination of all who don't fit the plan – Jews, gypsies, homosexuals. Sometimes I wish I were back in Oxford.'

Blanche shook her head. 'I don't want to hear any more of this. Tell me what it's like to be a fighter pilot.'

'We never talk to civilians about our work. Flying is no subject for a woman.' He went on to describe his schooldays, how he moved to Crelingen on the river Tauber when he was seven years old. 'Our family spoke the Swabian dialect and I was bullied by my schoolmates until I nearly killed one during a woodwork lesson. I was severely punished for it but they never bothered me again. That's how wars start – playground fights on a bigger scale.'

Otto drove her back to the chateau. Half-way down the drive the dog put its head on Blanche's shoulder and licked her ear. He stopped in the stable yard and they sat quietly watching the moon blinking through gaps in a slowly moving screen of cloud.

The kiss came suddenly, hungrily, and a hug so tight that she could scarcely breathe. She freed an arm and groped urgently for the door handle. 'I have to go now.'

'Let me walk you to the door.'

'No, please, I prefer to be alone.'

'Can we be friends?' He let go of her and reached over to fondle the dog's ear. 'If the weather is like this tomorrow we could take Seddy for a walk.'

The dog thumped the seat with his tail at the sound of his name and Blanche looked at Otto but couldn't see his eyes. 'I'll bring a picnic and a bottle of Madame Cazalet's wine. We could find a beach and pretend we're on holiday, rain or no rain.'

'Beaches are out of bounds to civilians but if you're with me it won't matter.' He got out of the car and held the door for her. 'Pray for rain before you go to sleep tonight and be at the hotel by midday. Ask for me at the desk.'

She stood in the cobbled yard listening to the rustle of branches and watched the headlights of Otto's car flicking from tree to tree as he drove away. When she raised her hands to her cheeks the flush had gone and her face was cold. 'Yes, I will pretend we are on holiday. Yes, I will forget about the war and ... *no, I will never forget Peter.*' She entered the chateau. Upstairs she lay in bed and closed her eyes against the fear. She turned over and the stalk of a feather scratched her face while rain drummed steadily on the lead covered sill outside her window.

CHAPTER SEVEN

The Amputation,
Sunday 5th of April 1942

Madame Cazalet spoke through a curl of steam rising from the coffee pot. 'A picnic for you and Otto, that's an inspired idea but let's not be too extravagant. Cold horsemeat and stale bread will remind him that we civilians are close to starvation.' She bustled into the larder and returned with a joint of meat. 'Now remember what I said to you, Lucette. Everything you see on that beach is important to us – the type of sand – is it firm or soft. Look for fortifications and fences, concrete gun-emplacements and anything else you see under construction.'

Her smile exaggerated the dimple in her cheek. 'Believe me, Lucette, I know Otto Stoeckl. When he finds a hollow in the sand dunes for you to lie in, try to judge if it's deep enough to give cover for soldiers coming ashore under fire. Make sure you keep your legs together. Tease him a little. Denial improves a man's appetite.'

Blanche left the chateau with the meagre picnic clutched under her arm. She was beginning to have doubts, thinking the whole idea was ridiculous when a cart turned into the drive ahead of her. She stepped aside to let it pass and waved at the driver.

The rain was wrecking her hair and smudging her makeup. Suddenly the prospect of a horsemeat picnic on a forbidden beach seemed like a bad idea. She was trying to decide whether to turn back when a faint shout made her stop and turn. Armande was pedalling furiously towards her, wobbling dangerously and skidding to a stop with her hair stuck to her cheeks.

'Lucette, thank God I've caught you. Give me your basket and take the bicycle. Madame Cazalet needs you, and for goodness sake be quick about it.'

'But...'

'I can walk back. Go on, hurry up.'

Blanche got on the bike and pedalled back, bouncing through the puddles. She skidded on damp hay strewn in the yard and nearly crashed into the back of the cart. Madame Cazalet emerged from a crowd of girls. An RAF Flight Lieutenant lay face-up on the paving amongst them. The sleeve of his jacket had been torn off and a bandage, dark crimson and encrusted, had been roughly wound around his upper arm.

She dropped the bicycle and knelt beside him. His breath was coming in shallow gasps. While loosening the top buttons of his

112

jacket she noticed his Distinguished Flying Cross ribbon and pilot's badge. Somebody came forward with a blanket and Blanche showed the girls how to lift him.

Painfully, yard-by-yard, six girls edged the unconscious man through the stone portal and along the path. When a squall of rain swept along the edge of the building the material became wet and slippery making it difficult to hold. The man was of medium build but progress was slow. Madame Cazalet went ahead to unlock the basement door.

Twenty minutes later the wounded man was in bed on the top floor of the chateau with Madame Cazalet tucking in the bed-clothes. Blanche was worried. The man's eyes were flickering – mottled skin, irregular breathing. She knew the signs. She said, 'Septicaemia has set in, it's well advanced. We must call a doctor.' Trying to stay calm she added, 'He's dying.'

'I understand your concern, Lucette, but we always rely on Monsieur Tibault in cases like this. I already telephoned him to say I need a new hinge for my Louis XV bureau when I realised the man was badly hurt. He knows what that means. He won't be long.'

'I don't understand. Is Monsieur Tibault a doctor?'

Madame Cazalet looked at her watch.

'Nicole is downstairs now, she's looking out for him – and no, he isn't a doctor.

'But surely…?'

'I know what you're thinking, Lucette dear, but even our local pharmacist is a Nazi sympathiser. Monsieur Tibault, however, is a staunch friend of the French Resistance.'

Blanche took the man's hand and compared his pulse against the second hand of her watch, trying to tell herself that his life was every bit as valuable as her own, and that the fact he would soon be dead made no difference to the effort she would make to keep him alive.

Madame Cazalet was standing by the window. 'I've told Marcel Tibault that we have a qualified nurse on the premises so when he gets here he will be relying on you to help him. If I know Tibault our patient will survive and your knowledge of the English language will be useful when he's strong enough to talk.'

'This man should be in hospital, it's his only chance.'

'Out of the question.'

Blanche held the man's hand – it was hot with fever. She spoke to him softly in English. 'Try not to worry. My name is Lucette Moreaux. I will take care of you. Squeeze my hand if you can hear me.' His response was the slightest pressure of one finger in the palm of her hand but his eyes were lifeless, like narrow slits in yellow parchment. Blanche ran to the bathroom, soaked towels in cold water and hurried back with them.

Madame Cazalet continued to watch from the window. 'Marcel Tibault. He obtained a scholarship to study medicine in London and was chosen to assist a famous surgeon over there, Lister or some such name. He qualified in 1880 and returned to France to run a thriving practice in Lyons. Patients flocked to him from all over the country, especially during the rabies scare. He was in such demand that he was forced to turn down an appointment as lecturer at the Pasteur Institute. In 1901, rather unfortunately he was accused of unprofessional conduct and was struck off.'

She glanced at her watch and shook her head. 'My God, what kind of war is this when we can't even get chloroform without arousing suspicion? While we wait I might as well remind you that whatever happens here today must never be mentioned outside this house – and you mustn't be too curious as to why our patient was found half-dead in a farmer's barn. As long as we are at war it's dangerous to know things that don't concern you.'

Blanche stripped off the patient's shirt, left the bandage in place and covered his body with wet towels. Madame Cazalet remained at the window where a grey sky showed itself behind rain-spattered glass.

The long wait ended with the sound of footsteps on the stairs. A group of RAF men entered carrying steaming cans of water and bundles of towels. An old man followed them – thin, bent, shock of white hair and breathing heavily after three flights of stairs. He closed the door with a bang, dumped his bag by the bed and extended a hand to Blanche. 'Enchanted to make your acquaintance, Mademoiselle. My name is Marcel Tibault. I understand you trained at the Hospital Saint Michelle in Lille. A long time ago I had a rather unfortunate experience there but I understand that it now enjoys a wonderful reputation, or did before the Boche took it over.'

He turned to the patient, took a watch from his waistcoat pocket and applied a varnish-stained index finger to the man's radial artery. After a few seconds he looked up and the smile had gone. 'This is serious.' Leaning so close that Blanche could smell alcohol on his breath he said, 'The English have an expression that I like to remember at times like these – *never say die* – are you familiar with it? Let's keep that optimistic phrase in mind while we proceed.' He handed her a pair of scissors. 'Remove the dressing please.'

Blanche cut into the blood encrusted bandage and carefully peeled it away. The wound was like an open mouth with blackened lips on either side. In its depths she could see splinters of bone like rotten teeth. Tibault took a magnifying glass from his bag and, holding a handkerchief to his face, took a closer look. 'We will have to be quick. Speed is the key in cases like these.' He took a bottle form his bag and dribbled some liquid into the cavity. 'Please follow my instructions as we proceed.'

Trying to keep her voice down, Blanche said, 'Do you think he can hear us?'

Tibault suppressed a chuckle. 'Maybe, but I've yet to meet an Englishman who understands our language.' Turning to Madame Cazalet he said, 'Henriette, would you be kind enough to hold the man's arm in an upright position while I prepare my instruments. I want to make as little mess as possible and holding it up like that helps to drain blood from the site of the incision.' He hummed quietly as he arranged the contents of his bag on the bedside table – dressings, bottles, bandages, scalpels, a tenon saw, kidney-shaped dishes, a bottle of brandy and a short wooden stick. He muttered to himself while preparing his instruments. 'Nervous system dulled. Reaction to pain diminished – oh well, let's see what we can do.'

Blanche filled the dishes with carbolic acid

and sterilised six needles. Remembering to speak in broken English she told the men to soak towels in carbolic acid and place them around the patient.

After asking Madame Cazalet to lower the wounded arm, Tibault squeezed his finger and thumb into the angle of the patient's jaw and peered at his tongue which had a long, bloodless cut behind the tip. He gestured for the brandy, took a quick slug himself, tipped a generous dose into the patient's mouth and picked up a bandage. Blanche watched him roll it to form a tourniquet, which he looped below the patient's elbow, twisting it with the stick before securing it with a length of string.

'I notice how closely you observe what I am doing, Nurse Moreaux, but you will have to forgive me as I'm a little out of practice.' He licked an indelible pencil and marked the patient's skin with a bold line. 'Old Doctor Lister taught us never to cut into diseased tissue – always make the incision at least three centimetres clear of the rot.' Gesturing for the men to hold the patient down he added, 'I'll make it four centimetres for safety.'

He cut boldly along the line. Blood spurted. The patient opened his eyes and screamed. Tendons sprang back from the blade like severed elastic and the stink of pus mingled with carbolic acid was like poison gas in the small room. Surges of vomit threatened to choke the nurse from Lille as she pressed dry sponges against severed arteries.

Tibault threw down his scalpel, gave the tourniquet another twist and re-secured the stick. He picked up the saw and, with his left hand on top of the blade, cut a guiding groove on the exposed bone. Then, shifting his stance and leaning forward, he sawed with a frenzy that sent gobbets of bone mulch spraying back behind his elbow. The men struggled to hold the patient who continued to scream as the severed limb angled away and fell heavily onto Blanche's foot.

Tibault loosened the tourniquet by two turns. 'A man who has the strength to sing like that deserves to live. Give him some more brandy.'

He loosened the tourniquet by two turns, deftly refastened the stick and nodded purposefully at Blanche who picked up one of the needles and started to join the edges of the radial artery with tiny stitches, pulling each one tight before starting the next. She pulled too far with the seventh stitch and unthreaded the needle.

Just as Tibault was mouthing something, and pinching the artery shut with his fingers to staunch the flow, Armande burst into the room. 'There's a German officer downstairs,

Madame, and I can't get rid of him.'

Madame Cazalet dropped the towel. 'What in heaven's name does he want?'

'He demands to see Lucette.'

Madame Cazalet stepped back from the bed and crossed herself with a quick movement. 'Tall, blue eyes, in his thirties?'

'Yes Madame.'

'Lucette knows who he is. She'll have to get rid of him.'

Blanche put down her needle. 'How am I going to do that?'

'Take him into the kitchen and make him a cup of coffee. Talk about the concert if you must but in the name of the Holy Virgin get him out of my house. You know the rules, how many times do I have to…?'

Tibault threw his hands in the air. 'Mother of Christ how can I be expected to…'

Blanche was already through the door with the banisters burning the palm of her hand and her feet barely touching the treads. Half-way down, she heard music, piano music, why, what the…?

She forced herself to pause in the hall and took a deep breath. *Mozart.* She recognised the piece – fluent and subtle and sensitive, loud and soft, surging then quiet.

Dear God. Standing outside the drawing room door she turned the handle, peered in and saw Otto seated at the piano. When she walked towards him he glanced up quickly but continued to play. She stood beside him and kissed him on the cheek.

He stopped in the middle of a bar, stood up and grabbed her wrist. 'What's going on here, I thought I heard somebody screaming when I came in?'

'It's nothing. The girls are playing a game upstairs.'

He gave a humourless laugh, 'And what about our day on the beach?'

'I'm sorry.'

'Is that all you can say?'

'Something happened.'

'What happened?'

'The weather, who wants to have a picnic when it's raining?'

He shook his head in disbelief. 'Pilots play when the weather is bad, you already know that, how many times do I have to tell you?'

'What was that piece you were playing?'

'Something I've chosen for our duet at the concert, it's the piano part that you will be playing to accompany me on the violin. You are the pianist, not me.' He touched her hair. 'I'm not angry with you but when it's raining the killing stops and we grab the moment. We talked about it last night. Don't you remember? Why didn't you let me know? Are you interested in me or not?'

'Of course I am – in you, the concert, and in you and me – us, but now I must ask you to…'

'To leave, I know.'

'Please don't be angry with me.'

'Why not come with me now? My car is in the yard.'

'I'm needed upstairs.'

'Needed for something more important than spending the afternoon with me? All right, I understand. If you've lost interest why can't you be honest about it?'

'Perhaps tomorrow?' Feeling suddenly weak she added, 'I'm sorry Otto but we have a sick girl upstairs and I'm a nurse and ... tell me, why did you choose that music?'

Otto stood up, quietly closed the piano lid and smoothed his hand over the walnut casing. 'It doesn't matter. But this is a fine instrument. I can't imagine why Henriette was so dismissive about it yesterday. Every key works, it has near-perfect tone and it certainly doesn't need tuning. That woman may be an expert at gourmet cooking but she knows absolutely nothing about pianos.'

'Please Otto, I'm sorry about the picnic. I had everything prepared but I have to go now.'

'Go on then.' Anger was on his brow as he turned away. She followed him down the corridor towards the front door. Pausing in the hall he said, 'Tomorrow then?'

She didn't answer, watched him go down the steps and waited until she heard him start the car. After running up the stairs she re-entered the room.

Tibault gave her an exasperated look. 'I've dealt with the arteries. Now please be good enough to close the wound and apply the dressings. I have to go now. Talk to him in English as soon as he becomes aware of his surroundings. Tell him not to worry and that lots of people go through life with only one hand, including a good friend of mine.' He threw his instruments into the bag. 'He's all yours now. Still bleeding a bit but I've left plenty of muscle tissue around the stump so you'll have no difficulty making a neat closure. I've also left you with spare dressings, my last reel of absorbable ligature and a full bottle of carbolic. Good luck.'

Blanche threaded another needle but the expressionless face, the parted lips, bleached cheeks and half-open eyes – in her mind – created another face, Peter's face, a white face inhaling seawater and being sucked down in the wreckage of a ditched aircraft. Dadan said he had been burnt to death but was he right about that? And was he right to say that Peter was dead – he could be still alive – or was this a premonition? Had some streak of feminine intuition brought these images from somewhere far away? She shuddered. What did it mean? Had some herald of death stolen into the room to warn her of…?

She pulled muscle tissue together with

neat stitches and when the wounded man groaned she was glad to hear it because it told her he was conscious and capable of struggling to stay alive.

Madame Cazalet entered the room without knocking. She put a handkerchief to her face and opened the window in spite of the rain. 'This business with the Major worries me, Lucette. I'm afraid you'll have to forget about him for the time being. The Café de Paris can go to hell until further notice now that you have somebody else to occupy your mind. I wish I'd never taken you to that café – and as for you volunteering to perform at the concert, God help us. If I know Stoeckl he'll be hanging around here every day if this weather continues. Somehow we have to keep him away from here.'

Blanche wiped her brow with the back of her hand and continued joining lips of muscle over the stump. She would have to let Otto go – in the same way she had let every other man she had known, every man apart from Peter.

When she had finished the suture Blanche sat on the end of the bed and finally gave way to tears that would not stop. She tried not to think about the other man, the man she had loved, the man who kept appearing as an image inside her head, burning to death or drowning in the sea. She lit a candle, placed it at her bedside and prepared herself for the first of many all-night vigils.

Several times during that first night the patient shouted unintelligibly and she had to fight to prevent him from leaving the bed. When patches of blood showed through the dressing she unwound the bandage, applied layers of carbolic-soaked gauze over the stump and dressed it again with a Mackintosh bandage. The patient's temperature remained high. He was sweating and she continued to apply wet towels to his head, chest and abdomen in a desperate attempt to keep him cool. Many hours later she watched his face turn pink in the light of a crimson sun that shone into the bedroom through the arched windows.

CHAPTER EIGHT

The Recuperation

Sometimes, when she sat by the bed looking into his half-open eyes, at his parted lips, his bleached cheeks, Blanche could see Peter's dead body lying there. A posthumous medal for gallantry – she could picture that too – worn by Pete's grieving mother on Armistice Day. But she promised herself that this flickering soul who had faced a different kind of death and who was now in her care would become strong again, return to England and live to see his grandchildren.

Return to England – the phrase occupied every corner of her mind. She wanted to get away from this place, turn her back on Madame Cazalet and go with this man to England. She remembered something that Otto said about the long awaited break in the weather coming soon – and now it had happened – uncounted days of brilliant sunshine. Otto was flying, killing his enemies and would be far too busy to suggest any further meetings. Every squadron of Butcher Birds that roared seaward over the chateau reminded her of it.

Dozing on the chair beside his bed, Blanche sometimes tried to guess what kind of man her patient was, if he had somebody waiting for him in England, a wife maybe, mother, father, friends. Tibault never promised a miracle – but the miracle was happening – gradually, day-by-day. The crisis had passed. The wound had healed. The patient accepted spoon-fed soup without choking but he would not speak.

Blanche lay naked on her mattress by the window with only a sheet covering her, half-listening to his breathing, half-dreaming that she was on the sagging camp bed in the musty summerhouse under the trees at

Tarvin Hall – long ago when her mother was still alive, before the accident or as Father called it, *the bereavement.* She was nine years old and it was her birthday. The housekeeper's carefully prepared cake was already cut, candles blown out, crumbs on the plate. Blanche could see herself on that day, wobbling down the gravel drive on a brand new bicycle, turning by the gate without putting a foot down and pedalling back. But why had Dad chosen that moment to explain how Mummy had died? The Trades Union Council called a General Strike in 1926 but Blanche was too young to understand what it as all about– but later she found out that it had caused the death of her mother. Only when she was fifteen did her father explain that Mum had been killed by a stockbroker's clerk driving a bus. Stanley Baldwin, the Prime Minister, would never admit that he had allowed people who were unqualified to…

A shout.

Blanche sat up.

'Run, Philip. Run faster, run.'

She grabbed her dressing gown.

'I failed, I failed.'

She leaned over his bed and looked into his staring eyes. 'How did you fail? What did you fail to do?'

'Philip is dead.'

Blanche squeezed his shoulder. 'Who is

127

Philip? Was he a friend of yours?'

'*We failed to steal it.*'

'What did you fail to steal?'

But he closed his eyes, sighed, fluttered his lips on an unintelligible word and went limp. Blanche felt his throat and found his heart-beat strong and steady, and his forehead cool under her palm.

The following day, while feeding him, Blanche said, 'You came here in a cart loaded with hay. We thought you were going to die. We put you on a blanket and...'

He spoke suddenly. 'What is your name?'

Blanche nearly dropped the spoon. 'Lucette Moreaux.'

'My name is Eric Blakeny.'

At last, finally, after endless days and nights of anxiety and worry Blanche wanted to yell and scream and hug him and kiss his lips. Instead he said in a put-on French accent, 'Hello Mr Eric Blakeny. Please forgive me. My English is not so good. I am your nurse. I will help you get strong.'

'What's happening to me? My right hand – my fingers are hurting like hell, but I haven't got a right hand.'

She put down the bowl. 'It is normal to feel pain like that. It will soon pass. Do not worry about it. Tell me, Mr Eric Blakeny, what was it you failed to steal?'

He pushed the spoon away. 'What are you talking about?'

'You tell me in the night. When you were a little crazy you tell me.'

'What did I tell you?'

'You say you fail to steal something and you were telling Philip to run very fast.'

'I can't talk about it, I'm not allowed to.'

As the days passed Eric Blakeny became more lucid and although Blanche found herself drawn to him, he never volunteered any more information about himself. Sheer curiosity, however, compelled Blanche to repeatedly lead him onto whatever it was he tried to steal and the man called Philip. Eric, however, seemed determined that this dream, if that is what it was, would forever remain a secret.

In spite of this he remained cheerful and enthusiastic about another subject. 'If somebody is born with a natural talent, that person should practise and improve his talent. Do you understand what I'm saying, Lucette?'

'Oh yes, talent, I understand.'

'You have a talent. You saved my life. What else can you do?'

'I play the piano. What can you do?'

'I try to be an artist in my spare time – that was before the war. I haven't picked up a paintbrush since.'

'So you are an artist and you are also in the Royal Air Force. When are you going to tell me what happened to you? Where did you hide after you were shot down? Who brought you to the chateau?'

'If I had two hands I'd give you a round of applause. Your English is improving.'

'Please tell me.'

'Let's talk about happier things. When this war is over I'm going to buy a cottage in England, keep a cow, grow my own food and paint pictures. My farm will have a river where I can fish and a studio with a north-facing window.'

Blanche sat on the bed and laughed. 'I will come to England and I will milk your cow.'

'Have you ever tried to paint, Lucette? It's not difficult, you might have a talent for it.'

She paused for a moment, remembering once again the pretence, and the promise she had made to Dadan never to reveal her true identity. 'I paint the wall and the cupboard, and the fence in my garden in Lille – never a picture.'

'Portraits are my favourite. Did anyone tell you that you have an interesting face and wonderful skin? You have a pretty nose too. If you can find me some paper I'll paint a picture of you, a portrait. Do you know what a portrait is?'

She nodded.

'Then find me a brush, some paint and a piece of paper and when your portrait is finished I'll take it to England and hang it on the wall of my cottage and I'll think of you every day while I'm having breakfast.'

'You are not yet ready to make a travel, Mister Blakeny. Only when you are strong can you go to England – and maybe I can come with…' She bit her lip. 'I will ask Madame Cazalet about the paint.'

'Perhaps I could practise on her first. She's not as pretty as you so it won't matter if I make a mess of it.'

'Monsieur Blakeny will make no messes. If he make messes he will clean them up himself, huh?'

Halfway down the stairs, Blanche was overcome with the strangest feeling. Peter was the man she wanted to marry, but where was he now? The banister rail was cold in her hand as she went down the stairs. Can you hear me Peter? If you are dead I know what you'd want to say to me – get on with your life. But suppose I never get out of this alive. Eric has been with me for a long time now. Is it because I saved his life that I feel this way about him – or is it because Madame Cazalet says that women get hungry for…? What I feel for Eric is only hunger, it has nothing to do with love.

Breakfast was already in progress when Blanche took her seat at the table and Madame Cazalet raised her hands in surprise when Blanche told her that Eric wanted to paint her portrait. 'So he's human after all. A picture of me? Now there's a surprise.'

131

'He needs brushes and paint and paper.'

Madame Cazalet removed a speck of dust from her cuff. 'It sounds like a good idea. Painting pictures will be good for Mr Blakeny, it will help to occupy his mind. Let me see. I have ink in the bureau, red, blue and green. Maybe you could find some charcoal in the grate. There might be a few old paintbrushes in one of the outhouses or even a tin of paint. Just imagine – a portrait of me by an English amateur amongst all my masterpieces. Oh well if it helps the poor man to pass the time, who are we to deny him the pleasure?'

Blanche was determined that her man was going to paint pictures, enough to fill a gallery if that's what he wanted. She went out through the main door, walked down the path and through the stone portico to start her search for materials in the stable block.

A light breeze ruffled her hair when she reached the place where Dadan had parked his van – how long ago was that? She started to count the weeks on her fingers, could it really be that long – ten weeks?

A familiar sound made her look up to see a flight of three aircraft roaring low over the trees. Was Otto up there? Blanche kept her hands firmly by her sides because nothing would induce her to wave at the enemy like Dadan had done. On the ridge of the coach-house a squeaking weathercock turned its beak towards England. *How much longer must I go on living in this place?*

She opened the first stable door and stepped into a small room with saddles and harnesses hanging from a rack on the wall. There was a tin on the shelf but it contained saddle soap. A range of empty loose boxes smelled faintly of horses and she saw Dadan's barrow, the one he had used for his box of fish. Next was a garage containing an enormous automobile, like a small bus with buttoned leather seats and a massive steering wheel. She went round to the back and blew dust from the maker's plate – *Sizaire-Berwick. 1918.*

The last door in the yard revealed a workbench, some tools and finally a pot of white paint and a medium sized paintbrush standing in an empty jam jar. She picked them up, closed the door behind her, left the yard, crossed the path, walked between the vines and entered the chateau by the side door and made her way back to the kitchen.

Madame Cazalet was alone, rolling pastry on the cold surface of the marble table. 'Ah there you are, Lucette. I see you have found some things for Eric's picture painting. Leave them here and come with me. I have something important to say to you. Shall we go to my study?'

Madame Cazalet stood with her back to the windows. Her face was in shadow. 'I need to know if Mr Blakeny is fit to travel.'

Blanche hesitated. 'The wound has healed. He's no longer in pain but … why do you want to know?'

'Because certain people in England want him back urgently. Dadan has received a message about it.'

'He's not ready yet. He hasn't been off the top landing since he came here. He seems well enough but I need to see how he feels after taking some proper exercise before I can declare him fit to make the journey.'

Madame Cazalet shrugged. 'Then you must take him for a walk immediately, but that needn't keep him from his pictures. I've found four sticks of artist's charcoal, and a box of crayons. Let's see what he can do with those until we know when the boat is coming.'

'What boat?'

'The British will send a boat for him as soon as we give the word. You will be guiding him to the beach but there's no need to tell him any of this, at least not yet. The boat will drop anchor close to the shore. You will signal with a torch at a pre-arranged time and wait for the answering flash. They'll send a small dinghy to make the pickup. No flash no pickup. I'll give you the detail in good time. We have a detailed plan of the beach and Dadan assures me it will be quite safe.'

'If Eric Blakeny is going to England, I'd like to go with him.'

Madame Cazalet took a step forward. 'What ever for, why in Heaven's name would the British want to take in a French girl? Your place is here with us, besides I have other plans for you when Mr Blakeny has gone. In any case what about the concert? Otto still wants you to play and he wants you to start rehearsing with him as soon as possible. If we're not careful he'll find somebody else to play the piano and all my efforts to arrange that meeting will have been wasted. I know I was a bit hasty in some of the things I said about Otto Stoeckl when he came here so unexpectedly, but I was terrified even if you weren't. Somehow you have to resume your friendship and perform in his concert. Make them clap and cheer you and make yourself popular with the men. Endear yourself to Otto and the Commanding Officer. Do these things and you will have a season ticket into the heart of Maupertus Aerodrome.'

She touched Blanche's cheek. 'Perhaps we ask too much of our little nurse from Lille but think of France, do it for your country. For the moment I suggest you go down to the cellar and find some clean wine case lids because I was unable to find any paper suitable for Mr Blakeny's pictures – and don't forget to take him outside for a walk, once round the chateau will do for a start.'

Blanche left the study. She lifted the trapdoor leading to the cellar and almost lost her footing on the steps. All was quiet under the low ceiling except for the beating of her heart in the stillness. She walked straight past a pile of unused wine cases, straining her ears for the sound of men but heard no talking and no laughing. She turned the corner at the far end and stopped. The cellar was empty.

CHAPTER NINE

The Execution,
Sunday 31st of May 1942

Blanche picked up four wooden wine lids, tucked them under her arm, left the cellar, climbed the stairs and found Eric looking out of the window. 'Will these do?'

'No paper?'

She looked at him bleakly. 'If only you knew what we French are going through – the shortages and the hunger. Do you realise that you're the only person in this house who is never hungry. And I'll tell you something else, you're the only one allowed to use proper lavatory paper.'

He stopped her with a kiss. 'I must be having a good influence on you. Your English is almost fluent.' She wanted to stay in his arms but somebody was knocking at the door.

Dadan entered and paused for a moment in the doorway. He crossed the room, kissed Blanche briefly on both cheeks and turned to Eric. 'My dear Mr Blakeny, what a pleasure it is to meet you at last. I understand you have been in the wars, as you English say. Forgive the intrusion but Lucette and I have some business to attend to. Will you excuse us?'

Dadan pressed his hand into the small of Blanche's back as they left the room. Halfway down the stairs he whispered. 'It's good to see you again. Everybody is full of praise for the work you're doing here, but I'm asking you to abandon your nursing duties for an hour or two. I need your help.'

'If it's another amputation, forget it.'

He laughed, took her arm and continued down the stairs. 'Henriette tells me that if it hadn't been for you we would have buried our English friend in the vineyard long ago. I expect she's already told you that the people in London want him back.'

They walked together along the path and

through the portico. Dadan opened the door of his van, and the smell of fish reminded her of the first time she came to the chateau. 'Before I agree to go anywhere you'll have to tell me what this is all about.'

'I want you to meet an Englishman, another shot-down airman. I think that you and he might have something in common.' He dropped heavily into the driver's seat and started the engine.

Blanche stood firm. 'I'm not leaving here until you explain.'

'He's a pilot – downed by German anti-aircraft fire during a photograph mission. For the moment that's all you need to know.'

Dadan was obviously hiding something and she wanted to scream at him. 'You said I have something in common with...' She stopped on the word. This man – something in common with this man – why did he say that, what does it mean? It has to be Peter, why else would he want to drag me away from Eric's bedside?

Driving away from the chateau, Dadan continued. 'You of all people know how long it takes to train men to fly – and women too, let's not forget them.'

Blanche covered her eyes. *Peter – it has to be.* 'What's the name of this man we are going to see?'

'Can't be sure, that's why I need your

138

help. On the shelf above your knees you'll find something that belongs to you. Come on – I said on that shelf you'll…'

'My Pilots' Notes, I was wondering when I'd see them again.'

'Put them in your handbag.'

During the following forty minutes Blanche asked herself a thousand questions before Dadan turned into a farmyard and stopped the van. He leaned back, put his hands together and snapped his knuckles without looking up.

'What happens now?'

Dadan said, 'You've been here before but you won't recognise it from the outside.' He got out and went round to open the door on her side.

She got out. The sun was dropping behind the roof of a large barn. 'You still haven't told me what you want me to do.'

'Do you have a handkerchief?'

'Yes, in my handbag.'

'I'm going to ask this man a few questions. When he answers I want you to listen carefully to what he says. I'll also ask you to put some questions of your own. If at any time you suspect that our friend is lying, get out your handkerchief and blow your nose. Got it?'

'Questions of my own – what sort of questions?'

'Don't worry. You'll catch on.'

139

'I don't understand.'

They went into the house. Blanche followed Dadan along a passage and it was the smell of damp plaster that told her where she was. She could feel the fear she'd felt when she was here before, when she was a prisoner in this place. But who was the Englishman she was about to meet? *You have something in common with him.*

Dadan took a key from his pocket, opened a steel door and Blanche immediately recognised the barred window, the bed and the chair. A man got up, tall, unshaven – and for one clock-stopping moment … but no – it wasn't Peter.

He threw his arms around as he spoke. He had a Scottish accent. 'How much longer are you going to keep me here?'

Dadan pulled a chair to the centre of the room, gestured for the man to sit down and stood behind him. 'This young lady speaks your language. She will stand in front of you where we can both see her.'

The man sat down, but only for a second. He got up again, crossed the cell and beat his fists against the wall. 'What is this? Either hand me over to the Germans or else help me get back to England.' He turned to face them and Blanche could see tears of frustration spilling onto his cheeks. Then he shouted – every word amplified by the featureless walls. 'I've told you my name, my bloody rank and my service number. I've practically told you my entire life story so will you get the hell off my back and get me out of here. I need to rejoin my squadron. I'm no use to anybody banged up in this place.'

Dadan pointed to the chair. 'Sit down please, William Summerfield, born on July the fourth 1922 at number seven Beverley Gardens in Aldeburgh in the English county of Suffolk, trained in Canada under the Empire Training Scheme and now a Flight Lieutenant in the Royal Air Force based at Benson in Oxfordshire. Sit down please. We are here to help you.'

'Then for the love of Mike get on with it.' He sat down looking at the floor.

'Tell the young lady what happened to you on the afternoon of the twenty-third of April this year.'

He looked up and heaved an exasperated sigh. 'Why don't *you* tell her? You know what happened as well as I do. A Junkers 88 came out of the sun and shot me down. I baled out, spent half a day hanging in a tree, cut my parachute straps and bloody nearly broke my leg when I hit the ground. After burying my parachute I wandered around in the rain – fell asleep and woke up knowing that if I couldn't find a friend I might as well be dead. I was cold and wet and bloody starving. When the sun came out I spread my clothes out to dry. I broke into houses to steal food. Three weeks ago I was cutting open a sack of wheat when a farmer found me. Told him I was a British pilot and he said he'd help me.'

Beads of sweat looked like tiny slugs on William Summerfield's forehead. He pushed a strand of damp hair out of his eyes and looked at Blanche. 'You look like a sensible girl. Would you kindly tell the man who's standing behind me to make contact with England and check out my story?'

Dadan said, 'Tell the young lady what type of aircraft you were flying.'

'A De Havilland Mosquito, registration R5W – how many more times do I...? And what does she know about it anyway?'

Dadan continued. 'How long have you been flying this type of aeroplane?'

'Questions, questions, questions. One hundred and seventy-three long, boring and dangerous bloody hours – what's that got to do with anything?'

'The young lady would like to ask you a question about your aircraft, it was a twin-engine type, I understand.'

Blanche looked up at Dadan. What? And then she was back in that upstairs room in a French farmhouse, remembering how he had made her answer his questions. Flying Officer Summerfield's one hundred and seventy-three hours could hardly compare with her own, single forty-minute flight in a Mosquito Mark Two, and wetting her knickers with fright while trying to force a jammed undercarriage lever during the approach to Castle Camps in Essex.

'Go on, ask Mr Summerfield some questions about the Mosquito.'

She hesitated, reflecting on how much more comfortable her life would have been if she'd stuck to her original belief that war was a sin – and never getting involved, never joining the ATA, never arriving in this hellish country where everybody suspects everybody else of treachery. She looked at the man and wondered what Dadan was trying to achieve. She said, 'What happened to your navigator?'

'I was flying solo.'

'Why?'

'My CO told me to go alone, don't ask me why.'

'Where is the undercarriage selector on a Mosquito?'

'Immediately below the turn indicator dial.'

'And the booster coil switch?'

'Bloody hell, what do you know about it? Top right of the dash – and for your further information there are four of them.'

She saw Dadan step forward until the bottom button of his waistcoat was touching the back of Summerfield's chair. He said, 'Ask him some questions about England?'

He half rose from the chair but Dadan pushed him down and said, 'Ask him about his aerodrome in England.'

Blanche looked at Dadan. 'Sorry, I've never been to RAF Benson.'

'Get him to name a popular programme on the BBC.'

She thought for a moment. 'Who is Tommy Handley?'

'Never heard of him.'

'What do the letters ITMA stand for?'

'What's the point?' I don't listen to the wireless. Anyway, what do you know about it?'

Blanche opened her handbag – *handkerchief, blow my nose* – but changed her mind. She pulled out her Pilots' Notes and flicked through the pages. 'Here we are – the De Havilland Mosquito. On take off what boost is required?'

Summerfield shook his head. 'That's classified information.'

'Where is Magdalen College?'

'Cambridge.'

'Who wrote Winnie the Pooh?'

'Noel Coward.'

'What is the nationality of Winston Churchill's mother?'

'Scottish.'

'What school did you go to?'

'Sherborne.'

'In what county is Sherborne?'

'Kent.'

Blanche opened her handbag, picked up the handkerchief and inhaled a scent that took her back to her family home in Northumberland, lavender, she wanted to go on smelling it and walk away – but instead she blew her nose violently through dry nostrils.

Dadan hit the man in the side just below his rib cage. Pulling his fist back for a second blow Blanche saw a bloodstained knife protruding from the side of his fist.

He stabbed again.

Summerfield opened his mouth on an unspoken protest and fell sideways onto the floor, head twisting on impact, eyes open.

Blanche closed her mouth to stop the scream. 'You've killed him.'

'Mr Summerfield was a German spy. Thank you for confirming it.' He took a handkerchief from his pocket and wiped the blade. 'I'm sorry you've had to witness this rather unpleasant and violent side of my work but we can't afford to take chances.' He folded the knife and put it back in his pocket.

Blanche knelt beside the dead man. There was no breath. The carotid artery was slack. The eyes were open, already drying.

She looked up. 'Who is this man? Tell me, damn you. Stop looking at me like that.'

'He's a member of the Luftwaffe Police.'

'How can you be so certain?'

'You just confirmed it. In any case we don't have to be certain about anything. Suspicion is enough.' Dadan drew a deep breath and passed a hand over his forehead as if trying to erase the frown. 'If you don't like violence, Blanche, why in God's name did you ignore your father's advice? You should have stayed in England working in a hospital full of wounded sailors and blitz victims. Instead you chose to be a pilot and find yourself in the middle of a secret war fought by people who've never heard of the Queensberry Rules. Go back to your Mr Blakeny and be thankful you're still alive – but don't you breathe a word to him about what you have seen here today.'

Blanche stepped over the dead man, sat down in the chair and clutched the incriminating handkerchief to her face. 'What about all those others – Madame Cazalet's airmen – how do you know *they* are genuine? What about Eric?'

'We check everyone. We check their identity with London in the same way that I checked on you – unfortunately we couldn't do the same for Mr Summerfield because of the radio ban. You must remember that every time we help an allied airman we risk our lives. Look at us, who are we? We are nothing but a bunch of enthusiastic amateurs who run a complicated chain of safe houses. Who are we up against? Trained soldiers with limitless resources, including the Luftwaffe police who have started using spies or should I say impostors – all fluent in English, all trying to beak into our network by claiming to be Allied airmen. This man gave me personal details about himself but unfortunately I was unable to check his story with London, that's why I called you in. Thanks to the Gestapo's new detector vans I've been forced to impose a ten-day silence on all our radio operators until we formulate a new plan. In the end our Mr so-called Summerfield turned out to be like my van. He didn't smell right.'

'How will you dispose of the body?'

'That's my business.'

They walked back to the van and set off towards the chateau. Dadan explained, 'I don't mind saying this now, but when I was called to cross examine you after your un-orthodox arrival, I was convinced I was about to meet a German infiltrator, and I wasn't even going to risk radioing London about it. I even warned the farmer's wife that she would soon have a dead woman in her attic. Maybe it was your sheer arrogance that saved you – and your story was so far-fetched that I began to think it might be true. Either way you sowed doubt in my mind, enough to risk a coded transmission to London.'

As Dadan drove, Blanche noticed how he continually looked in his mirror and moved his head from side to side as if searching for something. He said, 'By the way, what does ITMA stand for?'

'*It's That Man Again* – a programme on the BBC that's supposed to be funny. Perhaps Mr Summerfield was a British airman who preferred listening to the Third Programme.'

Dadan said, 'The Third Programme, what's that?'

CHAPTER TEN

The Concert, Sunday 7th of June 1942

Blanche walked onto the stage and looked down onto row upon row of faces stretching away beyond the lights.

Madame Cazalet's diamond necklace flashed a defiant message of normality from the front row and next to her was Oberst Wilhelm Schieder. The sight of them sitting together, chatting and laughing, seemed to emphasise the danger and the deception that was now dominating Blanche's life. So far infiltrating the enemy's lair had been easy enough, but where was it leading to, what was it doing to her emotions? A German agent calling himself Summerfield had been murdered because he couldn't answer simple questions – who would be next?

Bowing to acknowledge the applause Blanche wondered where Dadan was at this moment. Certainly nowhere near this place. She saw Schieder fixing her with a strange look – was it suspicion, distrust, derision maybe – or was it the same glint of cold-blooded murder that Dadan had shown while raising his knife to kill the impostor. Behind her smile Blanche reminded herself that *she* was an impostor too, an actress on a dangerous stage – and something serious had happened to her conviction never to kill a fellow human whatever the circumstances.

She sat at the Steinway, placed the score on the stand in front of her and, to a background of droning conversation in the crowded ballroom of Hotel de Fleuve, she reflected on how lucky she was to be at this concert – frightened but lucky because she had renewed her friendship with Otto and the chances of her access to the secrets of the Butcher Bird. After so many weeks without seeing each other, Otto had been unsure that a single week would provide enough time to prepare. Luckily she had managed to persuade him, convince him she was up to it, and now the big test was about to start. Madame Cazalet was right. Otto was indeed a virtuoso on the violin and his infectious confidence and lack of seriousness had given Blanche some happy moments during their four short rehearsals. They had laughed together and worked together, agreed on the tempo and the pauses.

She focused on five-lined staves through unexpected tears, flats and clefs looked like blurry dots and in her mind she could see Eric falling on the path by the vineyard on his first day of exercise in the open air. He had caught his toe on an uneven slab, put out a non-existent hand to break his fall, but luckily no serious harm had been done apart from a grazed chin. He was at last strong enough to go to England but if the boat didn't come, could a one-armed man unable to speak a word of French be able to slip unnoticed down the escape line to England? For several days now Blanche had been dreading the day when she would kiss Eric for the last time. Something more serious than simple friendship had grown between them over the past weeks, but why did Eric still steadfastly refuse to tell her why he had been sent to France?

Blanche could see Madame Cazalet blowing smoke through the wrinkled O of her lips. And yes, that lady had been right to describe the welfare of Eric Blakeny as a grave responsibility. As a French patriot she was also right to say that when Eric was safely out of the way there would be more time to concentrate on the man who now stood centre-stage in full regalia. Wheedle information out of Otto as only a woman can – that was Madame Cazalet's advice – press him for details about anything remotely connected with the Butcher Bird because valuable time had been lost and the British were becoming impatient for their precious information.

Major Otto Stoeckl's playful thrusts at the audience, as if fencing against an imaginary opponent with his violin bow, brought good-natured catcalls and applause. The lights dimmed. He took the silk handkerchief she had given him, tucked it into his collar and gripped his violin firmly under his chin. Adjusting his music with both hands, he gave Blanche an encouraging wink.

She watched him with her hands clasped together in her lap. It was hard to believe that Otto's hands could produce such sensitive music when those same hands would kill Peter without hesitation if they ever got the chance. *But Peter is dead, why can't I accept that?*

When the moment came Blanche's fingers found the springy touch she had failed to achieve during rehearsals. Otto played with her, leading her, following her, loud and fast, brightly – and sometimes with a touch so fragile and haunting that it brought a lump to her throat. The first movement brought

151

memories of childhood, but tonight there were no faltering fingers in this strange place, this place of entertainment deep inside the enemy's camp. It was music – and music was something that rose above politics and death and the dangers of war. As she played Blanche was able to forget the moment, able to enjoy being Lucette and feel flattered that Otto had chosen her as his partner in the duet.

Clapping broke like thunder as the final notes of the duet faded. Men were on their feet with arms waving. A heavy bunch of flowers whirled out of the darkness, bounced off the Steinway's raised lid and burst on the floor in an explosion of pink and green. With exaggerated gestures Otto gathered the broken bouquet, handed it to Blanche, kissed her on the lips and put his arm around her. They took the bow together.

Oberst Schieder released himself from Madame Cazalet's embrace, stood up and turned to face the audience and waited for the frenzy to diminish before holding up his hands for silence. 'Ladies and comrades-in-arms, we are privileged to have witnessed a truly magnificent performance, and it makes me happy to say that even during these urgent days of war, men of the Luft-waffe and their charming guests can still appreciate music of the finest quality – especially when played with such emotion and enthusiasm by two wonderful musicians. France and Germany are working together now, what better proof do we have of that happy fact?'

Otto led Blanche down the steps and they sat together next to Madame Cazalet and Schieder while Helmut Voss played a solo rendering of Eine Kleine Nachtmusic on his harmonica with his usual smile giving way to concentration.

Blanche sat in the audience with her eyes closed, thinking of Peter and Eric and Otto – three men, all so different. They were her Nachtmusik, her unanswered questions and her confusion, her anguish and torment. Was it possible to love three men at the same time even though one of those men was dead? But it was another girl called Blanche Longhurst who loved a Squadron Leader called Peter Mason, it couldn't be Lucette Moreaux because Lucette was French and she had never heard of him. If Peter was dead as Dadan claimed, Mr and Mrs Peter Mason would never live happily ever after. Two strange men had emerged to complicate Lucette's life – and she was falling in love with one of them.

An earnest youth recited two unintelligible poems in German. A lively trio of cooks played a medley of marches on cornet, trumpet and trombone while, all the time, Blanche felt increasingly nervous about what

153

was coming next.

At last she retook her seat at the piano to accompany the long-awaited finale of massed voices from the audience. She placed the songbook on the stand in front of her and opened it at the first marker – *BOMBEN AUF ENGELAND*.

Now it was different.

Her fingers that had done so well with Mozart were suddenly hesitant, lifeless, sluggish, as if the bones inside them had turned to rubber. She struggled into the first verse, missing notes and losing the rhythm. The audience seemed to sense her mood and the singing dragged, weak and out of tune. *Kamerad, Kamerad...* Where was the zest they had shown during that memorable evening at the Café de Paris?

Blanche kept her eyes on the music but her ears failed to shut out the words. *Comrades we have our orders. Advance on the enemy. Drop bombs on England.* My England. How can I sit here and listen to these people? Her hands froze. The singing stopped and long seconds of silence were broken by murmurs of discontent.

Helmut Voss the harmonica player, stood up. In a loud voice he said, 'Mademoiselle Moreaux, do you remember *Roll Out the Barrel*, that English song you taught us in Cherbourg? We like that song, Mademoiselle. Please may we sing it again?'

Schieder got to his feet and was about to protest but Madame Cazalet grabbed his arm and pulled him down. The men were cheering, thumping Heinrich on the back and chanting, *'Roll out, roll out, roll out.'*

Blanche stood up and put a steadying hand on the piano. The shouting got louder. *'Roll out, roll out, roll out.'* She gestured for quiet and with a sudden urge of confidence shouted back at them. 'Will somebody turn on the lights?'

Speaking slowly, so that every man could understand her faltering German, she said, 'My father was a soldier during the last war. In those days the French were fighting on the same side as the British and Americans. *Roll Out the Barrel* was one of the songs Papa taught me when I was a child. All right boys, Helmut Voss requests *Roll Out the Barrel* but let's start with another English song my father taught me. Remember how we do this? I say the words before every line and we all join in.'

She sat down and tried to imagine she was back in the public bar of the Old White Hart at Henley with fellow pilots grouped around the piano. She said the words of the first line in a voice that carried to the back of the ballroom – and started to play.

Private Jones came in one night, full of cheer and very bright. Madame Cazalet's soprano threatened to shatter the crystal chandelier

155

hanging directly above her head. Male voices swelled together. *He'd been out all day upon the spree.* Helmut's smile, half hidden behind his harmonica, produced a tremolo accompaniment that bore little resemblance to the tune. *Kiss me goodnight, Sergeant-Major, tuck me in my little wooden bed.* Heinrich Voss stood next to his brother and waved his arms like a conductor, but behind the Steinway's raised lid Blanche could see Wilhelm Schieder fixing her with a menacing stare.

More English songs followed but before Blanche's turn was over Schieder was on his feet calling for silence. 'That's enough. We will have no more of this traitorous rubbish not tonight or any other night. Let us see if the Mademoiselle can play a good German song.' He made a request of his own, sat down and pulled his arm away when Madame Cazalet attempted to pat his shoulder.

Blanche had played the request half a dozen times at the Old White Hart but had never heard it sung in its original language. *Werd' ich bei der Laterne steh'n, wie einst Lili Marleen...*

CHAPTER ELEVEN

The Portrait,
Saturday 13th of June 1942

Eric, with the empty sleeve of his shirt pinned up and the other rolled to the elbow, looked up when Blanche entered. 'So here you are at last sweet little Lucette. Does this mean you've decided to sit for me?'

'Madame Cazalet is happy with her portrait. You paint it very good. She hang it next to a picture of women working in a field.' Blanche was finding it difficult to keep up the pretence and today her French persona was wearing so thin it was almost transparent.

Eric cleared his throat. 'Now it's your turn, I hope you won't mind if I ask you to take your clothes off. It's very warm in here.'

'You painted Madame with her clothes *on.*'

'But you are different and this painting is going to be different and there's no need for you to feel shy. You've seen what I have to offer when I'm naked.'

'Funny man. Nurses do it all the time.'

'What do they do?'

'They always are seeing men with no clothes on – it is the job we do all the day long.'

'But we haven't got all the day long. If we waste any more time we'll lose the light. Strip off and kneel by the window.'

'I do not understand. What is this strip off?'

'Naked, nude, in the buff.'

'What is this buff?'

'Just get on with it and stop asking questions. I'm going to take my time over this one because I want to get a good likeness and because...'

'Because what?'

'Because tomorrow I leave France, and because you are much prettier than Madame Cazalet. Let's leave it at that. Do you understand what I'm saying?'

Blanche reached down, grabbed the hem of her skirt, peeled off her dress in one quick movement and left it in a heap. Kneeling by the window on bare floorboards she said, 'Are you happy now Mr Eric Blakeny because I am about to catch my death of cold.'

'Very good, that is an English expression.'

'Already my knee is aching.'

He grabbed a pillow from the bed and handed it to her. 'I can't paint you like that.'

She put the pillow under her knees. 'Like what?'

'You look very alluring in your underwear but I must have you completely naked.'

She undid her brassiere, rolled it into a ball and threw it at him – and suddenly she was no longer Blanche Longhurst, standing up and slipping off her knickers. She knelt on the pillow. *'Vous êtes un Anglais très vilain.'*

'For Pete's sake speak English.'

She watched him fitting his wooden board onto the makeshift ease. *For Pete's sake* – how strange it sounded coming from him. That was one of Peter's favourite expressions, but Peter was in another world now and in any case he was Blanche Longhurst's fiancé who had never met Lucette Moreaux, this French girl kneeling naked by Eric's bedroom window, a girl who had never suffered the negative influences of an English boarding school run by celibate nuns.

Eric was looking at her with his head on one side. He had a stick of charcoal in his hand. 'I'm going to miss you when I get back to England. If only we could...'

'If only what?'

'Go there together, live together and forget about the bloody war.' He paused. 'Shift your position a little, as if you were looking out of the window, then turn your head sideways to give me a profile – do you know what a profile is? Light and shadow is what I'm looking for and I want to capture the curve.'

'What curve?'

'The curve of your *retroussé* nose – it's a French word in case you didn't know.'

Lucette Moreaux knew what she wanted – maybe Eric wanted it too. She said, 'Why don't you tell me why you came to France?'

He came across and gently moved her head. 'Sideways, that's the angle I want.'

She watched him out of the corner of her eye – working with his good hand, glancing up at her and saying nothing. Without moving her head she could look through the window at the tall trees beyond the vineyard. No sound came from the direction of the airfield but after a day of good weather they would soon be flying in before the light failed. *Please God keep Otto safe.* She closed her eyes and felt the guilt of a traitor. Lucette Moreaux had her own deadly business to attend to tomorrow night. Madame Cazalet had told her what to do at breakfast that morning and now, in the silence of Eric's bedroom, a lump of fear was growing inside her stomach. Dadan and Madame Cazalet were strong and staunch even though the threat of death hung over their every action – but was Lucette Moreaux brave enough for tomorrow's task?

Eric was surveying her with the half-closed eyes of an artist, taking in every detail of her nakedness, but was he reading her

160

thoughts and seeing through the screen that obscured the lie she was living? Soon the painting would be finished and Lucette would stand up. She would put her arms around him and to hell with his precious picture, and to hell with Blanche Longhurst and to hell with all this pretence. Make love to Eric, on the bed, on the floor, feel him inside her and...

'For Pete's sake, just as I'm getting the shape of your left breast you start to wriggle.'

'I'm getting cold.'

'I know. You are catching your death.'

'Do not be talking about the death, Mr Blakeny. You would have been dead long ago if it hadn't been for me.'

She could see an old man progressing slowly between rows of vines, stooping to tie green shoots onto tight wires that flashed in the sun. 'I'm sorry, I shouldn't have said...'

The diagonal panes in the window rattled in their frames as three aircraft flew low over the avenue, wheels-down and dropping out of sight behind the trees.

Eric continued to work with his charcoal squeaking on the wine-case lid. 'Have you always lived here?'

'No, I have told you already. I was born in Lille. I lived there until the Germans invaded my city.'

'So why did you come here?'

'Why should I tell you? You never tell me

161

why you come here hidden under a load of hay.'

'It's an official secret.'

Blanche brushed a hand across her forehead. 'I'm tired of secrets and I'm tired of kneeling here by the window.'

'If you must know I came in a boat. It's a long story.'

'And you are going home in a boat. Tell me all about how you came here or you don't go home tomorrow.'

'How do you expect me to paint your lips if you keep chattering.'

'Tell me.'

'I can't.'

'You came here to steal something, you told me so yourself. When you were crazy with fever you told me.'

'I can't tell you why I came here but I can tell you that German soldiers chased me into a barn and I had to hide under a pile of straw. One of them stabbed me with a bayonet. Next thing I saw was a pretty creature with a turned-up nose telling me she'd look after me.'

'But who brought you to the chateau?'

'How should I know?'

'And I haven't got a turned-up nose.'

He narrowed his eyes and looked at the picture. 'You have now.'

'Can I see?'

'Not until you tell me what made you

decide to live in this house with Madame Cazalet.'

Blanche stood up, walked towards him, stepped over the discarded dress, put her arms around him and suddenly he was smaller in her embrace, thinner, shorter. Pinning his good arm behind his back she kept kissing him wetly on the lips until he pulled away to breathe.

'Why do you live in this place, Lucette, tell me why?'

'That is also a secret.'

Eric dropped the paintbrush and they fell together onto the bed.

CHAPTER TWELVE

The Escape, Sunday 14th of June 1942

The moon was directly overhead, blinking through gaps in an endless procession of cloud onto a flat sea that stretched to freedom one hundred miles away from the beach of Anse du Brick.

Memories of last night – his intimate touch – his breath in her ear and now his breath in her ear again. 'Come with me to England, Lucette. After last night I'd rather die on this beach than go home without you. What will happen to you if you stay here and go on living in the chateau? Madame Cazalet will go on making you do dangerous things like the task she is making you do now. I don't want you to die.' His good hand pointed into the darkness. 'Over there on the other side we could make a life together when this lot's over. I can see it now – the farm in Sussex, raising a clutch of bi-lingual children.'

Lucette pressed her chin into the sand. Blanche Longhurst's home was over there on the other side, lit by the same moon, a moon ignorant of the strife and the lies and the love and the danger and everything else that was happening on the Earth one quarter of a million miles away.

She inhaled a breath of uncomplicated air and held it in her lungs until the words came out in a rush. 'Bi-lingual children – is that a proposal? Do you want to marry me?' She rested her chin on folded arms waiting for his answer and thinking about what can happen to a girl's judgement under a bright moon. But this was real. Salty moisture was wicking into her blouse and making her itch.

So, Lucette Moreaux goes to England with a passionate man called Eric Blakeny and when she gets there Blanche Longhurst emerges to tell Eric who Lucette really is. And when Eric knows the truth will he still want to marry a silly girl who crashed a Mark Five Spitfire into a French field? But if Lucette leaves France she might never see her German pilot again.

Eric's nose nudged her cheek. 'You must make your mind up quickly. The boat will be here soon.'

She raised her chin and stared at the moon's rippling reflection on a black sea. She looked at her watch – nearly two o'clock – just half an hour to go, plenty of time to think about the day when Peter proposed to her. Yes, yes, yes, she had said yes without hesitating – and suddenly she remembered something that Otto had said. *In my job we don't tempt fate with reflections on mortality.* Dear God she wanted Otto to live and it didn't matter one little bit that he was on the wrong side of this stupid war. But, *oh God,* was it her need to return to England that made her fingers tighten around Eric's wrist?

The exact moment was approaching. Madame Cazalet had been very precise about the details of this mission, but she still didn't know the true identity of the nurse from Lille.

It was now exactly two o'clock under the moon and punctual men from England would be out there silently watching the beach, waiting for the signal. Blanche pointed the torch and dabbed the spring-

165

loaded button with her finger, dot-dash-dot, R for Ready.

For what seemed like an eternity nothing happened but then, from somewhere far out, a point of light stabbed dot-dot-dot, S for Standby.

Standby meant wait, it also meant stay alert and don't be afraid. She looked beyond moonlit ripples advancing and retreating along the shoreline, straining her eyes into the darkness.

Eric saw it first, a dark shape moving silently towards the shore. They ran hand-in-hand, stumbling on the soft sand towards a tall man standing by a rubber dinghy that bobbed in the surf. 'Two of you? Bloody hell, nobody told me that…'

In a microsecond the tall man's face turned white in a blinding flash. *Bang, bang, bang, bang* – pebbles flew like hail in the beam of a searchlight shining from the road.

Blanche fell on her stomach with grit in her mouth and the chatter of gunfire numbing her eardrums. Streaks of light fizzed over her head and, from far beyond the surf, a bright flash was followed by the deep boom of a heavy gun – and something exploded on the road behind.

Blanche glanced back and saw running men silhouetted by the yellow fire of a burning vehicle.

POP. Night turned to day for long seconds

while a white flare burst overhead to reveal two men scrambling into a rubber dinghy. She wanted to shout at them but bit her lip instead.

German voices were closer now. Brakes were squealing. Vehicle doors slamming. Hand held torches probed the darkness, their beams crisscrossing as they searched the beach.

The moon jumped out from behind a cloud to reveal soldiers swarming down the beach, alert and swinging their rifles onto imaginary targets.

Dear God – the rubber dinghy was already twenty yards offshore. *Yes, I'll come to England with you. I will have your babies.* She had wanted to tell him while his sex was inside hers but now it was too late. He was going to England without her. Do I love you Eric? If I die on this beach will you remember me?

Sand in the mouth. Wait. Lie flat. She didn't dare to move until the soldiers had left the beach and were back on the road.

To her right she could see a promontory of rock jutting seaward, its outline visible by the light of a moon that was dimmer now behind cloud. She ran, feeling vulnerable and exposed – but no shout came from behind, no challenge no rifle shot, no bullet in the spine, no sudden death. With every stumbling step the shouts faded and, glanc-

167

ing back, the torch beams were fainter against flickers of orange from a burning vehicle.

She stepped onto smooth stones at the foot of the cliff, skidded, fell down, hit her head on something. Leaning against a wall of vertical rock she pushed hair off her brow and felt a sharp pain and the stickiness of congealing blood. The enemy would never find her now.

She stumbled on blindly until the shock took hold and she sank onto her haunches with sharp edges of rock cutting her thighs. She knew the symptoms of shock. Look after yourself, stay calm, deep breaths – like she did on the day she found herself sitting in a field with her head resting on the crumpled aluminium of a crashed Spitfire. For God's sake, Eric, why did you leave me on this beach?

Blood oozing down her cheek now and tasting like rust. All was quiet in her narrow niche of rock. Wait. Don't move. Rest. Don't think about what might have been. Why won't my eyes stay open? The poem again: *Come sleep, o sleep the certain knot of peace, the balm of woe, the poor man's wealth, the prisoner's release...*

The wind woke her, strong and howling around the rocks, blowing her hair into drying crusts that stuck to her cheeks. The clouds had gone. The moon shone high.

Water was lapping at her crotch. Rising tide. Frantically she looked for a way out. The rock face behind her was vertical. A wave struck her in the chest, lifted her off her feet, filled her head with water and plunged her down and kept her under until her lungs were bursting. She fought to the surface, gasping and choking – but the current was strong and swirled her along past the rocks like flotsam. My God it's cold, waves in the face, head up, shock again – dreaming – a child again, swimming with Grandpa in Stokes Bay and hearing how he was ship-wrecked three times and bobbed up like a cork every time: When two shells hit my ship in the summer of 1916 I was sucked down with her. I took in a huge breath of seawater and went to sleep. Next thing I knew I was in a boat, somebody was thumping me back to life. Did Grandpa feel the cold seeping into his bones and brain, was he so chilled that he could barely draw breath?

At last. When she reached down for the hundredth time the sharp edge of a submerged rock struck her toe. She could see moonlight on the sand dunes and now there was sand under her feet. She waded towards the shore on trembling legs but the moon was moving sideways, the sky was toppling…

She sat up and blew seawater out of her nose, opened her eyes under sticky crusts of blood and, through the scratched glass of her Rolex, saw that it was twenty past four in the morning. She stood up, took one step, and another, made for the dunes and was soon crossing the road, following the path across last night's field, getting closer to the chateau with every step. Slushy mud pushed between her toes. I *will* return to England. I *must* return to England. Madame Cazalet may have plans for me here in France but somehow – in some way – by my own initiative if need be – I will make my own way home. But where is my home now? She looked at the sky and addressed her prayer to countless stars stretching across the sky. Oh God, will it be Peter, or will it be Otto – and what shall I do about Eric?

The chateau showed one single chink of light from an upstairs room when she crossed the stable yard – and the basement key was under its usual stone.

CHAPTER THIRTEEN

The Lesson,
Wednesday 17th of June 1942

Madame Cazalet looked up. 'Lucette dear, I'm so glad to see you're fully recovered. That cut above your eyebrow wasn't very deep. I don't suppose Otto will even notice it.' She wiped her hands on her apron. 'It so happens that you're just in time to help us make a leek flan.'

Blanche peered through the scratched glass of her Rolex and checked it against the kitchen clock. 'I'm expected at Maupertus at two o'clock. Otto will be waiting. I'd better not be late.'

Madame Cazalet put her hands on her hips. 'It's not yet midday, Lucette, and in any case why rush? There's not a gentleman who doesn't improve with waiting.' She turned to her work. 'Armande dear, I want you to weigh out two hundred grams of flour and you, Hélène, one hundred grams of fresh butter if you please.' She picked up a sieve. 'Put on that apron Lucette and shake the flour through this, it's not only full of lumps but these days we also have to

171

watch out for weevils.'

Blanche rolled up her sleeves, sieved the flour, pinched out the lumps and found no weevils. Half listening to Madame's instructions she added salted water and kneaded the dough into a ball. 'That's right, now spread your dough into this tin and make sure you press it well into the corners. Armande, wash those leeks and chop them ready for the melted butter.'

Blanche wiped her brow with her forearm, looked anxiously at her Rolex and then at Madame Cazalet who was busy cutting slices of ham into squares. It was an embarrassing question but she needed to know the answer but ... *I can't ask her here, not in front of the girls.*

Madame Cazalet removed her glasses. 'Now spread out the ham onto your dough while Hélène beats three egg yolks with a cupful of cream.' She wiped her glasses on the corner of her apron. 'Season with salt and pepper, pour the mixture over the leeks and by one o'clock we'll know if our efforts have been worth the effort – but perhaps it won't matter, the Royal Air Force is always hungry and I'm certainly not expecting any complaints.'

Blanche washed her hands in the sink, dried them and lowered her voice. 'Madame, I have to ask you something rather personal.'

Over by the window, where she couldn't

be overheard above the clattering saucepans, Blanche whispered, 'You have asked me to seduce Otto Stoeckl but I...'

'Don't be nervous dear. That frown, really, it's so unflattering. Never forget that I am here to help you. If you've something on your mind you must tell me all about it.'

'I'm worried that I might be...' *My God, perhaps I am already.* The thought of it – the possibility that she might be expecting Eric's child weighed heavily.

Madame Cazalet peered at her. 'What is it, Lucette?'

'Please Madame, not here.'

After giving final instructions to Hélène she tugged at Blanche's sleeve. 'Follow me.' In the privacy of her study she said, 'I think I can guess what's on your mind but you'll be quite safe if you have followed my advice.'

'Advice?'

'Don't tell me you've forgotten already.' Madame Cazalet opened the top drawer of her bureau. 'Mercifully, and in spite of wartime shortages, Dadan keeps me well supplied.'

Blanche shook her head. 'What do you mean?'

Madame Cazalet heaved a sigh. 'Such innocence and so attractive. If I forgot to warn you perhaps it doesn't matter because I don't suppose – well – how shall I put it? Tell me,

173

Lucette, have you already surrendered yourself to Major Stoeckl?'

'He hasn't touched me.'

'Madame Cazalet took six small envelopes from the drawer and fanned them like a hand of cards. 'You have a simple choice, large or medium and there are three to a packet. I suggest you carry a packet of each size until you know for certain. Dear girl, I must apologise if I failed to tell you this before.' She got up and wagged a finger. 'But I'll not warn you again.' She shook her head and then smiled. 'I'm very proud of you, Lucette. Both Dadan and I are grateful for what you've achieved so far. I must confess, however, that I was – well – I have to say that I was rather suspicious of you when Dadan first brought you to my house. Please don't take offence but you must understand that living like we do, under the threat of tyrants, makes me nervous and I'm constantly on the lookout for impostors trying to work their way into our organisation.' She pressed the envelopes into Blanche's hand. 'While living here, you and I have become good friends but you haven't opened your heart to me yet. Yes, I know that memories can be painful but always remember that while you are in my house you are never alone. We all have fears and we wouldn't be human if we didn't. My fears come in dreams. German soldiers force me to do unspeakable things and I wake up realising how easily it could all come true.'

Blanche could see a different light in Madame Cazalet's eyes, a new mood, something that reminded her of her mother who died while she was still a child. She pulled up her sleeve to consult her indestructible Rolex but could hardly see the dial through her tears. She said, 'I really must be going.'

'Of course you must, my dear. Now that Eric has arrived safely back in England you will have plenty of time to give Otto your undivided attention.'

'Eric is safe, are you sure?'

'Dadan has received a message from England, let's leave it at that. I shall miss him. He was a sensitive man, shy but passionate, just like a true artist should be. I feel certain that one day his work will rank with Winslow Homer and George Weatherill.' She glanced at her desk clock. 'Gracious me, is that the time? My latest batch of airmen has to be clear of these premises by Tuesday and we have a radio technician and three new agents arriving from England next week, Dadan will be marking out a suitable strip for the night landing. You also have something important to do so you'd best be going.' She sighed. 'I have to confess that I'm a little jealous of you, Lucette. If I were a few years younger I'd be the one to flirt with Otto. I know how to make friends with German officers but that's not to say that you are incapable. Go on, enjoy him but for the sake of the Holy Virgin *don't give in to his desires too easily.* Keep him keen, keep your ears open and whatever happens for God's sake don't forget the envelopes.'

Blanche went upstairs and stood in front of the bathroom mirror. With both hands on the edge of the basin she closed her eyes. She felt giddy and guilty and dirty but a plan was incubating inside her head, a mad idea that was only just feasible and as risky as hell.

She looked at her reflection. Was it Lucette who stared back at her as she washed her face and combed her hair? Was it Lucette who said, I will start today and Major Otto Stoeckl will help me?

Rain dripped off her hair and filtered down her neck as she walked down the avenue, counting the trees – eighteen, nineteen, twenty, twenty-one. When she reached the concrete road the idea was still growing.

Approaching the horizontal pole barring entry to the aerodrome she saw the sentry with his collar up against the rain. He stepped out from under a sheltering overhang and pointed his rifle at her. *'Halt.'*

Raising both hands in mock surrender she remembered the Café and the piano, the concert and the wonderful moment when this man's brother shouted his request for an English song.

'Hello Heinrich. I hardly recognised you under that helmet. Why don't you put away your gun and learn to play the harmonica like Helmut?'

'You are the musician, Mademoiselle. When you play all the lads fall in love with you.' He looked furtively over his shoulder, cleared his throat and sang a quick snatch: 'Kiss me goodnight Sergeant Major. You were wonderful.'

'That was because of you and your twin brother. Both of you knew that I was nervous and yet you shouted encouragement in front of all those people.' With the long pole still separating them she said, 'Do you remember that night in the Café de Paris when we first met? Helmut was playing his harmonica and Major Stoeckl told me that one day it would make him famous. But like him you are a mechanic. What are you doing out here?'

'Oberfeldwebel Milch gave me extra guard duty. He didn't like my hair, said it was too long and made me shave my head.' He pushed back his helmet to show her. 'When this war's over I'll slit his throat.'

Blanche leaned over the barrier and patted his arm. 'When the war is over the killing will be over too.'

177

'Why don't you write a song about it, Mademoiselle? The killing is over but the English must die. The boys will sing it in the Café de Paris and Helmut will accompany you on his harmonica.'

'Let me pass now, Heinrich. I'm meeting someone at the hotel.'

'Oh yes, Mademoiselle, I nearly forgot. I have a message from the Major.'

'Tell me.'

'Only if you promise to play for us again.'

'Come on, Heinrich. I'm getting wet and so are you.'

'Major Stoeckl has been delayed. He asks that you wait for him in the ballroom.'

Blanche took a step back. 'Take my advice and grow your hair.' He raised the barrier and she walked towards the hotel past rows of huts and hastily constructed buildings. The rain was in her face when she crossed the gravelled approaches and pushed in through the revolving doors of Hotel de Fleuve.

Feldwebel Haufschild got up from his chair behind the reception desk and put down his newspaper. 'The Major has asked me to say that he will join you shortly, Mademoiselle. Please find a seat in the ballroom.' He smiled. 'The piano stool perhaps?'

'No thank you Gustav. Oh, I nearly forgot to ask you if you are fully recovered after your wild birthday party.' Without waiting for an answer she walked along the corridor, entered the ballroom and found a chair by the north window. On the far side of the airfield a row of black hangars appeared like shapeless mounds behind a steady drift of rain. No more duets, no more concerts. Things were different now, the game had changed. Acquiring information in exchange for sex was a dangerous occupation and death would be the penalty if her pretence were discovered.

But the idea continued to grow in her mind and action was needed. It was no use hoping that the war would go away and fade out and blow away with the rain. She could imagine her father trying to defend the family home from German invasion with his shotgun and dying in the attempt. She needed to see him again and she wanted to see Eric too. Blanche shifted in her seat and watched the second hand of her Rolex ticking round the dial.

After a long wait, Otto entered the ballroom with the dog at his heels.

She pointed up at the gilded clock. 'Where have you been?'

'Forgive me. The young ones pick up these things in a flash but how can an old man like me absorb all this stuff about the new A-4 inside twenty minutes?'

'Twenty minutes? I've been waiting here for...'

'That's enough. Do we go for a walk or do we sit here arguing? It's the English who are obsessed with punctuality, what makes you want to copy them?'

She said, 'Let's walk across the fields behind the hotel, then we could cut back through the woods and follow the stream back to the aerodrome.' She could feel betrayal on her face, to hide it from him she bent down to fondle the dog's ear. 'You'd like that wouldn't you Seddy?'

Otto took her arm. They left the hotel and walked out in the country under a light fall of rain with Seddy running in front with his nose to the ground. Sodden fields stretched away on either side. Blanche wanted to keep the conversation sharply focused on the subject of flying but, at the same time, she couldn't help but feel happy when she was with this man. 'Is the Butcher Bird a difficult aircraft to fly?'

'Do we have to talk about flying?'

'I worry about you that's all. Can't you understand?'

'I have a lucky charm that keeps me safe so there's no need to worry. My last crash happened a long time ago, before I met you so forget it.'

'Tell me about it.'

He sighed. 'I had two bullet holes in my left wing and one in my shoulder. I lost control on landing and dislocated my left

180

knee – but that was nothing compared to the pain I had suffered twenty minutes earlier when I saw my wingman crash into the sea.'

'Was he shot down by a Spitfire?'

Otto laughed. 'Hey, yesterday you told me you knew nothing about aeroplanes.'

'I've heard of Spitfires, who hasn't?'

'It was a fishing boat. We approached too fast. I blame myself for it. Some of our fire raked the trawler but most of it splashed short. A long burst from the enemy's Lewis gun went straight into my wingman's engine. I could hardly believe that a Focke-Wulf 190 could fall to a weapon designed more than thirty years ago. I wrote my report in the sickbay.'

The rain was cold on her cheek when she looked up at him. 'The Channel is such a narrow barrier. Can we really prevent the enemy from crossing it? Surely you don't carry enough fuel to patrol our coast all the way from Calais to Cherbourg?'

'In heaven's name what's making you so inquisitive?'

'I'm anxious for you and I'm wondering what's gong to happen to my country when the war's over.'

He laughed. *Our* country.' He made a passable imitation of his commanding officer. 'Never forget that France and Germany are one country now, they are one-and-the-same and united forever.' He steered her towards the wood while Seddy hunted away in front. 'We need more aircraft but we'll never give in. We have a score to settle. All through my boyhood years and up to the present day I've never been able to forgive my enemies. Take the death of my wingman – I realise it was an act of war but it has to be avenged. Steinhover was my friend. An English fisherman deserves to die for killing him. Vengeance is mine, saith the Lord, I will repay.'

Blanche couldn't imagine herself wanting to kill an innocent man – and yet she had as good as murdered Mr Summerfield. She wanted to ask Otto why he wanted to murder an innocent fisherman but all she could think of was, 'I wish I could help you in some way.'

They stopped under dripping trees and stood close together. 'You've already helped me by performing at the concert and making it such a success. Last year Leutnant Gunther was the pianist and somehow he managed to persuade the men to sing *Hark, Hark the Lark* and *Come Thou Monarch of the Vine*. It wasn't a success.'

'Maybe a solo performance would be better suited to his style. Why didn't you ask him to play for you this year?'

'Because he's in England. His body is lying somewhere off the coast of Plymouth.'

They came out of the wood and continued

along muddy footpaths, crossed a field of green wheat and came closer to the aerodrome. Otto turned up the collar of his flying jacket. 'Perhaps the concert wasn't so important when you compare it to bigger events. Russia, Egypt and Africa, perhaps the whole world, will become part of the New Fatherland. The British will become part of it too whether they like it or not. This may sound strange to you, but I have fond memories of England. Oxford in the summer of 1930 and the river Cherwell, Magdalen College, cricket pavilions, cucumber sandwiches, open-air concerts on the quadrangle rudely interrupted by chimes from the clock tower. Hot afternoons long ago in another world and in another time – Oxford bells, the smells of good things in picnic baskets. Champagne corks floating in the river. I was awarded a degree in English but how can a modern person hope to understand the meaning of Chaucer? Shakespeare was different, he saw the lighter side of war through the stumbling English of a French king's daughter in Henry the Fifth. *Is it possible dat I should love de enemy of France?* My God, how apt is that question today?'

While watching the dog investigate the entrance to a rabbit hole, Blanche began to think again about her plan, but this time in a calmer more rational way. She put her arm through Otto's. 'While we were rehearsing for the concert you said something about an officers' ball. Have you thought any more about it?'

'I wanted to keep that as a surprise but, since you ask, Oberst Schieder has agreed to the idea and we plan to hold it next Sunday evening in the hotel ballroom. It should be a good party because coincidentally we will be celebrating a happy occurrence on the same night.'

'Don't tell me – your birthday.'

'Evil woman, don't you know that we never tempt fate by talking about birthdays in the Luftwaffe?'

'Why ever not?'

'I've told you already. The life of a pilot is short enough without tempting fate to shorten it further.'

'So what's the celebration?'

'It doesn't concern you.'

She could see a softening in his eyes, a smile and damp hair falling across his forehead. 'Please, Otto, please tell me.'

'What's the matter with you today?'

'I just want to know everything about you, what you are doing and what you are thinking – but you are a man. I can't expect you to understand such things.'

'Very well, we will be celebrating the arrival of the latest version of the Focke-Wulf 190. Three of them will be flying in from Bremen on Saturday morning.'

Something rose in her throat. 'It sounds like a lot of fuss for nothing.'

He took her gently by the shoulders. 'Will you be my partner at the ball?'

Don't give in too easily. 'What makes you think I'd want to celebrate the arrival of three A-4s?'

He pushed her away violently. 'Who said anything about A-4s?'

'You did. You said you were late because you'd been attending a lecture about the A-4, you told me so yourself. Don't look at me like that. Do you think I'm a spy or something?'

'I'm sorry. Please forgive me. I'm not myself these days, but I would feel honoured if you would be my partner at the ball. After your performance at the concert I won't be the only man to be disappointed if you don't dazzle us with your presence.'

Don't give in too easily. 'I want to be your friend but I don't want to go to the ball with you, and no amount of flattery will make me change my mind.'

'For goodness sake woman, what's got into you? First you love me then you don't. I'll never understand French people, especially the women. Would you prefer me to pick up some tart from the Café de Paris sand take *her* to the ball instead?'

Don't give in too easily. 'I'm a French cookery student and you are a German

185

airman who happens to speak my language. What makes you think we have anything in common?'

They walked along the edge of the stream and Otto threw a stick into the water. Seddy went in after it grabbed it in his jaws and sped away. *Don't give in too easily* – but playing hard-to-get with the man you were falling in love with wasn't easy, and she needed Otto for another reason. He was part of the plan. She slipped her arm through his and they walked together under the rain. 'What's that dog of yours doing now? He's got his head stuck.'

Otto laughed. 'He has a good nose for vermin. One day Scheider surprised me by suggesting that I lend him to the Luftwaffe Police to sniff out a man who went into hiding after trespassing on our airfield.'

'When was that?'

'Sometime in March if I remember rightly. There were two of them but one got away. They must have come ashore from an enemy submarine. Schieder was convinced he was the target of an assassination attempt but between you and me I don't think he's important enough for the enemy to mount such an elaborate plan. The dead man was carrying identity papers in the name of Philip O'Leary. We gave him a Christian burial and a headstone. You see, Lucette, chivalry is still alive in spite of this hellish war.'

The rain was like ice on Blanche's flushed cheek. *Run, Philip. Run faster, run.* Eric had shouted those words – and now she wanted to run too, away from danger away from everything. Otto's arms were around her and he was the enemy and she loved him – and – but – maybe – *Jesus help me.* The dog's nose was against her leg. Seddy was placing the stick next to her foot and throwing it as hard as she could helped ease the tension while the plan was developing inside her head.

'Why does the wet weather stop pilots from flying?'

He looked at her with tired eyes. 'It's not the rain. It's the visibility, or lack of it. Bad weather keeps wise pilots on the ground but our mechanics never stop. They repair our aircraft, strip down engines, patch, paint and test. Ten new A-3s flew in just before the weather clamped in and they need attention now – guns to test, bomb-racks to attach, compass-deviation cards to be written, windscreen de-icers to fit, and radios.'

Blanche looked across the airfield to where six aircraft were parked out on the grass under stretched tarpaulins. 'Were you a pilot before the war?'

'I served with the Kondor Legion in 1936.'

'What's that?'

'The Fuhrer sent us to Spain to gain combat experience.' He threw the stick again.

'They told us to attack Spanish villages, but I didn't enjoy murdering folk who had no wish to harm the German Nation. I was given a medal for it nonetheless.'

'Was that the one you were wearing at the concert?'

'Yes, I wear it on all special occasions, also when flying because I believe it brings me luck.' He gave her a quick glance. 'Now why should I tell you that? I don't even talk to my comrades about it.'

'What else don't you talk about?'

'What I think about the future. How people will judge Germany when this war is over. Are we criminals? It was a crime to kill Spanish peasants in a defenceless mountain village but I had no choice because a madman ordered me to do it. If I'd refused that painful duty my life would have ended in front of a firing squad.'

Blanche said, 'That's what war does to us. We all get caught up in it in different ways.' In her mind she could see Mr Summerfield falling sideways off the chair and it was as if her own hand had made the fatal thrust. She said, 'Why are you talking about war if it makes you feel guilty?'

After a long pause he said, 'Perhaps it will be over a lot sooner than you think.'

'Why do you say that?'

'Because Hitler might die. He might be killed before he has a chance to bring further disgrace on our nation. I have sworn to be loyal to the Fuhrer and risk my life for him but tell me Lucette – answer me this question – who is the real enemy?'

She searched his eyes. Was this a test? Was Otto testing her loyalty to the so-called alliance between France and Germany, or was he showing genuine shame for the crimes of the Third Reich?

He said, 'Don't look so scared, Lucette. We know each other and we like each other and that means that we have no reason to keep secrets from each other. Give me your honest opinion. If you were the dictator of Germany would you be persecuting Jews and suppressing freedom in every country you conquered?'

She said warily, 'I'll never understand these things so don't ask me about them.'

They walked arm-in-arm, getting closer to the aerodrome with every step. She said, 'Tell me about the Focke-Wulf 190.'

'It's a glorious aeroplane. It's not good that the English have christened it the Butcher Bird. And these are glorious times for fighter pilots, especially now that I belong to the Gruppenstab Trio.'

He stopped to ease the stick from Seddy's jaws. 'Did you know that this dog is your compatriot? I rescued him from an abandoned farmyard near Calais in the summer of 1940. Those were strange times. When we took over the local airfield we couldn't understand why everybody ran away. Farmers abandoned their homes. Cows were bellowing to be milked. Pigs were starving. Some of our men milked the cows and although Seddy was little more than a skeleton when I found him, he soon developed a taste for milk and grew strong on it. In those days a stagnant ditch marked the boundary of our airfield. Seddy used to swim there and come home stinking. It's a funny thing but whenever he gets wet the smell of him reminds me of those days – those ten-minute dashes across the Channel from Dover with the smell of wet-dog on my clothes. Imagine six Messerschmitts in a Schwärher coming out of a dive and separating into pairs, Rottenführer and Rottenhund roaring into Pegwell Bay over the fierce defences of Ramsgate. Put yourself in the cockpit. Imagine Manston aerodrome – little more than a cluster of huts – racing towards you and a green blur of grass three metres below your wing. A petrol-bowser is enlarging in your gun sight, parked Hurricanes are bursting into flames. Afterwards you curve away to fly back over the Channel with magazines empty and fuel tanks almost dry.'

They continued to talk about the Luftwaffe until they reached a line of parked aircraft. Blanche stooped to pick up a screwdriver stuck upright in the ground in front of the

190

first one. 'Somebody will be looking for this.'

He took it from her and pushed it back into the turf. 'It's there for a purpose. It shows a pilot that this aircraft has been re-fuelled, re-armed and is ready to fly.'

Blanche looked at the row of five hangars at the edge of the flying field. 'Ever since I was a little girl I've always wanted to be a pilot. I'm completely ignorant about aircraft but one day I'd like to fly my own plane round the world – like that English girl, what was her name? Amy something – Amy Johnson.'

He laughed. 'You wouldn't get very far in one of these. Seventy minutes flying time is the absolute limit on the fuel we carry but that's more than enough to create havoc over the Channel, but just imagine what will happen when Goering tells us to attack the English mainland.'

'How can you fight if you don't fly over the enemy's country?'

'Messerschmitts and Heinkels from other aerodromes deal with the British on their home ground. Our Butcher Birds attack ships and when British fighters come to de-fend the ships we shoot them down. The first Focke-Wulf pilot who flies over Eng-land will be a very popular man. He'll have the whole of the RAF after him.'

'But *why* don't you fight the enemy over England?'

'Because the FW190 is a secret. It must not fall into enemy hands, at least not yet.'

'What is so secret about it?'

'I'm not allowed to tell you so forget it.'

'I'd like to sit in the cockpit and imagine myself defending France.'

'You are a woman. Dealing with death is a man's game and dear God let it always be so. You are a strange person Lucette. I'll never understand what goes on under those curls. Forget about aeroplanes. Think about dancing and Strauss music, the rhythm and the magic and skirts flying. Think of Schieder getting drunk and everybody having a wonderful time. Go on, change your mind and accompany me to the Officers' Ball where you'll spread excitement and envy amongst my friends and make them realise that life's pleasures go beyond bottles of well-chilled Mumm de Cramant and the hard-working harlots of Cherbourg. Pin up your hair the way you wore it on the night we met in the Café de Paris. For one night at least you and I can pretend that the world is at peace.'

'What do German fighter pilots know about peace?'

'I remember it in the days when flying was just a game. We used to roar so low over French sunbathers that we could see them blocking their ears against the din. They'd look up and wave at our formation as we dashed along the coast between Dieppe and Le Havre. I don't suppose any of them realised how close we were to war.'

Blanche pointed to the nearest hangar. 'Is this where the mechanics work on your aircraft? Can we go in?'

'It's against regulations.'

'Please?'

'It is no place for a civilian.'

'I'd do anything to be allowed in there.'

'Would you sleep with me?'

'Maybe.'

'When?'

'After the ball.'

The hangar doors were open. Powerful lights lit the interior. They walked in together leaving wet footprints on the concrete. Fumes of oil, varnish and high-octane fuel hung in the air. Blanche counted seven aircraft. A man was sitting in the cockpit of the nearest one with only the top of his head showing. He looked up as they approached and raised an oily hand.

Blanche recognised him immediately as Helmut Voss, twin brother of the man at the gate.

Helmut nodded an acknowledgement to Blanche and said to Otto, 'The canopy actuator is engaging correctly at last, Herr Major, but the left runner is still slightly out of line.'

Otto shook his head. 'Don't you ever stop?'

'Not until everything is in working order, Herr Major.'

Otto turned to her. 'Hear that? This man and his twin brother are much more than mere mechanics. They are my loyal friends and will spend half the night if need be, fussing over my aeroplane to get it exactly right. Sometimes, when I leave the hotel and take a walk across the airfield in the middle of the night, I find them working. This mechanic and his brother are my comrade in arms, without them I would have been killed long ago.'

Helmut climbed down and wiped his hands on cotton waste. 'Mademoiselle Moreaux, welcome to Hangar Number Five.'

Before Blanche could answer Otto said, 'Helmut, how many times have I told you to keep the hangar doors closed? Even at night you leave them open. It's against blackout regulations.'

'It's the atmosphere in here, Herr Major. We would suffocate on the fumes if we kept the doors shut. Give me the right materials and I'll build an extractor system. Until then we'll have to keep the doors open while we're working.'

'I'll talk to Oberst Schieder about it. Now tell me this, is my DKW fit to drive?'

Helmut jerked his head in the direction of a small car that Blanche recognised immediately. 'I have made new parts for the magneto but don't try to make her fly. Spare parts are impossible to obtain these days.'

Otto turned to Blanche. 'When this war is over Helmut and his brother are going to join me in a business venture – that's if we survive.'

The two men began to talk to each other in German. Blanche tried to listen but something caught her eye and she wandered away for a closer look. A grease-stained book was lying on a workbench. *BMW 801-D Kommandgerat für Flugmotor.* Another book close to it was entitled, *Handbuch und Teilüberholungsanleitung für die Flugmotoren BMW 801-D.* She walked back and interrupted the conversation. 'A business venture together, what kind of business will that be?'

Otto said 'A repair shop, that's the favourite idea – motorcycles and classic cars. There should be a big demand when people can get their vehicles back on the road.'

She wandered casually towards the workbench and picked up one of the books. 'What's this?'

Otto moved across. 'Give me that.' He snatched it out of her hand, picked up the other book and put them out of reach on a high shelf above the bench.

Blanche tried to sound unflustered. 'Heinrich won't be much help to you today, not while he's on extra guard duty.'

Otto looked at her. 'How in God's name do you know that?'

'He was on duty at the gate.'

Helmut laughed. 'He's got three more days of it. Oberfeldwebel Milch did the same to me, gave me extra guard duty. In his opinion I was unshaven, he told me that in future I must always stand closer to the razor.' He squatted on his haunches and the dog ran to him. *'Guter Hund Seddy.'* He stood up. 'I've not yet had a chance to congratulate you on your performance at the concert, Mademoiselle.' He wiped his hands again, reminding Blanche of Wally Sugden and the Spitfire factory at Henley.

While shaking hands with him she caught sight of her reflection in the shiny Perspex of a cockpit cover – wet hair, bombed-out curls. She ran her hand along the smooth aluminium wing. 'Were you a mechanic before the war Helmut?'

'I learned my trade in the Bayerische Motorenwerke factory, that's where the engines of these aircraft are made, fourteen cylinder, double-banked radials. I was apprenticed to BMW at the age of sixteen.'

'Lucette doesn't want to hear your life history, Helmut.'

Her eyes were fixed on the engine. So that was how it was done. She glanced across at an aircraft that had its cowling removed. Yes, two banks with seven cylinders in each but

196

why doesn't the enclosed bank overheat, shielded as it is from outside air? Then she looked at the bookshelf above the workbench. Perhaps the secret was almost within her reach.

She heard Otto say, 'Lucette says she wants to fly around the world like that English girl, the one who flew to Australia before the war. Can you spare ten minutes of your time Helmut, to make a pretty girl happy?'

'You are the pilot, Herr Major, perhaps you should teach her.'

Otto laughed. 'Girls are good for many things but flying will never be one of them – but you never know, maybe Mademoiselle Lucette might prove us wrong one day. Go on, you show her how we do it.'

Helmut pulled down the entry step on the side of the fuselage. 'An aeroplane is like a young horse, Mademoiselle, easy to control once you get to know her. Put your left foot on the step and reach for the hand-hold.'

Blanche stepped onto the bottom rung and pushed her right hand into a spring-loaded flap half way up the side of the fuselage while Helmut guided her other foot into a higher recess. 'Now swing your free leg over the coaming.'

Blanche hitched her skirt a little higher than necessary, stepped over and settled into the seat. It was raked back to an almost semi-reclined position. Otto climbed onto the wing beside her and leaned over. 'Do you still want to do this?'

'More than anything.'

'Then put your hand on the throttle – no, no – that one closes the cockpit cover.'

Blanche curled her left hand around the stubby handle of the throttle and pushed it forward and back, noting how it moved easily but with just enough friction in the coupling to maintain its position under vibration. So this was it, the dreaded Butcher Bird, scourge of the RAF. Her thumb touched the roughened surface of a spring-loaded button mounted on the end of the throttle, and she pointed to it with her other hand. 'What's this for?'

'You tell her Helmut.'

The mechanic laughed nervously. 'Am I allowed to Herr Major? How do we know this young lady isn't an enemy spy?'

'God in heaven, Helmut, don't ever say that word again.' His voice reverberated under the curved roof. 'This woman is our friend. She is French, therefore we trust her. She is my friend and she is your friend, and she is a friend of Germany. How dare you accuse her of being a spy?'

Helmut raised both hands in surrender. 'Of course she is our friend, Herr Major. Forgive me. It was only a joke.'

'I'm sorry Helmut but let's not offend our guest with false accusations. Go on tell her about it.'

Helmut continued. 'It is called the Kommandgerat. It is an electro-hydraulic master control that responds to every movement of the throttle.'

'I don't understand.'

'I'll try to explain it to you. When the throttle is moved forward for more power or backwards for less power during flight or on the ground, this device automatically controls all other systems to suit that particular throttle setting. It provides the correct flow of fuel, it selects the right strength of fuel mixture, it adjusts the pitch of the propeller and alters the ignition timing to suit the engine speed – it also selects the correct gear for the supercharger. Do you understand? No other aircraft in the world has a Kommandgerat.'

'How do you operate it?'

'Just keep the button pressed while you alter the throttle setting and all other systems automatically adjust.'

Otto said, 'Come down from there, Helmut, it's my turn now.' He climbed up and pointed to the base of the control column. 'Before you fly you must free the controls. That red label is attached to the control-locking pin – it immobilizes the controls so they don't flap about in the wind when the aircraft is parked outside. Get hold of the pin and pull it out of the slot. That's right.

Now leave the pin hanging on its wire.' He took Blanche's right hand and gently placed it on the handle at the top of the control column. 'Now you can move the controls.'

With his hand covering hers they moved the controls together as he explained, 'Forward for down, back for up, right for a turn to the right and left for left.' He took his hand away. 'Try it for yourself. Move it, go on. Get hold of it. Don't be afraid. That hinged guard on top of the control column protects three small buttons conveniently placed under your fingers but I don't think you'll need to fire any guns during your flight around the world.'

'How do you aim the guns?'

'With this.'

'What is it?'

'It's the famous Revi reflector gun sight. It is always in alignment, so there's no need for the pilot to move his head to aim those twin MG 131 machine guns that are mounted in front of the cockpit, or the pair of cannon in each wing.' He flipped up a square of glass. 'It's called a reflector because the target is reflected onto this screen. The easiest targets are the ones that approach you head-on but once the enemy starts playing tricks you have to imagine he's a game bird and fire in front of the line on which he is flying. It takes practice. I can't imagine why I'm telling you all this.'

Helmut laughed. 'Maybe she'll need to aim her guns when she gets to England, Herr Major.'

Blanche felt a sudden cramp in her stomach and pretended to study her fingernails, willing it to go away. She waited until she was steady before asking her next question. 'How do I start the engine?'

Otto looked at his mechanic with raised eyebrows. 'Do you know something Helmut? I believe she really does want to fly around the world. You tell her but don't get too technical, remember she's only a woman.'

Helmut continued the lesson. 'Firstly you must select a fuel tank, it's that lever by your left knee. Push it into the notch.'

'Like this?'

'That's good. Now the fuel pump, it's that handle on the left, switch it on. Next come the cooling gills controlled by the lever directly in front of you, slide it one third of the way along the slot because it is the summer and I don't want you to overheat my engine.'

She made the movements slowly and deliberately, fixing everything in her mind as she did so.

'Now you will need to prime the engine.'

'Why?'

'You have to inject special starter fuel into the top two cylinders. A cold engine will not fire unless it's primed. Grab that yellow knob by your left elbow and pump it up and down. Now the Bosch magnetos here on the left, switch them on, both of them.'

'Like this, Helmut?'

He gave an approving nod. 'Now you are ready to press the starter button, which is by your elbow. Go ahead, the battery is fully charged so there is no need for an external generator. Keep it pressed and listen.'

She applied her thumb and heard the rising whine of an electrically driven flywheel. 'But the engine isn't starting.'

'You have to engage the clutch by pressing that pedal by your right foot. *Not now!*'

'Why not?'

'Because the engine will start inside my hangar. It's against regulations. The Major will have me sent to the Russian Front.'

She took her thumb off the switch and the whine died gradually to silence. 'What are all these other switches and dials for? I'll need to know about them if I'm to fly. What's this yellow lever for, this one on the right?'

Helmut shouted, *'Don't touch that.'*

'Why not?'

'If you pull that lever an explosive charge blasts the lid off the cockpit. It will make a hole in the roof of my hangar and I'll have to work in the rain.'

Blanche was trying hard to sound ignorant. 'Why would you want to blast away the lid of a cockpit?'

'Because if you crash or catch fire in the air you'll need to get out in a hurry – that's if you are still alive.'

Otto climbed up, touched her shoulder and pointed to various other items in turn. 'Wireless, flaps, undercarriage, altimeter, airspeed, ammunition counter, do you think you'll be able to remember them all?' He ruffled her hair with his hand. 'Now you are flying can you feel the wind? Come on I think you've seen enough for one day.'

'What are flaps?'

Otto gave a good natured sigh. 'Flaps provide more lift by enlarging the wing area.'

'Why would you want more lift?'

'So that you can fly more slowly without stalling. We use them on take off and landing.'

'How do I set the flaps for taking off?'

'Ten degrees, and don't forget to put the elevator rim to neutral. Then push the throttle forward and remember to thumb the Kommandgerat. When that dial shows 2,700 revolutions per minute, this one over here should read one-point-six atmospheres. When you reach 180 kilometres per hour on this dial you'll be flying. When your wheels stop bumping you are airborne. Retract your wheels with this switch, reduce throttle and press the Komandgerat again. Raise flaps at 230 kilometres per hour and climb at sixteen metres per second.'

Blanche could hear Helmut laughing while Otto continued, 'Do you understand all this or did I explain it to quickly? We don't want you to crash and burn before you've cleared the boundary fence. We don't want to see the Mademoiselle killed and cremated all in one go merely because she couldn't remember the drill.'

Blanche kept her smile in spite of the cruel note in Otto's voice but was reassured by the touch of his caring hand as she climbed down from the cockpit.

'The lesson is over now. Helmut has work to do.'

CHAPTER FOURTEEN

The Plan, Friday 19th of June 1942

Blanche put her head down and pedalled against the wind unaware that the front wheel was down on its rims and the slack chain was threatening to trap her skirt.

She had been through the plan over and over again in her head and every time it made her think of her fiancé because she was convinced he was still alive in spite of what Dadan had said. Peter was a survivor, the bad penny, the man who always showed

204

up. But suppose he *was* dead like in the visions she had seen – face melting in a blazing aircraft or drowning in the Channel? She had given herself to Eric, seduced him some might say, but did that mean she loved him? The confusion, the doubt, misgivings, the uncertainty of not knowing which one – or all three of them – would change her life when the war was over. She could imagine Eric stepping onto some jetty in an English port, pushing into a smoke filled pub and raising a glass of beer – but to whom? The French girl who saved his life or some other female who had been waiting for him to return?

But now it was Lucette Moreaux wobbling along the muddy path leading to Dadan's house and with every turn of the pedals she was glad that Blanche Longhurst had taken off from Henley in marginal weather and crashed her Spitfire in France. If she hadn't done that Lucette would never have met Eric and she wouldn't have found herself falling in love with Otto, and that was perfectly all right because Lucette Moreaux was not the girl who was engaged to Squadron Leader Peter Mason.

But the plan, the thought of it, the pitfalls and the imagined consequences had once again twisted into a knot in her stomach just as tight as the confusion in her head. The task Blanche had set herself was far more dangerous than escorting a one-off lover to a secret rendezvous with the Royal Navy.

She slithered to a stop and put her foot down. Through the low branches of a wind-bent tree she saw Dadan standing at the front window of his cottage and peering out. He was probably wondering why she had wanted to see him so urgently. She waited for a moment to rehearse her questions, and watched him turn and walk away from the window.

She wheeled Madame Cazalet's bicycle into Dadan's open shed and glanced up at low clouds racing each other under a high overcast. He was at the window again, peering out. This was the man who had mudered Mr Summerfield and for two pins would have done the same to her.

Dadan's lips were cold against her cheek. Leading her into a book-lined room he pulled chairs to the table. 'I owe you an apology.'

'What for?'

'Many of our beaches are watched by German night patrols. I was the one who picked Anse du Brick thinking it was safe. I risked your life by sending you there and I also risked the integrity of our escape line. But our man got away and you escaped arrest. Nobody gets a medal in our business but we could do with a few more people like you. Girls who know how to do things and keep their mouths shut about it. A kiss and a handshake is all I can offer. Now then, what's it all about, why the urgency?'

'I want to steal two books from the Luftwaffe. One of them is the overhaul manual for BMW 801-D aero engines and the other contains important engineering notes. As a pilot I know how valuable these books will be if I can get them to England.'

With an exaggerated lack of enthusiasm he said, 'Ridiculous, too far fetched.'

'I've seen them in Number Five Hangar.'

'What were you doing there?'

'Stoeckl invited me to sit in the cockpit of a Butcher Bird. The books were lying on a workbench.'

Dadan sat down. 'Tell me more.'

'The mechanics work all hours, day and night. They leave the hangar doors open because of the fumes.'

Dadan pinched the bridge of his nose. 'So the doors are open, that's wonderful but it doesn't mean you can just walk in and help yourself. You know what will happen to you if you are caught.'

'I'm not afraid.'

'But I am afraid. I'm afraid the Gestapo will force you to talk. I am afraid that this brave episode will mark the funeral of our escape line.' He stood up and put a hand on her shoulder. 'I know what you're thinking. I know how desperate the Allies are for information about the Butcher Bird but there are limits.' He broke off, sat down again, bent forward and cradled his head.

Blanche could see the reflection of his face in the polished table. She said, 'Madame Cazalet says that a radio technician will be arriving by RAF Lysander from England. I could return on that flight with the books.'

'Never.'

'Why not? I'll be able to explain everything I know about the Butcher Bird's cockpit when I get to England, and…'

'I won't allow it. It's too risky.'

'Maybe you'll change your mind when I tell you that Otto Stoeckl has invited me to be his partner at the Officers' Ball in the hotel on Sunday night, and it so happens that the Gruppenstab Trio will be in action over the Channel shortly after dawn the following morning. All three aircraft will be out on the grass, their mechanics will be making final adjustments before the mission, the hangar doors will be open and I hardly need to remind you that the hotel overlooks the airfield.'

Dadan got up. Pacing the room he said, 'Let's see if I've got this right. You go to the ball on Sunday. You spend that night in the hotel and in the early morning you walk calmly across the airfield, enter one of the hangars, pick up some documents and return to the chateau.'

Blanche nodded. 'That's exactly right.'

He threw up his hands in despair. 'The whole idea is utterly ridiculous. Don't you realise that all civilian guests will have to leave the building when the ball finishes?'

'But what if Major Otto Stoeckl invites me to spend the night in his bedroom?'

Dadan examined his fingernails. 'Tell me Blanche – or should I say Lucette – how certain are you that your gallant officer will invite you into his bedroom. How far are you involved?'

'Our relationship is unconsummated if that's what you mean.'

Dadan shook his head and a sudden look of weariness took the sparkle from his eyes. 'I can see you pulling back the bedclothes on Monday morning and getting out of the Major's bed. But what makes you so certain that he won't wake up and ask you what the bloody hell you're doing?' Dadan wiped invisible sweat from his brow. 'I have to say this is a new one on me.' He paused. 'Wait a minute. Perhaps there is a way.'

He crossed the room, knelt down, peeled back the edge of a carpet and took a knife from his pocket, which Blanche recognised immediately. He prised up a floorboard. 'Maybe your plan isn't quite as ridiculous as I thought. I have something here that might improve your chances.'

Dadan brought a tobacco tin to the table and opened it to reveal a tiny phial wrapped

209

in cotton wool. 'This is what the Americans call a Mickey Finn. When my father was a young man working in the stockyards of Chicago he met a gentleman called Micky Finn who ran an establishment known as the Lone Star Saloon.' Dadan held up the phial. 'This is the stuff that Micky used to lace the drinks of his customers who would later find themselves stripped naked in some dark alley wondering how they got there. Chemists call this stuff Chloral Hydrate and as you can see it looks like water but let me assure you it's been putting people to sleep since 1832. Snap off the top of the phial, pour the liquid into the Major's drink one hour before he takes you to bed, and he'll be asleep before he's had time to touch you – and he'll go on sleeping until well into the afternoon. When I tried this stuff in a German sentry's coffee the poor chap didn't wake up for fifteen hours. I understand it's doubly effective when mixed with alcohol.' He re-wrapped the phial and put it back in the tin, which he handed to Blanche.

'Now let's look on the dark side and everything goes wrong and the Gestapo get hold of you. At first they will be friendly and curious but when you refuse to answer their questions they will remove your clothes. They will then shove high-voltage electrodes into every orifice of your body and

210

switch on the current – a small dose at first because they want to be able to hear what you have to say. At first you'll resist and then you will scream. After a few minutes what is left of your sanity will be cursing your mother for having given birth to you, at which point they normally switch off the current and allow you to recover. Then they will question you again but now you can't scream because your vocal chords are ruptured – but you can whisper, and whisper you do until they know everything.' He looked her in the eyes. 'Risking your sanity and perhaps your life for the liberation of France is the act of a brave woman but you also need to know how to kill yourself *before* the questions start. Every British agent who parachutes into France carries a cyanide capsule – death within twenty-three seconds if bitten or half an hour if swallowed. Unfortunately we have no cyanide.

'Here's the deal. If you get hold of those books I will allow you to go to England in the Lysander but only if you promise to kill yourself if things go wrong.'

'But how?'

He got up, crossed the room, took down a thick, leather-bound volume from the bookshelf and placed it on the table in front of her. 'Take a look.'

Blanche picked up the book with both hands, it was heavy. She read aloud from the gold-embossed spine: *'Promenades Dans les Nuages*. What's this?'

Dadan said, 'Promenading amongst the clouds has come a long way since 1818 but as an aviator I thought this book might interest you.' There was a spark of humour in his eyes. 'I'm sure you'll agree that it's not only engineering manuals about modern aircraft that concern us. You will find that this ancient book about hot-air balloons also has its uses. Go on open it.' Blanche lifted the cover and blinked.

Dadan gave his fingernails a cursory glance. 'Rather neat don't you think? Go on, pick it up.'

A miniature pistol lay in a deep recess cut into the pages. She picked it up and read the words engraved on the side of the barrel, FABRIQUE NATIONALE D'ARMES DE GUERRE HERSTAL-BELGIQUE BROWNING'S PATENT DEPOSE. 'So I'm supposed to shoot myself with this, is that it?'

Dadan nodded and said, 'Don't be put off by all that fancy engraving, it's a deadly weapon. I didn't know they made pistols as small as that one until I removed it from the pocket of a Gestapo agent. As you can see it's barely ten centimetres long and no wider than the thickness of my finger. Right-handed women usually tuck miniatures like these into the top of the left stocking as close to the groin as possible so that it doesn't make too much of a bulge. Stand up and I'll show you.'

Blanche raised an eyebrow and remained seated.

'All right, but for the sake of the Holy Virgin let me show you how to use it.' He picked it up. 'The magazine contains six rounds of ammunition but before it will fire you must lift the safety catch with the ball of your thumb – like this. After each shot it will cock and reload automatically, but that won't concern you. One shot is all you require.' He handed it to her. 'When capture is inevitable, hold the pistol in your right hand and place the muzzle against the side of your head just above and slightly in front of your ear.' He came forward and touched the side of Blanche's head to show her the exact place. 'It's very noisy but you probably won't hear anything. If all goes well you can return it to me on Monday, and if I never see it again I'll know you're dead. If you decide to go ahead with this plan of yours nobody must suspect that you are carrying a weapon, and that includes Madame Cazalet and the girls.' He laughed. 'And certainly not Otto Stoeckl.'

Blanche curled her fingers around the mother-of-pearl handle, slipped her finger through the guard and lightly touched the gold-plated trigger before putting the pistol back on the table. 'I don't want it.'

'No pistol, no flight home.'

'So I have no choice.'

Things were different now. She was in a different kind of war and there was no room in it for pacifists. She re-checked the safety catch and lifted her skirt.

Dadan averted his eyes. 'If you place it correctly nobody will know it's there.'

CHAPTER FIFTEEN

The Ball, Sunday 21st of June 1942

Blanche entered Madame Cazalet's smoke-filled bedroom and found her already dressed for the ball, sitting at her dressing table and applying makeup. A green cigarette smouldered on an ashtray by her elbow and a glass of amber fluid showed evidence of lipstick on the rim.

Madame Cazalet spoke to Blanche's reflection. 'Your dress is on the bed, Lucette, it's the one I wore on my wedding day. I've lowered the neckline a little and added some ribbons.' She drew on the cigarette and emitted a smoky chuckle. 'We mustn't make you look too much like a bride – we don't want the Major to get the wrong idea. Oh, and I want you to keep the handbag and the hand-embroidered Madeira handkerchief and silver powder compact that are inside it.' Madame Cazalet took another puff. 'Now my dear, prepare for some bad news.'

Blanche felt her heart jump.

'The Lysander from England has been delayed. We aren't expecting it until next week.'

'Why, what's happened?'

'They haven't given us any reason but Dadan and I want you to go ahead with the theft of the books as planned. One of our shot down airmen will take them to England next week.' She patted another layer of makeup under her eyes. 'Now we have the ball to think about. Flaunt yourself tonight my darling. Flirt with your German officer and have a wonderful evening. Above all make sure he invites you to spend the night with him and bring those books to me after breakfast on Monday morning.'

'I can't do it.'

'What can't you do?'

'Steal from the Luftwaffe. I'm sorry but if there's no reward I'm not prepared to take the risk.' The words were out before she was able to stop herself.

Madame Cazalet stood up abruptly. 'Reward? Dadan never said anything to me about a reward.'

'He said I could go to England in the Lysander and deliver the books myself. That was to be my reward.'

'You want to leave France just when you're doing so well? Think of your father who remained in Lille to face the enemy. You are French. Your country needs you to help fight our secret war. What would your mother say if she knew you were running away? You are staying here whatever happens and you are going to the ball. When you're waltzing with Otto try to look happy even if you don't feel it – and make sure you bring those documents to me on Monday.'

Beads of sweat had somehow managed to struggle through her layers of make-up and were forming tiny drops on Madame Cazalet's cheeks. 'These people barged their way into our country and now they invite us to a sumptuous ball. Even in my worst brandy-soaked dreams I could never have imagined anything like this – but we are going to do it in grand style, Lucette. Like Cinderella we are going to the ball in a fine vehicle, not one of Wilhelm's lorries. Now go and get dressed or we'll be late.'

Blanche picked up the dress and the handbag, climbed the stairs, undressed and conjured enough water from the hot tap to have a bath. Wrapped in a towel she returned to her room, put on her suspender belt and stockings, opened a drawer and grabbed the pistol. Mother-of-pearl felt smooth and cold against her thigh as she pushed it down. She took the tobacco tin from its hiding place, stowed it in her handbag next to the powder compact and stood combing her hair for several seconds in front of the mirror. Stepping into Madame Cazalet's wedding dress she wondered if the irregular stitching in the neckline would be strong enough to resist the pressures that lay ahead.

On her way downstairs Blanche heard Madame Cazalet's voice cut through a bustle of girlish excitement. 'Armande dear, don't forget to ask your man what type of aircraft he'll be flying after his posting to Morlaix.' She walked across the hall to join the others and Madame Cazalet held up her arms in genuine surprise.

'Who is this? Do we know this girl? Lucette dear you look beautiful. Now you know what you have to do, but I also want you to get Otto onto the subject of beach parties because we still know next to nothing about the Atlantic Wall.' She turned to address the others. 'Everyone please remember why we are going to this ball – I mean the real reason – and why we make friends with these people.'

Madame Cazalet gave a muted 'oh' of delight when she saw the Sizaire-Berwick out in the yard. 'You've done well, everyone, that car is cleaner than new.' The wire spokes of the car's enormous wheels looked like webs of silver, rows of rivets caught light from the evening sun and the starting handle was like a bar of gold under the tombstone radiator.

Madame Cazalet opened the rear door and offered a steadying arm to each of her girls as they stepped onto the running board and squeezed together on the all-embracing Moroccan leather seat. 'Not you, Lucette, I want you to help me start the engine.'

Madame Cazalet sat behind the wheel, turned on a brass tap, set the timing lever and whispered to Blanche confidentially. 'Our family chauffeur taught me to drive when I was fourteen but I've hardly driven since. Marcel was a wonderful driver but now he works in a Boche munitions factory. Swing the handle for me Lucette dear and once we've got her started come and sit next to me.'

Blanche gripped the handle and jerked it up in a swift half-turn. On the seventh attempt the massive engine ended its long hibernation with a deafening backfire followed by a steady rumble. Blanche climbed up with her naked armpits damp with sweat and sat beside Madame Cazalet who released the handbrake with both hands and crunched into gear. Lurching down the drive Blanche remained silent, counting the trees as she always did, half wishing that after the ball she would be returning to the safety of

218

the chateau with the others. Twenty-two, twenty-three... The automobile bumped over potholes and the smell of exhaust failed to mask a headier blend of pre-war perfume evaporating off five nervous girls squashed together on the back seat.

Once clear of the drive the car gathered speed and tracked dangerously close to a long drainage ditch bordering the road. Madame Cazalet, looking small and frail behind the steering wheel, managed to maintain a continuous babble of conversation. 'Three more airmen to deal with next week and you'll be leading them. It will be a Cherbourg fishing boat this time. When the war is over we might go over there ourselves. You can be my interpreter. Have you ever been to England?'

While Blanche was wondering how to answer she felt something pop out of the top of her stocking. 'Only once, I went by ferry from Calais.' She felt under her skirt and found the pistol on the seat between her legs. 'I went there to practise my English.' When she tried to pick up the weapon it slipped noiselessly to the floor, cushioned by the thick carpet.

Madame Cazalet glanced across and the Sizaire-Berwick swerved dangerously. 'Have you dropped something my dear?'

Blanche deliberately allowed her handbag to fall, leaned forward, picked it up, opened

219

it and crammed the pistol inside in one swift movement.

After an erratic journey the car halted with a squeal of brakes. Otto was there waiting for her. Was it elation, fear or love that made her tremble? Wilhelm Schieder was standing beside him on the newly raked gravel in front of Hotel de Fleuve. As Otto opened the door on her side his diamond-studded medal caught points of light from the dying sun.

Blanche smiled nervously. 'What have you done with Seddy, is he coming to the ball too?' She took a quick glance across the airfield and far away across the grass the corrugated iron hangars showed squares of light through their open doors. She took a deep breath and put her hand through the crook of Otto's arm.

He said, 'Helmut is looking after Seddy. He'll find a bed for him in the hangar when he starts work.'

'When will that be?'

'Three in the morning.'

They entered the hotel by the revolving doors and Otto's arm tightened around her shoulders as he steered her towards the mirrored ballroom. Small tables circled the room with linen tablecloths heavy with silver and dazzling white under the chandeliers. Two violinists, a pianist and a drummer played Strauss waltzes to a floor already crowded with whirling couples while Oberst Schieder, with Madame Cazalet on his arm, led Otto and Blanche to a table for four.

Blanche was about to sit down but Otto led her quickly onto the floor. He spread his right hand across her back and, as they danced, she felt his outspread fingers spanning the butterfly-mark in the groove of her naked spine while they waltzed to music from another era. She shut her eyes to help savour the moment – or was she ashamed to look him in the eye? Betrayal, falsehood, lies – she tried not to think of them. Instead she would enjoy the evening and wait for the dawn.

The handbag, burdened with half a pound of gunmetal, bumped heavily against Otto's back and tugged at her wrist during the spins. Flickering light from the chandeliers, through closed eyelids, brought visions of Peter and a burning aircraft. Had Dadan been right after all? Was a one-armed portrait painter trying to burn Peter out of her memory? Was Lucette Moreaux falling in love with an enemy pilot?

She opened her eyes to a clash of cymbals. Otto steered her to the table where Madame Cazalet, slurring her words slightly, was working her witchcraft on the Commanding Officer. 'Have you forgotten what it feels like to swim in a rising tide that has been washing over sun-heated rocks? The sun will shine again, Wilhelm darling, you'll see. Can't you forget about killing your enemies for five minutes and listen to me for a change?'

Schieder muttered something unintelligible and refilled her glass until it overflowed. 'Sometimes you seem to forget that we are at war, Henriette. How many times do I have to tell you that all beaches are out of bounds to civilians? Is that all you people think about, pleasure and parties?'

'I don't like your tone, Wilhelm. We are not you people not even your people and we never will be – but that doesn't stop me loving you. This party was one of your better ideas and may I say that you are making my girls and me very happy. We are all very grateful.'

Schieder drained his glass and kissed her on the ear. 'Enjoy it while it lasts. Otto and I are hosting another party tomorrow morning, one in which we intend to drown all our guests. Young Hartmann over there is also involved. Let's hope he stays sober for the seven o'clock take off.' Schieder leant across the table and punched Otto's shoulder. 'And make sure you wake up in time. With your Oxford education you know better than any of us that the English are a punctual race. We wouldn't want the Gruppenstab Trio to disappoint its guests.' He turned to Madame

Cazalet. 'If we weaken the enemy and keep on hitting him, he will never invade France. The English have an expression for it – *little by little*. But you're right about one thing, the weather is lifting. But picnics on the beach and frolics in the sand dunes must wait until the war is over.'

While waiters brought assiette de fruits de mer and artichauts vinaigrette, Madame Cazalet took a long draught of chilled champagne. 'You must unbend a little, Wilhelm – a bit of sex amongst the dunes might smooth your edges and help you to relax.'

Perhaps it was the word sex that made Blanche go suddenly wet between the legs with anticipation, but at the same time she knew that going to bed with Otto was a vital part of her plan to shorten the war.

Madame Cazalet broke an uncomfortable silence by tapping Otto on the shoulder and asking him for a light for her cigarette. She fluttered her eyelids at him. 'I recognise that lighter of yours, American isn't it? You told me that it always lights first time but I've often found that attractive men are prone to exaggeration.'

'Try it for yourself.'

Madame Cazalet took the lighter, successfully rolled the flint and winked at him through a haze of smoke. 'You are a truthful man after all.'

'You can keep it.'

'I couldn't possibly…'

'It's yours. If it fails to light first time I'll take it back to the factory and lodge a complaint. The Spanish surgeon who set my leg in 1936 spent an hour of his time persuading me to stop smoking so now I only use it to please elegant ladies such as yourself.'

'I shall see your face in the flame every time I use it, Otto darling, and I shall always remember this wonderful evening. One of these days I'll repay you in a way you'll not forget.' She caught Blanche's eye for a long second before slipping the lighter into her handbag.

Schieder gave a disapproving grunt and glanced at his watch. 'Have you heard of those German authors, the Brothers Grimm?'

'Of course I have.'

'Then you must know all about Cinderella.'

Madame Cazalet smacked his thigh. 'It was a Frenchman who wrote that story.'

'French, German, what does it matter? In any language she went home at midnight and so must we.'

Lucette Moreaux was in Otto's arms again, whirling to the music with her half-covered breasts pressed to the front of his uniform – sweeping, circling, laughing to the flying beat of the Trish Trash Polka. She said, 'I pray for bad weather tomorrow, and

224

storms and fog so thick that they'll keep you on the ground forever. I want to spend every day and every night of my life with you.'

They came out of the spin and stopped facing each other in the centre of the dance floor. Red-faced and breathing heavily, like an adolescent, Otto said, 'I love you, Lucette. I gave a trinket to Madame Cazalet just now but I have something more valuable for you.'

She could feel herself blushing: 'But I don't smo…'

He stopped her with a kiss. 'You'll never light a cigarette with this.' He led her to the edge of the floor and, partly shielded behind a giant fern, he unpinned his medal.

Blanche shook her head. 'You are a generous man, but…'

He took her hand, opened it, pressed the medal onto her palm and closed her fingers around it. 'It's my Saint Christopher, my Grimm's fairy tale, my lucky charm that has kept me alive long enough to meet a beautiful girl. You are my protector now, Lucette. I have no further need for my Spanish Cross.'

Blanche opened her hand and looked at the diamond-studded cross with eagles and swords arranged around its central swastika. 'Why Spanish?'

'That civil war I was telling you about. Adolf Hitler awarded me with this medal.

We paraded through the streets of Berlin and crowds cheered us all the way. Here, let me fix it for you.' He opened the pin. 'Keep still or I'll prick you.'

'But if it protects you, how can I accept it? You'll be needing it tomorrow.'

He laughed. 'It's mere superstition, one that ended thirty seconds ago. I award this medal to the beautiful Lucette, my brave and steadfast friend, the beautiful lady who never leaves my thoughts. I have no further need of lucky charms. You are my charmer now and will always be so.'

She blinked back a tear and looked away. 'I will treasure your Spanish Cross but you must take care of yourself tomorrow.' *Oh God, I mean it. What is happening to me?*

'We have the whole night ahead of us.'

'But you are flying in the morning.'

'Don't remind me.'

'If you don't go to bed soon you'll never wake up in time.'

'A steward will wake me, he'll knock on my door, *our* door. Remember what you said?'

'What did I say?'

'When I showed you how to fly the Butcher Bird, surely you remember.'

'Tell me.'

'You promised to make love to me after the ball.'

She put a hand to her face to hide the

blush. 'What time will the steward wake you?'

'Five thirty, but I'm used to getting up early. You can stay in bed as long as you like.'

Blanche looked up at the gilded clock, it showed exactly twenty-five minutes past eleven. She thought about the phial of chloral hydrate and Dadan's words boomed loud inside her head: *he'll be asleep before he's had time to touch you, and he'll go on sleeping until midday.* But she wanted him to touch her but knew that if he woke up too early her plan would fail.

Sitting at the table again, Madame Cazalet said, 'What did you do to deserve that? You are a devil, Otto. You gave me a lighter but Lucette goes home with diamonds.'

The music started again but Blanche smiled at Otto and shook her head. 'Not just now if you don't mind? I'm feeling rather faint and anyway I don't like American fox-trots.'

'Faint? Can I get you a glass of water?'

'No really, I'm perfectly all right. I'll sit this one out if you don't mind. Ask Madame Cazalet to dance with you. I won't be jealous.' But Otto held Madame Cazalet so close in the dance that Blanche was soon feeling more than a twinge of jealousy. Schieder tried to start a conversation with her but lost interest and got up to talk to a comrade at the next table.

227

Blanche immediately slid Otto's glass towards her, reached under the table, opened her handbag, prised open the tin, broke open the phial and emptied its contents into Otto's champagne. After returning the empty phial to her handbag she noticed that her finger was bleeding and hurriedly left the table. In the powder room she ran cold water onto the cut and returned to the table with her thumb firmly pressed to it. She found Otto, Schieder and Madame Cazalet sitting together deep in conversation and saw that Otto's glass was dry. She gave him a searching look, which he took as a signal for more dancing.

The Emperor Waltz went at a reckless pace while the hands of the gilded clock progressed towards one o'clock. Otto showed no ill effects and whirled her with such speed that the handbag tugged painfully at her wrist. Without warning the strap broke. The handbag shot away, skidded across the polished floor cannoning off dancers' feet like a billiard ball and ending up out of sight under a table.

Blanche escaped from Otto's grip and ran after it but a man was already on hands and knees half-hidden by the tablecloth. He emerged with the bag and Blanche held out her hand. 'Thank you.'

He was about to hand it back but snatched it away. 'Let me guess what you have in here.'

He appeared to weigh it in his hand. 'Far too heavy for such a slender wrist.' Blanche made a grab but the man held it beyond her reach. 'Shall we solve the mystery?' he undid the clasp and raised his voice. 'Who would like to know what French girls carry in their handbags when they go dancing? Spare knickers, contraceptives maybe? It's heavy, could it be a bomb?'

Otto leaned past her and grabbed the man's wrist. 'That's enough, and I think you have had more than enough to drink for one evening. Give it back to the lady and get yourself out of my sight.'

Contraceptives? Hell. Blanche remembered Madame Cazalet's advice. *N'oublie pas ta capote anglaise.*

Otto steered her back to the table through whirling couples. Schieder was acting strangely. His eyes were glazed and lifeless. He was rapping the table with his knuckles, failing to keep time to the music. Without warning he slumped back in his chair, slid to the edge of the seat and grabbed the tablecloth as he fell to the floor amongst flying glass and a coincidental clash of cymbals from the orchestra.

Dancers ran to cluster around the table. A junior officer lifted the tablecloth and peered at his chief who was breathing heavily with eyes closed.

The medical officer pushed through the

throng, loosened Schieder's collar, took his pulse and called for a stretcher. Blanche knelt beside him. 'Can I help? I'm a nurse.'

He looked at her quickly. 'He's certainly not drunk but he's breathing with difficulty. I don't like the look of him. Under any other circumstances I'd say he's been poisoned.'

Madame Cazalet looked anxiously at the doctor. 'Three glasses of Champagne, that's all he's had the entire evening.' She peered into her lover's face and smacked his cheek. 'Wake up Wilhelm.' Getting no response she sighed deeply and left the table in search of more robust company while Blanche, Otto and the doctor stayed with Schieder until men hurried him away on a stretcher.

At two o'clock Madame Cazalet assembled her party for the short car journey back to the chateau. Watching them go made Blanche realize that she would never see them again. The musicians packed their instruments. The last couples left the ballroom. Overflowing ashtrays, empty bottles, glasses and crumpled table linen emphasised in some strange way the mixture of excitement and dread that fluttered in her stomach.

They climbed the stairs together. Was this a dream, this sound of her heels clicking on the mahogany staircase?

In the bedroom they stood together by the

window looking at the stars, and it was Lucette Moreaux – not Blanche Longhurst – who felt the last traces of resistance leaving her like an ebbing tide.

PART TWO

CHAPTER SIXTEEN

The Advice, Wednesday 15th of April 1953

I wake up screaming. I sit up in bed and my ten-year-old son bursts into the bedroom, jumps onto my bed and clings to me so tightly that I can hardly breathe.

I hear my father's heavy feet on the landing. Standing in the doorway he says, 'Another nightmare Blanche?'

'Sorry Dad.' Sometimes I wonder if my father deserves a daughter like me.

At breakfast a few days later, after Jamie had left the table, Dad says to me, 'I think you'll like Doctor Pritchard. He'll cost me a fortune but he happens to be the best shrink in the north of England.'

'If you're talking about psychiatrists, Dad, I'm not interested.' But my father is an old soldier and although he's ill and nearing the end of his days he still expects unswerving obedience from his daughter. It's no use my arguing.

Charlie Chaplin without the hat and cane, that's Doctor Pritchard, clipped moustache and smiling at me as he extends a hand and he doesn't flinch when he sees my fire-scarred face. At first I'm suspicious but quite soon I warm to him and find myself laughing at his unfunny jokes.

Dad paid a lot of money to get this expensive man to make the eighty-mile round trip to our house in Northumberland but I'm glad he did because during my thirty-five years of life I've seen more than my share of clinics and hospitals – and I don't want to end my days in one.

Doctor Pritchard starts by asking questions that are easy to answer – my full name and so on, the age of my son whom I christened Jamie.

'Who is the father?'

'I don't know for certain.'

Doctor Pritchard takes a notebook from his pocket. 'Does Jamie ever ask you who his father is?'

'He started asking that kind of question shortly after his sixth birthday and hasn't stopped. I tell him quite truthfully that his dad was an accomplished pilot, a wonderful and caring man who would love him to bits if he knew he had a son.'

'And what do you say to Jamie when he asks why his dad isn't here?'

'He believes his father is dead. He wants me to marry a stepdad he can be proud of, somebody he can introduce to his friends at half-term. He often asks me to describe his

236

father but the truth is I can't because Jamie's father is one of two men and I don't know which. Sometimes I lie awake at night wondering if the two men I was involved with are still alive. What am I supposed to tell my son, that I lost touch with both of them before I realised I was pregnant? I feel bad about it and yet I want Jamie to know the truth.'

When Doctor Pritchard probes further into my past I find myself describing what it felt like to see the Birdman falling to his death onto a crowd of spectators, a vision that has haunted me ever since that terrible event that happened before the war. It made headline news at the time and Doctor Pritchard says he remembers reading about it, but I can't bring myself to tell him what people said about me after that dreadful tragedy. *I blame the girl who took him up. Only eighteen but surely old enough to notice the smell of alcohol on a man's breath.*

I tell Doctor Pritchard that my father persuaded me to give up flying to become a nurse and I tell him how I took up flying again very soon after the outbreak of war and, wonder of wonders, he shows no surprise when I tell him that I ran out of petrol and landed in occupied France on the sixteenth of March 1942.

Doctor Pritchard is proving to be an understanding man and not easily shocked, but I suppose that's to be expected in a psychiatrist. Gradually I open up to him. I tell him how Eric Blakeny's arm was amputated by a cabinet maker, and how I still think about Eric nearly every day because he made love to me after I had nursed him back to health. He could be Jamie's father.

My war had a dark side. I try to describe that too, like seeing Dadan stabbing Mr Summerfield to death because he couldn't answer my questions. The war ended eight years ago but sometimes it seems more like eight days, and it's all so fresh in my mind that I decide that Doctor Pritchard isn't going to hear *everything* that happened to me. I won't tell him that I also had sex with an enemy officer in the summer of 1942, but I will tell him about the eccentric lady who owned the chateau and how she taught me to prepare food for Allied airmen hiding in her cellar.

Doctor Pritchard listens to me like a priest at confession. I try to explain that it wasn't Blanche Longhurst who had sex with two different men in June 1942, it was somebody else, not me at all but a French girl called Lucette Moreaux. Did these men seduce Lucette or did she seduce them?

Doctor Pritchard understands. I see it in his eyes. I tell him how Lucette Moreaux was nearly shot to death after guiding Eric to a beach; how she played piano in a Luftwaffe concert; how she flirted with an enemy pilot who seemed unsure about the cause he was fighting for and who owned a dog that he'd rescued from a deserted French farmyard. I describe the Officers' Ball but my story ends when Lucette is on the staircase that leads to Otto's bedroom.

Doctor Pritchard nods wisely. 'Do you suffer from hallucinations?'

'Only when I'm dreaming.'

He laughs. 'I only ask to confirm that you're not showing symptoms of schizophrenia. What you have is a much less complicated condition, which I've christened the Bilingual Syndrome. I'll try to explain. Multilingual speakers often display more than one personality, a different one depending on the language they are speaking. In your case, when you are speaking English, you find yourself reserved, perhaps a little shy. In French you are more outgoing and far less inhibited. The explanation is simple. When we are babies we try to imitate our parents' speech and gradually we become fluent in our native language. During these formative years we acquire a lot more than the ability to speak. We learn what is acceptable and what is not. When we did well we were praised by our loving parents, and when we kicked over the traces or spoke out of turn they restrained us and

239

guided us and taught us how to behave. This is how language and character become inextricably woven together in a child's developing psyche. When Blanche Longhurst speaks French she becomes somebody else, but don't be ashamed of it, you are not alone. When you were in France during the war you became somebody else who in reality had never had French parents to teach her about limits and boundaries. Although Lucette Moreaux never existed in real life, she has become part of you and will always be different to the well brought up Blanche Longhurst.'

The doctor is trying to help me but I'm almost relieved when he changes to the delicate subject of my hideous appearance.

'Your face, forgive me but you haven't told me what caused the disfigurement.' He washes his hands with invisible soap and I can see him hesitating. 'Please, I don't want to know if you don't want to tell me.'

I look at the floor because I don't want to tell him. I also don't want to tell him what happened to me after the Officers' Ball.

He put his elbows on the table and his hands come together under his chin. 'I'd like you to do something for me. When the summer term starts and your boy is back at boarding school, I'd like you to get away from here for a week or two, maybe longer.' Looking at me over the top of his glasses he says, 'Take Eric Blakeny for example, why don't you go and find him, talk to him, tell him you have a child. Get things into the open and see what develops. Eric might need you and perhaps you need him. If that doesn't put you on the right track get your-self over to that French chateau. Seek out Dadan and Madame Cazalet, talk to them, share old memories. Ask the good lady to remind you how to cook a leek flan. There must be hundreds, probably thousands of people who are still suffering from the traumas of war, and horrors that will only go away if they face them and recognise them for what they are, nothing more than events in their past lives that can never return.'

He unclasps his hands. Focusing on his fingernails he says, 'When I was a student my professor told me that memories of fear and shame should be treated like damp clothing. Hang your shirt on the line, he used to say, hang it out and let the wind do the rest.'

Doctor Pritchard gets up from his chair, folds his notes and puts them into his briefcase. 'Have you ever been to Poole?'

I shake my head.

'One of my patients tells me that it's now possible to drive your car up a ramp and park it inside a new kind of cross-channel ferry. At the other end you drive off in

241

France. Goodness knows why they called it *Southern House,* it's a funny name for a ship.'

I see him to the door and watch him drive away.

Doctor Pritchard has made it all sound so simple. If I face my demons everything will be fine. Let's hope he's right.

CHAPTER SEVENTEEN

Finding Eric,
Wednesday 29th of April 1953

It's still dark when I open the garage doors. I put my suitcase behind the back seat, I climb in, sit behind the wheel and breathe smells of old leather and petrol. The planned route of 330 miles, prepared for me by the AA on five closely typed pages, is beside me on the passenger seat of my fifteen-year-old MG Tourer.

The ignition light shines like a red eye when I turn the key. The petrol pump ticks. I pull out the choke, press the starter button and listen to a rumble that makes me wish I were back in the ATA, about to take off, fly for eighty minutes and land in the field next to Connie's house and share her favourite breakfast of scrambled eggs with Worcester sauce. That's where I'm going now, Rock Cottage, but it won't be the same without Connie, not like the old days. She worked in a munitions factory during the war, which is a far cry from her present job as a receptionist at the Savoy Hotel in London. When I got back from France, Connie was the first to visit me in hospital. That voice, I'd recognise it anywhere. My eyes were bandaged and I could hardly speak but I wasn't deaf. I told her what I could – about the Spitfire and how I found myself in France, but when she asked after Peter I didn't know what to say, and I never told her how I got myself back to England. How could I when I can't even bring myself to think about it?

Connie will always be my best friend. We run up huge telephone bills talking to each other. And letters, we write to each too, that's why her latest scrawl is in the glove compartment of the car. Just like her to remind me where she hides the key of Rock Cottage, and then write out all those instructions about how to get to it – as if I didn't know.

I drive through the crowded streets of Newcastle and cross the Tyne Bridge. Poor old town, empty gaps in the terraces look like missing teeth. War war, war, how did a pacifist like me get mixed up in it? I'm not like my father who seems to have actually enjoyed being a soldier in spite of the things he had to endure during the First World War.

Doncaster, and according to my Rolex it's breakfast time. The roads are choked. I wait patiently in traffic. Patience is something I do rather well these days. In August 1945 people who had been patient for six years danced in the streets, but I was in no mood to celebrate the end of the war with my face hideously scarred and a fatherless child. It was Dad who insisted that he started boarding school when he was nine, and he's paying for the Dragon School in Oxford so that the boy can follow in his illustrious grandfather's footsteps and get a proper education.

I have lots to think about during the long drive to Wiltshire, time to take stock while I get away from my well-meaning father. Mr Pritchard says that meeting Eric will help me see things differently but what kind of person is Eric now? And what about visiting France and the chateau? Even if Madame Cazalet has survived she might prove to be yet another friend who fails to recognise the real person behind my burnt face. And it will be a different France because I'll be Blanche Longhurst this time and I'll have my own transport – and that reminds me of the DKW that belonged to... I can hardly bring myself to say his name. After all these years the chances of meeting Otto again are almost non-existent. Germany lost the war. The Luftwaffe was destroyed.

The Great North Road runs close to the railway line and reminds me of my journey home in 1942 with my head completely covered with bandages except for four small openings. Father walked right past me at the station and it was only after I'd flung my arms rather painfully around his silly neck that he knew who I was. But the sense of relief at being home at last was overwhelming.

My homecoming had its problems. As the weeks passed the worry increased until finally one Monday morning in the autumn of 1942 I took the train to Newcastle because I was too embarrassed to confront our family doctor. It was an unknown doctor who asked me the dreaded question after I'd spent half the day in his waiting room.

'Does your husband know that you are consulting me?'

'I haven't got a husband.'

'When did you last have intercourse?'

'On the twenty-second of June.'

The doctor gave a clinical nod. 'No bladder on this earth can withstand the pressure of an enlarging womb – no doubt you've noticed changes in the frequency of urination. Loosen your clothing and lie on the bed.'

After a swift examination he told me that what I already knew. My nipples were enlarged and the swelling of my abdomen was typical. He added rather flippantly, 'You'll be a mother by April Fool's Day unless I'm very much mistaken.'

Pedalling home from the station I was wondering how best to break the news to Dad. In the end I decided to walk boldly into his study and confront him.

He peered at me over the top of his newspaper. 'What is it Blanche?'

'I'm expecting.'

'Expecting what?'

'I'm pregnant.'

He dropped the paper and looked at me for ages without saying anything – then it was, 'I don't believe you.'

'It's true, Dad.'

'You stand there telling me that you're pregnant? Who's the father?'

'I don't know.'

'What? My daughter's about to give birth to a bastard in the middle of a war and she doesn't even know who the father is?'

That was eleven years ago and now I can't get Eric out of my head as I drive down to Sussex. He never kissed me goodbye, not even a handshake but that was hardly surprising with German bullets whistling over our heads. Is it ignorant of me to imagine that I can rekindle the spark that flashed between us while he was painting my portrait? But it wasn't me was it? Lucette Moreaux was the subject of his picture and it was she who had the orgasm that turned out to be little more than a taste of sugar compared to... Oh God – Otto again – there were two men in my life in those days but it seemed perfectly all right at the time because Lucette Moreaux didn't have a fiancé called Squadron Leader Peter Mason waiting for her in England.

No, I don't want to think about Peter because I'll never come to terms with what I did to him. But I *am* thinking about Peter as I drive through London's bombsites and rebuilding work, bump over tramlines and hear Big Ben chiming four o'clock. It must have been about four o'clock when Eric made love to me in the chateau but what will he think of me now when he discovers that Lucette Moreaux was a fake. Sunlight flickers through urban trees as I head west out of the city.

I cross into Sussex with the AA route open at the last page. A thick fog is forming and I can barely see where I'm going, like that desperate climb through cloud in Spitfire W3297 – yes I can still remember the number. It's too thick to drive safely but I can't be far from Eric's place. I see the outline of a large hotel and drive into the car park. I might have to spend the night here but that depends on how I get on with Eric.

In the public bar somebody with his hat askew asks me if I want to bet on a horse as I push through the tight throng of late-afternoon drinkers. The barman smiles at my question 'Sorry madam, no rooms available.' But his answer to my next question is more helpful. 'Do you mean Eric's place?' He makes a diagram on the back of a beer mat and, as I leave the bar I hear a sudden burst of laughter.

I nearly miss the turning because it's little more than a gap in a hedge bordering the road. Now I'm driving down a track, blindly feeling my way with the MG's exhaust pipe scraping the ground. As I descend the fog thins until I'm under it, under the cloud as if I were in Wally's precious Spitfire gliding down to that French farm. Raised banks either side of the steep path are missing my mudguards by inches and then, out of the mist a lake appears on my left and ahead of me I see a chimney half obscured by trees.

Am I ready for this? I stop the car, switch off the engine and hear rushing water. I'm on a bridge over sluice gates taking the overflow from the lake. I drive down off the bridge and stop in a muddy yard next to a barn-like building with an enormous rotting water-wheel attached to its side. The house is across a muddy yard, brick and timber under a sagging roof. I get out of the car and look at the house. The door is shut and the windows are closed. A sudden clap of pigeon wings makes me jump and an equally sudden smatter of rain comes out of the oppressive cloud above the smokeless chimney. I turn up my collar and look at my watch – half-past-five on a bleak afternoon according to my trusty Rolex.

'*Hello there.*'

I spin round. A man is striding down from the bridge. Who is it? Tattered overcoat, mud-spattered boots – yes, same old smile. He comes closer and his smile changes to an expression I've seen a thousand times over the past eleven years. 'Looking for somebody?'

I stand there, stupidly, wondering what the hell to say. I saved this man's life, he was dying, I nursed him back to health but Eric Blakeny hasn't the faintest idea who I am. He doesn't recognise the girl who led him to a French beach, the one he promised to take back to England with him.

The rain comes suddenly and Eric pulls up his collar. He grabs my arm and we splash through poultry-trodden mud towards the house. When he opens the door I almost miss my footing as I step inside and while he goes to fetch a towel I try to calm myself and look around.

The room is like an art gallery. Every wall is

covered with landscapes, portraits, abstracts, watercolours, pencil drawings and I remember him saying, 'If somebody is born with a natural talent, that person should practise and improve his talent. Do you understand what I'm saying, Lucette?' He may be an artist but the pile of unwashed dishes by the sink looks like the leaning tower of Pisa. Quite obviously he's unmarried. No woman on this earth would tolerate a mess like this.

He comes down the stairs, shoves a towel at me and pulls out a chair. 'Far be it from me to be the bearer of bad news but I have to tell you that this road is a dead end so you'll have to turn round in the yard and go back where you came from. We can have a cup of tea while the rain blows over.'

I sit down and try to dry my hair but I need to wash my face because the thick layer of makeup that I like to hide behind has turned to mud. We go upstairs and he shows me where the bathroom is.

When I come down again Eric is pouring the tea. He gives me a cup with his good hand and says, 'What brought you here, did you take a wrong turning?'

By now I'm ready for anything. 'No, I didn't take a wrong turning, I came to find you.'

'Why would you want to do that?'

'Because a long time ago you were my friend.'

'What? You might claim to know me but I haven't the remotest clue who you are.'

'My name is Blanche Longhurst, don't you remember me?' He looks totally blank and then I remember that he always knew me as Lucette. 'Does the name Lucette Moreaux mean anything to you?'

He puts down his cup with a clatter. 'I knew a girl called Lucette but that was a hell of a long time ago. She lived in France. Don't tell me you knew her too.'

'I see her every day.'

'What, here in England? That's wonderful news. I'm desperate to get in touch with her again. I wouldn't be alive now if it hadn't been for her. How long have you known her?'

'All my life.' His enthusiasm is encouraging even though he can't bring himself to look at me for more than two connected seconds. In spite of that something makes me want to tease him and something else tells me to get up off this chair and say goodbye. Behind Eric's left shoulder I can see a schooner with tattered sails sinking in a storm, and next to it is a charcoal sketch of a herd of cows with bulging eyes. I say to him, 'You wouldn't recognise Lucette if you saw her today.'

'If course I'd recognise her. Tell me where I can find her.'

I make a show of looking at my watch and

251

try to sound casual. 'Time I was going.' I get up and make for the door. He follows me.

Outside the rain has stopped and I try to ignore the touch of his left hand under my elbow as I settle into the driver's seat. Stupidly I forgot to put up the hood. Damp from the seat is invading my underwear. I switch on the ignition, pull the starter – and nothing happens.

Eric says, 'The rain must have got to it, short circuit more than likely, your battery's flat as a pancake. Let's push her into the barn and I'll see if I can find some jump leads. Failing that you can spend the night here and we'll sort it out in the morning. I have a spare room, an unused toothbrush, acres of clean sheets and I can lend you a pair of silk pyjamas but they'll be far too b...' He stops on the word. His eyes widen with surprise. His hair is still wet.

'I've brought my own pyjamas.'

He leans over and peers at me. 'I must be blind not to have recognised that retroussé nose – but what happened to the rest of your face?'

'It got burnt. It could have been worse. Please don't ask me about it.'

Suddenly it seems ridiculous. Here I am sitting in my car with a wet bottom knowing that I'll never be able to tell him what happened to me in France or how I made my way back to England. I shrug my shoulders. 'I thought it was about time we saw each other again. I went to the library and just as I was beginning to think the name Blakeny didn't exist I found an E. Blakeny living at Watermill Farm in the Sussex telephone directory. I knew it was you by the unusual spelling, coupled with the fact that you once told me you wanted to live on a farm when the war was over. I was on the point of ringing you when I decided to visit you instead. I thought I'd give you a surprise.'

'You did that all right.'

We go back into the cottage and Eric sits down shaking his head. 'What happened to the French accent?'

I tell him that I became trapped above cloud in a Spitfire, found myself in France and became involved with the French Resistance and couldn't use my real name so became Lucette Moreaux.

Eric is amazed. 'You had me completely fooled. Were you still at the chateau during the Allied invasion in 1944?'

'I was back in England by then. I read all about it in my father's newspaper.'

'So during all the time you were looking after me in France you were deceiving me.' Then he asks the question I've been dreading, the one I can't answer, the question that makes me realise that I must be crazy to have come here at all. I turn away.

Through the window I can see trees swaying in the wind on the far side of the river. 'It's a long story. I lot of things happened to me after we parted on that beach, things I can't face up to any more, the memory of them. I've been seeing a psychiatrist. He told me to face my demons. Something like that.'

'Am I one of your demons?'

He looks so serious that I can't help smiling. 'You bet, you're one of them but there are others, and when I leave here I'm going over to France to find them.'

'You could fly.'

'Funny man. The very thought of piloting an aeroplane fills me with dread. This time I'll do it the safe way. I'm going to Dover and then I'll drive my MG into a newfangled ferry called *Southern House*.'

'I meant as a passenger.' He goes over to an old fashioned bureau and rummages in a drawer. 'I kept this magazine because of an advertisement that caught my eye. Here we are. This is the February edition of *Flight Magazine*.'

He brings it the table and reads aloud. 'Since experimental services began in 1948 with one Bristol Freighter aircraft, traffic on the Lympne to Le Touquet services operated by Silver City Airways Ltd has steadily increased. During last summer's season 13,000 vehicles were carried and forty-two round trips were flown daily. As heavier demands are expected in 1952 a similar service between Southampton and Cherbourg is already operating.'

He shoves the magazine across the table and I'm looking at a simplified map of the Channel with a dotted line connecting Southampton to Cherbourg's Maupertus airport. Eric says, 'Play your cards right and old mother Cazalet might be there on the airfield to meet you.'

The tension between us is easing and soon we become more relaxed. It seems I'm stuck here for the night whether I like it or not so I help cook supper. The wine flows and during the meal we talk about France and about Madame Cazalet and the incredible cabinet maker Mr Tibault – and I want to believe that Eric is the father of my child because he's laughing and happy and so am I – but that thinly disguised look of revulsion is on his face every time he looks at me.

I say to him, 'You never told me the reason why you went to France in 1942. You never said anything about it during the entire time I was nursing you back to health after that awful amputation.'

'That's because they made me sign the Official Secrets Act.'

Perhaps it's the intimate atmosphere of the farmhouse, or his half-lit face in the flickering oil lamp, or old memories of a friendship that grew between us in a dangerous place that makes me say, 'To hell with the Official Secrets Act. Just tell me.'

'It all started on a spring morning in 1942. I was at my desk in the drawing office of the Vickers factory working on a new version of the Spitfire when...'

CHAPTER EIGHTEEN

Preparations,
Friday 6th of March 1942

Eric Blakeny heard a motorbike. He looked up from his drawing board and, through the window, saw Captain O'Leary riding across the airfield at his usual reckless pace. For goodness sake what does he want now?

The door opened. He came in and Eric said, 'Hello Philip, if you've come about table tennis I don't want to play this evening. There's a war on in case you hadn't noticed.'

Philip threw his cap and missed the chair. 'I've come about the Butcher Bird.'

'For goodness sake man, can't you see what I'm trying to do in this boring little office?'

'That's why I'm here. Do you remember

that evening when we called a halt because it was too dark to see the sixth hole?'

'You're talking about golf again, please don't confuse me.'

'While we were having a drink in the clubhouse you told me that the Luftwaffe's latest fighter aircraft was giving you a headache because the RAF didn't have a plane capable of matching it.'

'Come to the point Philip.'

'You said you'd sacrifice your nonexistent fame and wealth in exchange for any technical information on said aircraft however meagre or small.'

'Explain yourself.'

'How would you like to meet a Butcher Bird pilot?'

Two days late a sentry was checking their identity cards. 'Welcome to RAF Station Tangmere, gentlemen. The Officers' Mess is the last building on the right at the end of this road. I hope you have a pleasant evening.'

They were greeted by an older than average Flight Lieutenant with a bullet wound in his cheek. 'I'm Jimmy Moss the mess secretary. I hope you two don't mind sharing a room but it's the best I can manage at short notice. We're dining in tonight so it's drinks in the anteroom before dinner and for reasons as yet unknown the two of you are required to

257

be in RAF uniform.'

A steward led them upstairs. He put down their bags in a twin-bedded room and opened the wardrobe. 'Flight Lieutenant Coldwell's personal effects have been sent to his mother but his uniform is still in the wardrobe. He won his Distinguished Flying Cross for a low-level job over Antwerp, post-humous unfortunately. This other uniform belonged to another deceased officer who had rather short legs but the trousers should be all right if you slacken off the braces.' He tilted his head at a framed photograph of a showgirl wearing two tassels and a gold star. 'When I heard you was coming I left Veronica on the wall, Mr Coldwell would have wanted me to do that being the hospitable kind of gentleman that he was. It's a rum old world we live in today and no error. It's here today and gone tomorrow in this business. The ablutions is at the end of the corridor and if there's anything else you want from me just touch the bell.'

Changing into his uniform Philip said, 'He's right about the trousers.'

Eric looked at himself in the mirror and wondered if he'd ever have the courage to be awarded a DFC.

They went downstairs and the Wing Commander intercepted them as soon as they entered the anteroom. 'Delighted to welcome you aboard and glad to see you're properly dressed. I'm afraid our honoured guest will be in flying clothes.'

The visitor was wearing a leather jacket, a silk scarf, riding breeches and long boots. Two armed guards escorted him into the room. The Commanding Officer shook hands with the stranger and addressed the assembled company. 'In spite of the fact that our guest, Maximilian Steinhover, is an enemy pilot he no longer flies for the Fuhrer thanks to the brave actions of a British fisherman. Tonight I expect you all to demonstrate that the age of chivalry is not yet dead. Enjoy the evening and you have my permission to treat our guest as a friend while he is here in our mess.'

Steinhover was of less than medium height. He had a boyish look about him but his impeccable hair and upright stance gave him a certain air of authority. He said fluently, 'I trust I will soon have the honour to return your hospitality as guests of the *Jadgeschwader II, Gruppe III* after your Spitfires have been shot down in flames over France.'

Evidently the interpreter sent down from London would be enjoying his soup and fish under false pretences.

The Wing Commander took a tumbler of whisky from the steward's tray and handed it to his guest: 'To the Third and Last Reich, may its downfall be swift.'

259

Steinhover took a massive gulp and the steward immediately topped up his glass. In the dining room he sat next to the Commanding Officer with Eric on his other side. Between ladlefuls of peppery soup the Wing Commander told how he had shot at a wild boar in Bavaria that had seemed none the worse for it, and Steinhover reciprocated with a solemn account of a stalking holiday in Scotland that resulted in a stag weighing eighty-nine kilograms.

Throughout dinner the steward kept topping up Steinhover's glass and afterwards the German pilot readily accepted an invitation to sit in the cockpit of a Spitfire.

Members of the hangar party soon became more relaxed in the absence of their boss. They patted their guest on the back, laughed at his so-called jokes and *heilhitlered* him and goose-stepped with him across the blacked out aerodrome. In the cold atmosphere of the hangar, however, Steinhover reached for the nearest wing to steady himself. It was easy to see that his stomach was in turmoil after such generous treatment at dinner. Eric remained sober and alert.

The German pilot put an unsteady foot on the wing-root of a Spitfire and, to English cries of *jawohl* and *achtung,* was lifted into the cockpit. Settling himself onto a fitter's cushion he looked up at Eric who was leaning over him.

'Do I have sufficient fuel to return to my base in France?' The question provoked cheers and thumps on the back. 'Which one of you gentlemen will teach me how to fly your Spitfire?' He pointed forward and belched loudly. 'Will somebody open the hangar door a bit wider please.'

The response was a series of catcalls and more rude gestures while Steinhover squinted at the controls through eyes that appeared to be glazing over.

Eric started his carefully worded comparison between the Spitfire and the Butcher Bird with starting procedures, engine settings, climbing and stalling speeds.

Steinhover placed his hand across the three levers on the throttle quadrant. 'What are these for?' Eric pointed to each in turn: 'Boost, pitch and this one here is the mixture control.'

Steinhover pushed the levers backwards and forwards and shook his head sadly. 'In the Butcher Bird we have the Kommandgerat.'

'The what?'

He looked up at Eric. 'It is smelling very bad in here. Please open the hangar doors a little wider.' In response to more whistles and two-fingered gestures Steinhover gave a cheery wave and farted loudly. 'When we fly the Wurger – the Butcher Bird as you call it

– we do not have to worry about propeller pitch, revolution speed and what the bloody fuel-mixture is supposed to be.' His face was the colour of chalk.

Eric said casually, 'Tell me about the Kommandgerat.'

'It's a secret. Only when the war is over will I tell you about it. You English, you make me bloody drunk and you explain everything very bad. For the love of Winston Churchill will somebody tell me how to start the engine?'

Eric leaned in and gave Steinhover a re-assuring pat on the back. 'Let's see how it compares with your Butcher Bird.' He flipped up both magneto switches, turned on the fuel cock, nudged the throttle forward half an inch, adjusted the mixture control, pushed the propeller speed control forward, opened the radiator shutters and looked into Steinhover's half closed eyes. 'Starter on the left, booster coil on the right, you have to press them simultaneously.'

'Simul-what?'

'Both together, and…'

Steinhover's fingers hit the buttons with the speed of a striking snake. Shouts of panic were lost in the engine's roar. Men scattered but Eric clung on, leaning into the cockpit and lunging at the ignition switches while the Spitfire made a curving sweep towards the half-open hangar door. Frag-

262

ments of propeller flew like shrapnel.

The following afternoon Captain O'Leary was in his office. He took several sheets of paper from a drawer in his desk, shook a bottle of blue-black ink and filled his fountain pen. The plan was clear in his mind so all that was needed now was to get the details down on paper in a style that could be easily understood by the thickest of senior officers.

PROPOSAL

1. OBJECT:
To bring back to this country, undamaged, a Focke-Wulf 190.

2. FORCE REQUIRED:
a) One Motor Torpedo Boat (MTB), equipped with Direction Finding apparatus to carry a collapsible canoe to within two miles of the coast of France. **b)** One collapsible canoe equipped with wireless transmitter. **c)** One officer of commando. **d)** One specially selected pilot.

3. METHOD:
<u>Day One:</u> **a)** On the night of Day One the MTB carrying the officers and canoe will leave England after dark and proceed at best speed to within two miles of a selected beach in France. **b)** The canoe will be carried inland and hidden in a wood or buried in dunes. The two officers will lie up during

263

the following day.

Day Two: **a)** The officers will move inland at nightfall until they are within observation range of a fighter aerodrome. **b)** The officers will keep the aerodrome under observation and plan the attack for the start of nautical twilight on day three. **c)** During the night the officers will penetrate the aerodrome defences by stealth and will conceal themselves as near as possible to a selected Focke-Wulf aircraft.

Day Three: **a)** At the start of nautical twilight, when the aircraft are being warmed up by ground mechanics, the two officers will take the first opportunity to shoot the ground mechanics of the selected plane as soon as it has been started up. **b)** The pilot officer will take off in the machine and return to England. **c)** The commando officer will first ensure the safe departure of the aircraft and will then withdraw to a previously reconnoitred hide-up. **d)** During the night, the commando officer will return to the concealed canoe.

Day Four: **a)** Before nautical twilight the commando officer will launch the canoe and be picked up by Motor Torpedo Boat. **b)** The MTB should be off the coast for two hours before nautical twilight on Day 4, Day 5, or Day 6 providing the weather is calm. **c)** If the weather is unsuitable the returning MTB should come on the first suitable morning. **d)** The commando officer, after launching the canoe, will paddle on a pre-arranged bearing. The MTB, making due allowance for the day and the consequent set of the tide will proceed on a course to intercept the canoe. In addition the officer will make wireless signals, which will be picked up by the MTB using Direction Finding gear.

4. SELECTED AERODROME:

a) The selection of an aerodrome will be dependent on intelligence not at present available to me. The requirements are: **1)** Within 20 miles of a landing beach that is not too strongly defended and which has a hinterland of dunes or woods offering a hiding place for the canoe. **2)** Within observation range or close to the covered approach of a wood or other place of concealment. **b)** It is thought that possibly Maupertus aerodrome might be suitable. It is close to a suitable beach making the need for cliff climbing unnecessary.

5. RETURN OF THE PLANE:

Arrangements must be made with Fighter Command to ensure that the pilot officer is not shot down by our fighters on returning with the captured aircraft. It is suggested that these arrangements should not be dependent on wireless or on the officers taking distinctive markings or signalling apparatus. Possibly Fighter Command could be instructed not to shoot down any single Focke-Wulf 1909 appearing over the coast during speci-fied times on the selected days. In addition, the undercarriage could be lowered for identification.

6. DATE:

The beach landing should be made on a rising tide to cover footprints and also on a dark night to achieve surprise.

OTHER CONSIDERATONS:

a) Food: The officers will be equipped with 10 days compressed rations. **b)** Preparation: The officers should have ample time to train together for a period which need not exceed 10 days. **c)** Security: The officers suggested in the accompanying letter frequently go sailing together. The commando officer owns a double canoe which is used daily.

O'Leary read his plan through twice, put it into a buff envelope marked MOST SECRET and thought carefully before writing the accompanying letter…

To: OC No 12 Commando.
MOST SECRET and URGENT
From: Capt. P.H. O'Leary
'E' Troop. No 12 Commando.

Sir,
I understand that, as a matter of great urgency, a specimen Focke-Wulf 190 is required in this

country. I attach my proposal for procuring one of these aircraft.

I have the honour to request that this, my application, be forwarded as rapidly as possible through the correct channels to the chief of Combined Operations. I further propose that the pilot to accompany me should be Mr Eric Blakeny, a close friend of mine, a skilled test pilot of fighter aircraft and well qualified to bring back the plane. He is also young and active and a man in every way suitable to carry out the preliminary approach by land and sea.

I am most anxious to be allowed to volunteer for this operation.

I have the honour to be, sir
Your obedient servant
P.H. O'Leary 9/3/1942

As the day drew nearer Eric could neither sleep or eat. Dying for his country might be an honourable thing to do but suicide was still a crime in the eyes of the law. The dreaded comparison between honour and suicide was plaguing him while he waited with Philip for the train and it was still on his mind when they arrived at Kingswear station.

Dartmouth harbour was blacked out, so dark that the MTB was barely visible alongside the jetty. *What the hell am I doing here?* They crossed the gangplank and an officer

267

greeted them, gnome-like under the hood of his duffel coat.

'Welcome aboard gentlemen, I'm Lieutenant Ronnie Seaton.' He lit his pipe and quickly pinched out the flame. 'At least the weather's on our side.'

Eric wasn't so sure. The small ship was rocking, bursts of spray spattered the deck like handfuls of gravel. The skipper checked his watch. 'Six hours from now we'll be standing two miles off the French coast with our main engines stopped. We'll be putting to sea in twenty minutes.' He led his guests below where Philip had to stand with his head at an angle.

Seaton pushed back the hood of his duffel coat and removed his cap. 'Welcome to the wardroom, gentlemen.'

Eric asked, 'What happens if we meet a German E-boat?' and immediately regretted asking.

Seaton laughed. 'We run like hell in the opposite direction. Instead of torpedoes we carry the equivalent weight in extra fuel in our tubes. In plain language it means we have unlimited range but no balls.'

'Have you dropped passengers before, in France I mean?'

'I'm not supposed to answer questions like that.' He undid four wooden toggles and threw his duffel coat across a chair. 'Leading Seaman Blend has prepared supper for us.

Meanwhile will you join me in an aperitif?'
He found a bottle and squinted at the label.
'I have to admit I'd never heard of *Waidla
Geist Schnapps* until three weeks ago. This
was given to me by a young lady who had to
leave France in a hurry. There, I've said it.
Of course I've been to France – do it all the
time.' He found three small glasses and
wiped them with his handkerchief. 'Here's
to us, Navy, Army and Air Force and the
spirit of cooperation in Allied Fighting
Men, how does that sound? That last time I
got involved in one of these combined service operations I caught five soldiers with
blackened faces frying eggs in my wardroom.'

Eric sniffed his drink cautiously. Philip,
after downing his in one-go said, 'Blakeny
here is a civilian.'

Seaton raised an eyebrow. 'The uniform
had me fooled.'

Eric took a sip of his drink. German
schnapps tasted all right, so at least something good was coming out of that country.
The irony of it made him smile. Seaton took
his leave, went up on deck followed by
Philip. Eric was still finishing his drink when
the engines started with vibrations that
shook the floor. Soon he was on deck too,
looking in the direction of the receding
harbour, invisible except for one solitary
pinprick of light shining like a glow-worm

from somewhere in the blacked out town as they headed seaward.

The wind was fresher now and the small craft butted past the dim silhouette of a ruined castle guarding the harbour mouth. Six hours, one hundred miles of open sea, plenty of time to eat supper and plenty of time for Eric to run through in his mind everything he knew about German aeroplanes, which wasn't very much following the chaos at RAF Tangmere.

While lying under a blanket on a thin mattress, more thoughts pushed in during the long period of inactivity. How long did Elizabeth stay alive before her body was pulled from the rubble, and the dreadful business of arranging her funeral, in a rush, with the urgencies of war making it difficult to come to terms with the bereavement. His wife was dead and life seemed cheap without her, perhaps that's what had made him agree to take part in this suicidal mission. Philip was a good chap in spite of the questionable influences of Eton and Cambridge, but he was a typical Commando type – gung-ho and press-on come what may – able to laugh at the prospect of death, one had to admire him for that. But what did he know about the difficulties of flying a foreign fighter aircraft? The whole thing was a gamble and it was insane to think that it would be easy to just climb into the cockpit of a Jerry plane and fly it away. Yes, life after victory was the only thing that really mattered – and love. What was that Spanish song that Elizabeth used to sing, something about doves chattering to each other on a rooftop? *There is no love like the first love,* that was it, and it must have been the gunboat's rocking motion that made Eric dream that he was sleeping with his late wife on the top bunk of a cross-channel ferry on the way to Le Touquet to play roulette...

'Time to go.'

Up on deck Philip was flexing his limbs, trying to dispel the stiffness. The sea was calm. Eric pulled back his sleeve – twelve minutes past four in the morning and still dark. Three sailors were unlashing the canoe from its stowage and the gnome was there too with Leading Seaman Blend at his elbow. Somebody came on deck with bags continuing sten guns wrapped in oilcloth, clips of ammunition, grenades, wire cutters and food for three days.

Eric shook hands with the skipper and whispered something about hoping to meet again. He stepped into the canoe and settled into the narrow seat behind Philip.

After paddling for several minutes Eric looked back. The gunboat was barely visible, melting into the darkness with its auxiliary shut to a barely audible mutter. A warm wind was on their backs. Eric dipped his paddle and tried to keep time with Philip whose back made a dark shape against the cliffs of *Cap Lévy*. As they got closer he heard waves breaking on the shore. Closer still and the canoe scraped to a stop.

They got out of the boat and stood in the surf, knowing that the rising tide would soon obliterate their footprints. All was still. Taking an end each they carried the canoe into the cover of trees and removed the struts exactly as they had rehearsed on a quiet river in England. The undergrowth was thick enough to hide the canoe, and there it would stay until the Butcher Bird was flying towards England and Philip was ready to paddle out in the canoe to meet the torpedo boat.

They lay hidden throughout the following day. Eric was exhausted yet at the same time keyed up and unable to rest. Small sounds cut the silence, a creaking tree trunk, the rustle of a small animal and from far away the drone of aircraft. He again tried to picture the cockpit layout of an aeroplane that he had never seen before and when night fell they picked up their weapons and moved on silently towards the airfield, feeling their way with Philip O'Leary in front squinting at the luminous dial of his compass. Eric winced at every crack of twig or crunch of stone until at last they came to the boundary fence.

Dawn's first light showed and Eric wondered how long he had slept. He wound his watch and after a hurried meal of biscuits and corned beef that was to lie heavily on his stomach, he checked his sten gun, checked it again, fitted the magazine, made both grenades secure in their pouches, loaded his revolver and checked his binoculars.

Philip cut the bottom wire. They crossed a drainage ditch and lay flat in a slight hollow about one hundred yards from the nearest aircraft.

As the dawn continued to lift, men appeared, walking towards the long lines of aircraft, ten, twenty of them, thirty. The aircraft were just beginning to show their camouflage paint, black crosses and swastikas in the rising sun. The mechanics, dressed in black overalls, talked and joked with each other as they found their respective machines and extinguished their cigarettes in the damp grass.

Eric watched through his binoculars while the men dragged up accumulator trolleys and connected them to plugs under spring-loaded flaps set just behind the engine cowling of each aircraft. A retractable entry step was pulled down from a housing on the side of each aircraft and Eric could see handholds and more steps positioned higher up on the fuselage. He rehearsed the movement in his mind – step, handhold, step, handhold, bend the knee. Would there be time to strap in before take off?

Radial engines, compact and streamlined, started up noisily and ran smoothly at the tick-over. How could an air-cooled engine with such a small frontal area stay cool in flight? And what about the Kommandgerat, had these people really invented something to eliminate three separate levers to control boost, pitch and mixture? Would there be time to work it out before taking off under a hail of bullets?

Eric continued to watch, waiting for the sky to brighten sufficiently to make a safe take-off in an unfamiliar aircraft. He glanced at Philip lying next to him and listened to the steady hum of warming engines. Keeping his head well down, Eric put his binoculars to his eyes and panned across the airfield look-ing for obstacles and noting the angle of the windsock. He focused on a concrete struc-ture, low and flat-topped with a horizontal slit – a gun emplacement, machine-gun probably. Focus on the slit.

What was that? A flash? A glint? Some-thing made of glass? A lens? Maybe a pair of binoculars?

Next to it he saw the barrel of a gun swing-ing to its target...

CHAPTER NINETEEN

Watermill Farm, 29th of April 1953

At Watermill Farm, April showers have turned into a storm. I hear thunder booming. Lightning flashes and the wind is almost strong enough to break the windows.

Eric pours another coffee. 'After that everything became confused in my mind. Pain is what I remember most, it was shooting up my arm like an electric shock. I vaguely recall running towards an open barn and feeling straw on my face and in my eyes. Dogs were barking. Men were shouting in German. Something like elastic snapped inside my arm and I must have bitten my tongue to stifle my screams and I was almost choked by a river of blood that tasted like rust. The next thing I knew I was in bed looking at a strange mark on the ceiling shaped like a map of Africa. A face appeared but I couldn't make out the features. Somebody was looking down at me and the hand on my brow felt like ice.'

I want him to go on. I could listen to him all night because during all the time I was nursing him back to health in Madame

Cazalet's chateau he never told me a single thing about why he came to France in the spring of 1942.

'That's where I come into your story, *n'est-ce pas.*'

'My God, yes, I suppose it must have been you.'

'So you came to France in the middle of a war and failed to steal your Butcher Bird?'

'It's not a happy story. I never saw Philip again and, during all the confusion on that bloody beach I failed to take you with me to England.' He leans back in his chair. 'When I arrived back, safely thanks to you, I tried to pick up where I'd left off. Some of the things I'd seen while I was in France made me even more determined to find an answer to the Butcher Bird problem so I took a small room on the first floor of the Cricketers Arms just a short walk from my drawing office and set to work. I'll always remember the first night I spent in that bedroom. I went upstairs, undid my tie one-handed, took off my shirt and trousers one-handed, squeezed tooth-paste one-handed and pulled back the bed-clothes one-handed. When sleep finally came an air raid siren woke me but I stayed in bed thinking about the new Spitfire. All hope of getting a Butcher Bird for comparison had gone so I was left with the prospect of beefing up the airframe of the Mark Five Spitfire to accommodate the mighty Griffon engine

276

– that was our only hope. The following morning I was back in my drawing office when...'

Vickers Aircraft Factory, Tuesday 23rd June 1942

'Sorry to disturb you, Mr Blakeny – telephone – you'll have to come through. Your extension is out of order.'

Eric went down the passage to the switchboard and picked up Number Two telephone. 'Blakeny here.'

'Fancy a trip to Wales?'

He didn't recognise the voice and why on earth go to Wales of all places when he had barely settled in after returning from France. 'What's up?'

'Can't tell you over the phone but we have something here at Pembrey that might interest you.'

The following day Eric was in a train on his way to Oakington and, as always in quiet moments, he managed to forget about work and reflect on his French nurse, Lucette, her beautiful face, black hair, pale skin and a smile that used to linger at the corners of her mouth. Where is she now? How long would she be able to survive with her country overrun by Nazis?

A different girl was waiting for him on the

platform at Oakington station and at first glance she appeared to be little more than fifteen years old.

'I'm Kitty Brady, your pilot. I understand you need to get to RAF Pembrey. It so happens that I'm ferrying an old Albermarle that's been patched up after a crash. They need it at Pembrey for target towing. I've only just arrived myself. I'm glad your train was on time because we are due to take off at thirteen-hundred hours.'

They climbed into a mud-coloured Hillman. Kitty crashed the gears, drove recklessly onto the airfield and parked next to the Albermarle. Why Armstrong Whitworth had relied on a pair of Hercules XI engines to lift more than ten tons of steel and wood into the air, and then call it a viable weapon of war, was still a mystery.

Eric took the right-hand seat while the girl produced a ring-bound booklet from her pocket, opened it at a marked page and said, 'I've never flown one of these before and I'm new to the Oakington runway.' She kept referring to her book while starting up and preparing the aircraft for take off. 'They tell me it's rather like a Mosquito to fly apart from the tricycle landing gear.'

Eric, aware of a touch of dampness under his shirt, said nervously, 'And three tons heavier. I'll take her if you like.'

Kitty looked down at the metal hook

protruding from his sleeve. 'Sorry sir, passengers aren't allowed to take the controls,
it's against regulations and anyway I need
the experience. I've clocked up seven hours
on Mosquitoes so we should be okay.'

From the meagre comfort of the right-
hand seat Eric noticed that the runway
sloped upwards to a point about halfway
along and then dipped out of sight beyond
the summit.

The girl turned another page and opened
the throttles while Eric kept his eye firmly
on the airspeed indicator. He knew what
was going to happen but was too courteous
to interfere.

The aircraft ski-jumped off the brow, sank
back with a tooth-shattering bounce and
wobbled over the boundary hedge on the
brink of a stall. Kitty shoved the controls forward and gave Eric a quick smile. 'Nobody
told me about that hill.'

Eric wanted to give her a reassuring pat
but resisted the temptation. Instead he
looked down at the silvery curve of the river
Cam and the colleges of Cambridge sliding
under the port wing. When this war was
over he would go over and find Lucette and
fulfil the promise he'd made on that dangerous beach in France – take her to England, marry her, live happily until death, his
death or her death – somebody would be
left alone at the end but that was a million

years in the future.

After half an hour he could see Dunstable Downs and the wide boundary fence surrounding Whipsnade Zoo. What do animals think about all day, do they have souls? Will God condemn them to hell if they don't believe in Him? Does He punish a wolf for disobeying the sixth commandment? He looked at the girl, cooler now and more confident – and her turned-up nose reminded him of Lucette.

After two hours the Albermarle was dipping towards the south coast of Wales. The girl said, 'Our approach speed should be exactly one hundred miles per hour – that's quite a bit slower than a Mosquito.'

The aircraft descended towards a triangle of tarmac, touched down heavily in a nose-up attitude, bounced airborne again but settled safely. She steered off the runway, taxied towards the control tower and was shown where to park by a beckoning airman. After undoing her harness she rubbed dust off the dashboard clock with her fingers. 'If I'm quick I can catch the three-forty-five from Llanelly station.'

Eric's relief at feeling firm ground under his feet was tempered by his anxiety about Kitty's train. A car arrived and a young man in uniform stepped out. 'Eric Blakeny I presume.'

Eric squeezed the girl's shoulder.

'Thanks for the ride.' As she climbed into the front seat next to the driver he noticed how the dividing seam of her trousers tightened into the cleft, and suddenly the clock wound back eleven days and he was in a bedroom on the top floor of the chateau, walking across a creaking floor, shirt open, helping Lucette to her feet, trying to ignore the stabbing pain in his non-existent arm and saying, 'Take a look, what do you think?'

Lucette came towards him, holding her dress. She stuck out her lip. 'You painted my birthmark.'

'I saw a butterfly on your back – it's part of you.'

'I don't like it.'

He put his half-arm around her waist and reached past her with a stick of charcoal to sign the picture. 'Your English has improved.'

'That's because you talk too much, about anything and everything but never about what brought you to France with half your arm hanging off.'

Eric cupped her right buttock with his good hand and when she turned to face him her dress fell to the floor and he could feel her breasts against his chest. Her face was flushed to a colour that would have been impossible to capture on the lid of a wooden wine case using soot and red ink.

He said, 'Tomorrow night, when you lead

me to the beach, we may never see each other again.'

She kissed him. 'Don't talk about tomorrow, don't think even about it.' Her hands were behind his head.

Eric lifted her off the floor and carried her backwards until the edge of the mattress was behind his knees. They fell with Lucette on top. Oh God... She straddled him. He arched his back. She bent forward and took the lobe of his ear between her teeth and...

'I'm Pilot Officer Ronald Bellshaw, glad to meet you Mr Blakeny. I gather you want to take a dekko at our Butcher Bird... Mr Blakeny? Are you feeling all right?'

'I'm sorry – yes of course I am. What did you say? Did you say Butcher Bird? Do you mean to tell me that you have one here?'

'Didn't they tell you? It's in Hangar Number One. Our CO, cautious man that he is, has ordered an armed guard around the clock. God help anyone who lets the pilot escape.'

'The pilot?'

'In the guard room.'

While walking towards the hangar, Pilot Officer Bellshaw seemed glad to talk about his prize. 'I was on duty in the control tower swallowing the last of my tea and watching a group of idle airmen sitting on the grass playing cards. All of a sudden I saw an odd-

282

looking kite approaching the airfield from the direction of the Gower Peninsular. At first I thought it was a Typhoon but it wasn't radioing so I guessed it must be some ferry type. I hoped it would be an ATA dolly rather than some hairy-arsed old codger dating from the flood. I grabbed my binoculars for a closer look. That's never a Tiffie, I said to myself. The aircraft was side slipping with wheels down and heading for runway two-eight without so much as a by-your-leave. Didn't even bother to do a circuit. It had to be a woman – these ferry types you know, no sense of airmanship – I'm surprised you got here in one piece. Anyway I picked up my flare pistol and ran out onto the balcony intending to make her go round again, radio or no radio. Only after the kite had landed did I recognise the markings. A Jerry, can you believe it? Bold as bloody brass and there was Leading Aircraftsman Hodge marshalling it towards the refuelling area cooler than a cucumber. I ran down the steps, crossed the grass at a sprint, vaulted onto the wing and pointed my flare pistol at the pilot's head. You should have seen the surprise on his face. Luckily he gave himself up without a fuss.'

Eric had been watching Bellshaw's face for signs of a leg-pull. 'Does he speak English?'

'Not a flaming word, but we've been promised an interrogator – a not unattractive woman, or so I'm led to believe. She'll be here tomorrow.'

When they reached the hangar, the airman on guard snapped to attention and presented arms. Bellshaw saluted with a pair of brown leather gloves still clutched in his right hand and stood aside for Eric. 'On you go.'

There it was. Shiny and new, a prize fallen from the sky. Could it really be as easy as this? Eric went round to the front end and immediately noticed an impeller fan set behind the three-bladed propeller. Interesting – a double bank of radial cylinders, one behind the other and an impeller to suck in cold air to stop everything seizing up with the heat. No heavy glycol tank and no coolant to spew out of bullet holes during a dogfight.

Eric pulled down the entry step, climbed into the cockpit and surveyed the instrument panel. What a difference to the captured ME 109 he had flown at Farnborough last year. The seat was reclined back so far that he was almost lying down. He put his feet on the rudder pedals, noticing how the flange at the lower edge of the pedal fitted under his heels to take the weight of his legs. He put his right hand on the controls and looked down at Bellshaw.

'I'd like to meet the pilot before he's lost without trace in a POW camp.'

I'm upstairs at Watermill Farm, lying on my back in an unfamiliar bed, wondering why a German pilot would want to land an undamaged Butcher Bird in England. Eric needn't have gone to France at all, and he would have two arms instead of one if he he'd stayed in England – and if Philip O'Leary was dead, he died for nothing.

Sun streams in through the window. I hear movements downstairs and a door slams. I get out of bed, go to the window and see Eric walking across the yard towards the lake.

After washing and dressing I go downstairs into the untidy remains of last night's supper. The least I can do for this man, whose life I once saved, is to prepare his breakfast.

A simple wash-and-line painting hangs in a dark corner of the kitchen, that's why I didn't notice it before. It's of a girl with her head half turned. She has a birthmark shaped like a butterfly in the groove of her spine. The artist has signed it in the bottom right hand corner: *LUCETTE by Eric Blakeny, June 1942.*

CHAPTER TWENTY

Back to France,
Tuesday 31st of May 1953

I'm shivering on a canvas chair in a Bristol Freighter. Is it the draught from an ill-fitting door, or is it because of the fear and excitement I feel?

I'm also feeling a little sad because it didn't work. No, it didn't work but I have no regrets. Eric still talks about his dead wife and wonders how long she lasted, trapped under the rubble of a bombed building. How long would it last if I married Eric? Not long, I know that now, it would be no use trying to settle down in an isolated valley with an artist who can't even look me in the face. The spark that once flashed between a French nurse and her wounded patient has fizzled like a spent firework. Maybe he isn't the father of my child after all.

With a mug of coffee in one hand and a half-eaten sandwich in the other, I'm looking through a square window at fishing boats as we let down towards the coast of Cherbourg. I can see the shadow of our

286

aircraft as it crosses the beach and I can hardly believe that we are about to land at Maupertus airfield. But there's no doubt, I can see the curved roofs of five hangars and I can see Hotel de Fleuve's gravelled approaches exactly as I remember them.

My car is unstrapped and I drive it down the ramp and onto the airfield. A man in uniform checks my passport and, as I drive towards the road, I'm becoming aware of what is possibly the worst of my demons. I can picture him in the grass with a hole in his face and he's lying on the exact spot where he fell. *Dear God, was I wise to come here, am I ready for this?*

I drive into Cherbourg, park the car, walk by the harbour wall and breathe sea air mingled with a faint smell of French tobacco. Nothing has changed. I exchange a friendly word with a fisherman who stops loading nets into a multi-coloured boat, shrugs his shoulders, chats to me and laughs. He's waiting for the tide and I'm waiting to find the courage to turn my head and look across the street.

The illuminated sign is still there, gilt letters painted on glass over the doorway. I cross the cobbled road and push my way in through swing doors. Nobody is singing. No uniforms, no laughs, no banter. The piano is still there but there are no mugs of beer on top of it. I straddle the stool, put my hands on the keys and hear Helmut playing his harmonica, other ghosts are crowding me as I play a chord. *Kiss me goodnight Sergeant Major.*

A waiter comes. I order espresso coffee and remain seated at the piano thinking back to the moment when I saw Seddy lapping water from a glass ashtray. Stupid tears test my carefully applied make up. Why am I sitting here, is it because I'm half expecting a German officer with a dog at his heels to walk in through the door?

I drive east along route D901. The sun is in my eyes as I enter the village of Carneville and I park close to an ivy-clad inn. Inside it is dark and cool.

A boy cleaning windows steps down from a chair when he sees me. Luckily I'm able to book a room but I decline his offer to let me inspect it first. Help is what I need. 'May I see a copy of the local telephone directory?'

The boy produces a well-thumbed edition and I take it to the window. Dessoude, the entry is there but the initials are wrong – no G for Gilbert, no M for Marie. I give him a tip for reminding me how to get to the farm and after a short drive I'm looking at the barn and the house. They are unchanged I can see the field where I landed the Spitfire. I remember bursting through low cloud and seeing the ground rushing up at me. I can hear wind in the trees and the angry shouts

288

that made me dash for cover.

I get out of my car, open the gate, cross the cobbled yard and find a hand bell in a niche by the farmhouse door. I don't recognise the woman who comes, young, blonde, quite pretty but overweight and she doesn't smile as she stands in the doorway with her arms folded. I tell her who I am, where I've come and why I'm here.

She stares at me for several seconds then shakes her head. 'They are both dead.'

I try again. 'Mr and Mrs Dessoude used to live here. Is your name Dessoude?'

She steps back into the house and closes the door in my face. I'm left wondering whether I should ring the bell again, but the sound of a distant tractor gives me a better idea and I walk away from the house along a muddy track. Through a gap in the hedge I can see a tractor working its way towards me and when it gets closer the driver switches off the engine, climbs down, comes over, removes his cap and asks what I want.

'I'm looking for Marie and Gilbert Dessoude.'

He scratches his head. 'I'm afraid they are both dead. I am Charles, their nephew. I inherited this farm from them.'

I wonder if this man has any idea what happened here eleven years ago and try hard to sound casual. 'A British plane landed in this field on the sixteenth of March 1942. If you know anything about it I'd be glad if you'd...'

Charles Dessoude doesn't flinch at my burnt face. 'You mean the Spitfire? What do you know about it?'

'I understand it was flown by a woman.'

He laughs. 'A woman, that's impossible, but it was a Spitfire and it did land here. Come with me please.'

As we pass the house I see the blonde woman watching us from an upstairs window. When we reach the barn Dessoude pulls two wooden battens from their keepers, heaves the door open and ushers me inside. I follow him and as my eyes adjust to the dim light I see stacks of bags, piles of hay, a plough and farm implements of every description. At the far end we clamber over piles of scattered timber to a place where specks of dust swarm like flies in light beaming down from five slits set high in the stonework.

Dessoude steps forward and tugs at a tarpaulin covering a long bulky shape in front of me and through a cloud of settling dust I see a large shark-like object with battered protrusions, an opaque windscreen, peeling paint, shredded rubber on the tail wheel. I step forward and wipe away the dust with my hand and there it is. The registration number W3297 is still legible. I touch it again, wing-less, wheel-less and stupidly wonder what

Wally would say if he could see his precious Spitfire now.

I'm wondering just how much Dessoude knows about it. 'Does anyone know what happened to the pilot?'

'My uncle never said a word about this.' He picks up a wooden crate and places it against the aircraft and I step up, lean in and look at an array of familiar dials now hiding their obsolete functions under layers of dust. Prompted by a gentle push I grab the top of the windscreen, step over the broken hinge of the entry flap and lower myself into the seat.

He says, 'I never knew it was here until a few months ago. One day I noticed that the outside of this building was longer than the inside by about five metres. Do you see those ventilation holes in the stonework. They were only visible from the outside, they'd been blocked off by an inner wall that turned out to be nothing more than a temporary structure, no load-bearing properties and clearly erected in a rush. When I broke through the wall I found the Spitfire.'

I hardly notice the hard lip of metal pressing into my thighs. 'The pilot must have had a parachute. I wonder what happened to it?'

'Perhaps Gilbert took it. Perhaps he met the pilot. Maybe he knew why this plane landed here.'

When I tell him that the parachute was probably made of silk, he looks at me and raises a finger. 'That might explain why my mother received pair of silk culottes for Christmas, hand-stitched they were. She always wondered how her sister could find pure silk in the middle of a war.'

I put my hand on the spade-like handle and try to remember how I felt when I last sat in this cockpit. I curl my fingers around the frayed binding and reflect on the mix of circumstances that brought me here, and have brought me here again eleven years later. If I were to tell him that I was the pilot he wouldn't believe me, so I'll let it rest. Instead I say, 'Do you know a lady called Madame Cazalet who used to live near here?'

He nods. 'Big house about six kilometres away, she lives with a gentleman friend. They sold off most of the land.'

CHAPTER TWENTY-ONE

The Reunion, Sunday 31st of May 1953

The high arch of trees is denser and darker than I remember. Low branches whip the windscreen and the chateau looms above me with green stains streaking the walls like spilled paint. Some of the top-floor windows glint in the sun, but others are like the empty sockets of stags' skulls, like the ones that used to adorn the corridor inside.

I park on the same spot where Dadan parked his van when he brought me here for the very first time. Getting out of the car I feel familiar cobblestones through the thin leather of my shoes and I think of Dadan with his wheelbarrow loaded with fish. I was afraid then and I'm still afraid. I left France without saying goodbye to Madame Cazalet and I want to stay a moment longer, here, on the spot where I first saw Eric lying in this yard while the nurse from Lille caught a stench of septicaemia strong enough to convince her that the man was dying. And now Lucette Moreaux is back where she belongs, in France – and she remembers the smell of a dog sitting behind her in a DKW car and Otto's lips on hers and the things that might have been if only … if only, if only – how many pilots have uttered that despairing phrase after a crash?

The garden portal is now a careless jumble of broken stones piled on either side of the path and, as I walk towards the chateau, I imagine that I'm listening to the drone of Butcher Birds climbing from Maupertus and turning north to fight their losing war. I tread the overgrown path and remember the unshakeable Dadan walking with me, no wheelbarrow this time, and no fish.

I give three loud raps with the knocker. After a short wait the door swings inwards and I take a cautious step over the threshold and hear a voice that I instantly recognise. *'Bonjour mademoiselle.'*

Can it be, this bent figure stepping forward into the light with haggard face and dabs of rouge like fever on her cheeks? She touches my sleeve and her smile shows a gold tooth that dispels all doubt. I've come a long way to see her. Now I'm not sure what to say. It's clear that she doesn't recognise me but I don't want to tell her who I am, not just yet.

'I'm from England. I've been talking to Monsieur Dessoude about a British Spitfire that crashed in his field. I'm wondering if you know anything about it.'

Madame Cazalet dismisses the question

with a shrug. 'Many aeroplanes crashed in my country during those sad times.'

'But this one was flown by a woman.'

'What does Dessoude know about it?' She looks at me closely and ushers me inside. I follow her and yes, the stags are still on the walls of the corridor but now the big drawing room is a scene of decaying elegance with a large crack in the alcove mirror and gold leaf flaking from its frame. Plaster mouldings on the ceiling are broken and yellow and a dangling chain shows where the chandelier used to be. No Meissen figurines. The walls are bare. No tapestries, not a single picture except for a portrait of Madame Cazalet over the fireplace that captures how she looked all those years ago. I cross the room for a closer inspection and see a scrawled signature in the bottom right-hand corner, Eric Blakeny, June 1942. The Napoleon Clock no longer dominates the mantelpiece and a long row of framed passport-style photographs had taken its place.

Madame Cazalet stands beside me. 'What makes you think that Dessoude's Spitfire was flown by a woman?'

Before I have time to elaborate, she steps forward and picks up one of the photographs. 'Do you like my boys?'

'Yes, who are they?'

'They are airmen, many of them were English like you but none stayed here for more than a few days. Nearly all of them got safely back to their sweethearts and mothers. An important member of the French Resistance managed to convince somebody equally important in London that every airman flying over my country should carry photographs of himself so that we could make forged identity cards for them. You couldn't trust anybody in those days, not even the local photographer.'

Has she recognised me? I see watery reflections in Madame Cazalet's eyes as she continues. 'I gave them love. I gave them food and money. I gave them clothes and shoes for their big feet and as you can see I kept some of the photos.' She goes down the line touching them and picking them up for a closer look and saying their names out loud. At the end of the line she picks up a larger photograph of a happier group of eight young women in less formal poses. 'They were all so young.'

Looking up at the portrait of herself she says, 'Perhaps you will think me vain but that picture was always my favourite. It was painted by a good friend of mine. I had to sit for many hours but painting pictures was good for him because it helped build his strength and give him something to occupy his mind.' She picks up another photo from the mantelpiece. 'And here he is, Eric the artist. He was unlike the others, older than most. Nobody knew why he came to France. Can you imagine what it felt like to make love to a man with the talent of Rembrandt? Poor Eric, he suffered terribly while living here in my house. The screaming, so terrible it was. No chloroform, no modern antiseptics and when he left for England it made me very sad. Often I wonder if he still loves me.' Madame Cazalet lifted the photo to her lips and kissed the glass.

I decide that now is the time. 'My name is Blanche Longhurst.'

'And I am Henriette Cazalet.' Her repeated blinks squeeze a drop of moisture from the corner of her left eye. 'Is this your first visit to France?'

At that moment I hear footsteps, the door opens behind me and I turn to see the unmistakeable figure of Dadan striding across the room. He stretches out his arms. 'Blanche, my dear girl, is it really you, can it be? My God what happened to your face?'

Before I can answer, Madame Cazalet says, 'Claude, do you know this woman?'

'Of course I know her and so do you. Surely you remember Lucette Moreaux.'

She takes a step forward and a dawn of recognition rises on her sagging cheeks. 'I do believe – no, can it be true, the nurse from Lille, here again?' She takes my hands in hers and suddenly the old, caring Madame Cazalet has returned, and she is speaking French to me again. 'My darling girl, welcome back. I'm so sorry I didn't recognise you. You must spend some time with us now that you are here and tell us all your news.'

I explain that I have already booked a room at Carneville but they both insist that I stay the night.

While Dadan telephones to cancel my booking, Madame Cazalet says, 'We had quite an adventure and so did you. After you left Dadan told me things about you that I knew nothing about. When he told me that you were an English pilot and how you arrived unexpectedly in France I could hardly believe it. You are a very good actor, perhaps you should be on the…' She looks at my face and breaks off.

After a pause she continues. 'There is something we have been asking ourselves for a long time. What happened to you after the Officers' Ball?'

I look away.

'Never mind my dear. I don't want to know if you don't want to tell me. We were friends then and that's what we'll always be. Now I have to leave you for a minute, so you stay here and have a drink with Dadan. I still have my vegetable garden. Leek pie, remember?'

Dadan is on his knees rummaging in a

298

cupboard with his back to me. I say to him, 'Do you remember Mr Summerfield?'

He doesn't even turn his head. 'Who?'

'You killed him. I blew my nose and you stabbed him to death.'

Dadan rises. 'Oh yes, I was thinking about him only the other day. I still have the knife. I use it for weeding the path.'

'Was he really a spy? I mean, did you ever find out for certain?'

Dadan opens a bottle of calvados, pours generously and we clink glasses. 'Let's drink to his memory even though the poor wretch was working for the enemy. He failed to answer your questions. That was enough for me.'

'I've been worrying about that episode, in fact it's been bothering my conscience for years. Call it feminine intuition if you like. How can you be certain he was working for the enemy? Just because he failed to...'

'My dear Lucette – or should I say Blanche – I didn't *need* to be certain. Mere suspicion was enough. Remember our first meeting, in that attic at the farm? It seems rather brutal to say it now, but I would have broken your neck without hesitation if I had thought for one minute you were a spy.'

I walk over to the window. How can Dadan live with himself, shrugging off the death of Mr Summerfield like this as if it meant nothing? God knows what it has

299

done to me. I try to think about Otto again, something I always do when the demons come to haunt me. I can smell his dog. I can hear his laugh. I can feel him ruffling my hair. I can picture him teaching me how to fly a Butcher Bird. If only I could turn back the clock.

Thank God for Madame Cazalet. She comes into the kitchen carrying a handful of leeks. 'Talking of old times? Has Dadan described what happened to us after you disappeared?' And while making her famous leek flan, she tells me...

Chateau Chatelain,
Thursday 25th of June 1942

Madame Cazalet paced backwards and forwards across a vast Persian carpet. 'Four days and still no word from Lucette.'

Dadan sat with his head in his hands. 'I gave her my Browning and told her what to do with it if the Boche caught her. She's dead, I know it, but we can't afford to hang around any longer. We have to leave at once. It's all my fault. When she came to me with some stupid notion to steal documents from the Luftwaffe I encouraged her. I must have been mad.'

Madame Cazalet glared at him. 'Only an idiot would encourage her to pull a stunt like that with no proper planning.'

He stood up. 'Idiot or not we must leave here now before they come looking for us. Tell the girls to…'

The sound of squealing brakes made Madame Cazalet run to the window. An army lorry was parked in the yard outside. Uniformed men were leaping from the tailgate. Another truck arrived, Dadan made a bolt for the door.

She shouted after him, 'Come back, where in God's name are you going? Don't leave me now.'

Five girls burst in through the door and Madame Cazalet held up her hands. 'Everybody keep calm, whatever happens we must maintain our dignity.'

She opened the window and shouted so loud that her voice turned to a high falsetto. 'Go away. There is nothing for you here.' But she could already hear running boots inside the chateau and, within seconds, six soldiers pushed into the room and formed up in an orderly line stamping their feet. An officer followed. One glance at the skull and crossbones above the peak of his cap was enough.

'Good evening Madame. Good evening ladies. Your house is surrounded. You would be well advised to do exactly as I say.' He turned to his men. 'Two of you guard the door of this room. The rest of you will join the others. Bring any man you find to me, here in this room.'

Madame Cazalet put her head back. 'How dare you people come bursting into my house uninvited?'

The officer eyed her from head to toe and strutted round the room with his hands clasped behind his back. 'You already know why we are here.' He continued to strut but stopped abruptly by the mantelpiece.

'What have we here?' He touched the clock and stroked the brass eagle and ebony sphinxes on either side of the dial with a gloved hand. 'This is an extremely unusual piece if I may say so. A thermo-compensating pendulum is rare in a mid-eighteenth century clock.' He glanced at his wristwatch. 'Accurate too, it would appear that we have something in common, Madame Cazalet. I am also a lover of precious artefacts.' He glanced around the room. 'I have to say that I am most envious of your collection.'

The sound of breaking glass from another room made the officer turn quickly and shout at one of his soldiers. 'Tell those imbeciles that if they destroy anything of value in this house they will be severely punished.'

A short burst of gunfire came from the direction of the vineyard. Madame Cazalet took a step towards the window but the officer drew his pistol. 'Who gave you permission to move?'

After a short standoff the door opened and a man wearing RAF uniform staggered into the room, white-faced and with blood oozing between fingers that clutched his thigh. Two more airmen followed, pushed and goaded by soldiers with fixed bayonets.

'What have we here?' The officer looked at the men in turn then leaned forward until his nose almost touched Madame Cazalet's powdered cheek. 'Would you be kind enough to introduce me to these gentlemen?'

She pushed against the officer's chest with both hands and drew herself up defiantly. 'You find me at a disadvantage. A troop of armed soldiers against a handful of girls and three unarmed men.'

'Damn you woman. These men are wearing RAF uniforms.'

'And damn you too. No doubt you will do what your warped mind thinks right and I hope you live long enough to regret it.'

The women were hustled outside and told to climb into one of the trucks. The men went into another truck. Screened from the outside by a canvas cover and in semi-darkness, Madame Cazalet sat huddled with her girls in the speeding lorry, staring unblinkingly at two soldiers who sat opposite. Nobody spoke. The taller man avoided eye contact but the other removed his helmet, placed it between his feet, pushed back his

303

hair and surveyed the women with lips parted and the tip of his tongue protruding.

Fear at last – the fear of torture and death. Madame Cazalet wanted to ask where they were going but a sense of pride and defiance prevented her. After twenty minutes she knew that it wouldn't be the Gestapo head-quarters in Cherbourg. She wanted to grab both men by their collars and shake it out of them but dignity prevailed because that was her only defence. Death, thoughts of it bun-ched in her chest. Shot, hanged or worse. Would dignity abandon her when the mo-ment came?

Armande leaned back with head tilted side-ways and eyes closed. Hélène wept silently into her handkerchief. Madame Cazalet stared at the canvas, trying to interpret the swerves and turns of the speeding truck. Where are they taking us?

Yvette, never shy, made her request in a surprisingly steady voice. 'I need to urinate.'

One of the guards laughed, got up, made his way forward and banged his first on the back of the driver's cab. The truck slowed and stopped. Somebody peeled back the can-vas. The sun was low in a crimson sky. One of the guards beckoned the girl to follow him but others made it clear they needed to go too. 'All right, everyone out stay where we can see you.'

Madame Cazalet squatted over damp

earth thinking about Dadan and wondering why he had run away. One of the guards relieved himself, facing her unashamedly.

The journey resumed in darkness. Could Lucette be a traitor? Is her disappearance at this time mere coincidence or has she betrayed us? Where is she now?

The truck rattled on through the night until they heard the shriek of a train whistle and the squeal of brakes as they pulled to a stop. The officer peered in with face obscured by the peak of his cap. 'You will all remain here until I give the order.'

An hour passed with the silence broken by the occasional sob from Hélène. Madame Cazalet checked her watch and immediately one of the guards grabbed her wrist. 'Give me that or I'll tear it off.'

She snatched her hand away and the other guard laughed. 'One of these girls will be giving me her knickers if they keep us waiting here any longer. They're as good as dead anyway so let's show them a thing or two before they die.' He grabbed at Armande, ripping three buttons off the front of her dress in one quick tug. Madame Cazalet's kick went straight to the fork of his breeches and the man doubled up with a half-suppressed yell of pain. At that moment the officer banged on the tailgate. 'Everybody out.'

The guards picked up their rifles and

jumped down. The women followed, sitting on the edge of the tailboard before dropping to the ground. They were lined up and marched into the station. Some bystanders turned away from the pathetic group while others ogled.

The party approached the trucks by stepping over railway lines that were barely visible in the blackout. One of the guards opened a sliding door in the side of one of the trucks. It was already crowded with silent women. The stench was terrible.

Madame Cazalet climbed in and the girls followed. 'How long...?' But the door slid shut with a rush.

In pitch darkness Madame Cazalet could feel sweating bodies pressed against her in the crush, moaning, crying, somebody vomited and the stink of it on the straw was like poison in the airless truck. A whistle wailed. The train jolted but the women were so tightly packed that nobody fell. Picking up speed the train chattered over the points as it headed out into the country.

How long would this journey last? How long could women last under these conditions? Questions and doubts came to Madame Cazalet like steel on steel. She pictured leather-covered benches and brass rails, mirrored walls, a coffee machine and the slow rotation of a ceiling fan ruffling a single strand of hair that had escaped from Lucette's curls. Yes, she remembered entering the Café de Paris with Lucette and she could see the look the girl had given Otto Stoeckl when he came over to join their table. Something about the swaying press and the rhythm of the train reminded Madame Cazalet of the concert and how German airmen had cheered and clapped until a blush had crept upwards from Lucette's throat to colour her. Was it shyness or was it guilt? Lucette had fallen in love with a Boche violin player and she must have fallen into a trap where she would either be tortured until she told all, or else forced to ingratiate herself with these people. A long blast from the engine's whistle seemed to carry a message of betrayal and death.

Madame Cazalet was almost asleep on her aching feet when she heard the sharp crack of a distant explosion. Brakes were squealing. The train was slowing and tilting and tipping. She heard crunching wood, crushing metal, screams. Arms flailed in the darkness, straw was in her eyes. And suddenly there was damp earth against her face, fresh air in her lungs and a bright moon overhead. Men were shouting and bullets whined to accompany the cries of wounded men.

She picked herself up, wiped something from her eyes and through a screen of gushing steam saw the train angled down the embankment like a wounded snake. Hélène was lying still with her head at an unnatural angle, mouth open, mud in her eyes and on her lips.

Screened from view by the protecting bulk of an overturned truck, Madame Cazalet climbed up the embankment. Thank God. Lois, Armande and Brigitte were alive and Carmen was trying to say something between sobs. Men appeared, backlit by the night sky, stepping over railway lines. As they came closer she recognised Albert, Jacques, the stooping figure of René and young Pitou whose real name she could never remember. And then a man's arms were squeezing her so tight she could barely breathe. His stubble was on her cheek, the smell of his sweat in her face.

'Dadan, thank God you're safe, thank you, thank you. I love you.'

He slung his rifle across his back. 'All the guards are dead. Now we must get the women away from here.'

Chateau Chatelain, Tuesday 31st of May 1953

We sit together, the three of us, and suddenly it feels as if the past eleven years had never happened.

Madame Cazalet says cautiously, 'Now you know our story but what happened to you after the Officers' Ball? We won't be angry if you did something you are ashamed of. The war is over now.'

I hesitate because I'm still not ready. She follows with, 'Perhaps you will tell us tomorrow after you have spent the night here, in your old room if you like. How do you say it in English – *for old times' sake?* Dadan and I live alone now, just the two of us in this great big house.'

I go out with her to collect my suitcase from the car. I know what I want to ask Madame Cazalet but for the moment it will have to wait.

While sitting at the kitchen table eating leek flan, Madame Cazalet puts down her fork and reaches across to squeeze Dadan's shoulder. 'This is my man now. What a fool I was to doubt him when he ran out of the house.'

Dadan smiles. 'Derailing a train is quite easy when you know how. A fog signal attached to a hundred grams of gelignite blows out a metre of track as neatly as if it were cut with oxyacetylene.'

Madame Cazalet smiles. 'He's bald and overweight but he's always been a brave man – he needs to be now that he's taken me on.'

I say, 'What happened after you'd escaped from the train?'

'Thanks to Dadan, three barges were waiting for us on the canal. And thanks to a co-operative Mother Superior we were able to lie low in the convent at Pinoir until the heat was off.' Madame Cazalet dabs her eyes with a tiny handkerchief. 'My boys and girls were very brave, many of them gave their lives. The lucky ones were spared to rebuild a peaceful world from the ruins.' She sat back in her chair and drained another full glass in quick gulps.

While listening to her story I've been asking myself if I was right to leave France when I did – and in the way I did, without telling anybody about my real plan, not even Dadan. I remember him explaining how to use the miniature pistol and how I... No, I can't face that demon – not here – not yet.

Madame Cazalet chatters on while she makes coffee. 'Imagine what it felt like coming back to this house after the war to find it completely ransacked. All my possessions had been stolen and what remained had been smashed. The chateau was in a terrible state, far worse than the comfortable decay that surrounds us now. Do you remember my Napoleon clock and all the family history it had witnessed? Of all of my treasures that is the one I miss the most – and all I have now is the key to wind it up because they forgot to take it.'

Doctor Pritchard was right. If Madame Cazalet can talk freely about the horrors she has faced, why can't I? Perhaps now is the moment to unburden what happened to me after the Officers' Ball. I won't tell her everything, but at least I can describe what happened after I woke up and left Otto's bed. Thinking about it makes me feel like Lucette again and how she was worried about sleeping with a German officer without getting pregnant.

I take a sip of coffee and replace the cup carefully in its saucer. 'I'm a mother now.'

Madame Cazalet fiddles with her cigar and drops a long sausage of ash onto the tablecloth. 'That's wonderful, my dear. Who is the lucky man? Did you leave him in England?'

'The lucky man, as you put it, could be one of two men.'

Madame Cazalet smiles knowingly. 'I always suspected that you had something going with Eric, but what we want to know is what happened to you. You never came back to us after the Officers' Ball.'

'I wanted to return to England because I was convinced my fiancé was still alive in spite of what Dadan had said. But you both wanted me to stay here so I had to plan my escape.'

Dadan makes an intense study of his fingernails. 'During our first meeting at Dessoude's farmhouse you told me the name and rank of your fiancé and yes I have to admit it, I was lying when I told you he

311

was dead. I reckoned that if Blanche Long-hurst believed her fiancé to be dead she might not be quite so anxious to return to England. We needed women like you, attractive, courageous and bilingual – and women have certain advantages over men in some aspects of the secret war we were fighting in those days. I don't need to re-mind you that it is sex that motivates the human race, and Boche personnel stationed in France were far from home and hun-gering for a bit of female company. That's why I told you that Squadron Leader Peter Mason was dead, to keep you in France.'

Attractive girls, courage, is Dadan talking about me? In the silence that follows I can hear Doctor Pritchard advising me for the umpteenth time to face my demons. Perhaps now is the moment to tell him about the deaths, and I'm on the point of confessing when Madame Cazalet comes to my rescue with a knowing smile.

'You, Dadan and me, and let's not forget, our old friend Otto Stoeckl, were thrown together. That's what we have in common. Thrown together into a conflict over which we had no control. I blame the politicians and the ambassadors – those are the people who changed our lives. Dadan told me that you were a pilot. Are we to assume there-fore that you made your escape to England in an aeroplane? And if so was Squadron

Leader Mason waiting for you when you arrived?'

'Peter died. He was shot down shortly before I got to England.'

Madame Cazalet says quietly, 'I know what it feels like when a girl falls in love with a man only to find he's been killed before they've managed to crease the sheets together. But never lose hope. Things can change. I'm in love with this wonderful man who will always be my hero although I have other names for him when we quarrel. If he hadn't derailed that train I wouldn't be sitting here now and nor would he. We found happiness together. Why don't you try and do the same? Find the man who really loves you.'

'But Peter Mason is dead.'

'I said, the man who *really* loves you.'

'I visited Eric two days ago. He doesn't love me.'

'Never mind about Eric and you must try to forget about Peter. What about Otto, perhaps he loves you.'

'Sometimes I dream about spending the rest of my life with him.'

She smiles, taps out a cigarette and plants it between her lips. After several unproductive sparks from her lighter she manages to suck on a tiny flame. 'I should have thrown this thing away ages ago.' She snaps down the lid and pushes the lighter across the table.

I look at its engravings, a British crown and the head of an Indian chieftain. I pick it up and close my fist around it and remember Otto explaining that it had belonged to an American fighter pilot shot down over France in 1940, a member of one of the Eagle Squadrons operating from England before America came into the war.

I open my hand and look at it again. 'This was Otto's lighter, his Zippo. I saw him give it to you at the ball.'

'It's yours now. If you want to you can give it back to him.'

'I will if I ever meet him again.'

'I should have given it to him when we had coffee together three weeks ago. He was asking after you but of course we couldn't tell him anything, we hadn't the faintest idea what had become of you. It was good to see him again even though he was a Boche pilot, Otto is living proof of something I've known for a very long time – men improve with age.'

Otto alive? And suddenly it's as if I'm with him in his bedroom in Hotel de Fleuve. I can feel his hands tearing my dress, his tongue between my lips and my hand sliding down his sweaty back over the joints of his spine to the cleft of his buttocks. But it isn't me. It's Lucette who falls backwards onto the counterpane. It's Lucette who flexes her knees and opens herself to him and tastes the sweat in his armpits. It is Lucette who feels Otto's

314

hands in her hair and it's Lucette who whispers. *'Je t'aime'* over and over again as she grabs him and guides him knowing that she will always remember this moment. Always – how long is always when a girl believes she could die tomorrow?

Madame Cazalet looks at me strangely. 'Is something the matter, my dear?'

'Where is Otto now? Is he in France?'

'He's German, why would he want to live in France?'

'Does he live in Germany?'

'No.'

Hours later I'm lying in bed and looking up at a dark patch on the ceiling that looks like a map of Africa. I reach for the bedside table and pick up the card that Madame Cazalet gave me and read it over and over again. *Classic Car Restoration. Prop. Otto Stoeckl, Coneyhurst Road, Billingshurst, Sussex. Telephone: Billingshurst 351.*

CHAPTER TWENTY-TWO

Finding Samiah Cable,
Wednesday 1st of June 1953

I'm in the Bristol Freighter again, leaning back in my canvas chair and looking down at the sea.

We'll meet again, don't know where – but I know when it will be and I also know where. I take Otto's card from my pocket just to prove that it wasn't a dream. But *who* will meet him again? Will it be Lucette Moreaux who played piano at his concert and went for walks and threw sticks for his dog and wore his Spanish cross at the ball? Or will it be Blanche Longhurst who will embrace him and kiss him and hope that he will be able to look her in the face, the woman who will always be a stranger to Otto because she was an impostor who tricked him and betrayed his trust and is now so hideously scarred that only the bravest of men can look at her.

A voice is reminding me of something and it's so realistic that for a moment I wonder if I'm going mad. *You have one more demon to face before you go and find Otto.* Yes, I have another demon and I know a man who will help me to face it. I must find him now because once I make my peace with Otto I may never seen Samiah Cable again.

To a background of droning Bristol 734 engines I remember peacetime days, Dad teaching me to swim when I was a child. But as I look out of the window at the endless stretch of grey water with no land in sight, I'm filled with horror. I feel myself going numb, lungs half paralysed and blood so cold that it's almost congealing in my veins – and I relive the tight grip of panic that slowly turned to despair when I realised I was going to drown. But I was lucky. I survived that day and almost every day since I have thanked God for allowing me to live through it.

We land at Southampton and I drive off the aircraft. Heading towards Connie's house in Wiltshire, I switch on the car radio. *This is the BBC Home Service and here is the news. France has appointed General Henri Navarre to lead the campaign against Communist forces in Indo-China. John Foster Dulles, US Secretary of State, predicts that if Viet Minh forces drive out the French and set up a Communist system, the whole of south east Asia will fall under Soviet domination.*

Here we go again. Another war against Communism threatens while the conflict in Korea still rages on with no end in sight. Am

317

I still a pacifist? The war against the Nazis ended in 1945 but another one against Russia is about to start, another war to make hell of people's lives. Otto once told me that not all German people applauded the Fuhrer whose plan was to murder everyone who didn't fit his policy. Could it all happen again? Considering this question helps to stop me thinking about my own personal brush with death in 1942 in the cold water of the Channel that's below me now.

It's dark when I arrive at Rock Cottage. I drive the MG through the gate and park in front of the garage. The lights are on. I can see Connie through the window. I need her now more than anything and it's by some lucky chance she's here. I'll look forward to catching up on her news and I'll stop worrying about my own problems for a change. Doctor Pritchard would approve of that. He'd also approve of what I plan to do tomorrow.

Connie is thirty-five, the same age as me. She's a beautiful blonde, the kind men go crazy for but she's still searching for her ideal man. I'm soon reminded that she is also practical. Half expecting me to turn up a the cottage she has acquired two fillet steaks and a bottle of Beaujolais by courtesy of the Savoy Hotel, which is little short of a miracle considering that the paltry meat ration is one shilling and sevenpence worth per person, per week.

While Connie grills the steaks under the gas I try to persuade her to come with me to Devonshire. 'You've told me a million times how demanding your boss is, but surely he can run the most prestigious hotel in London without you for a few days. Just ring him up and tell him you're ill. A trip to the West Country will do you no end of good. It's high time you blew some of that London smog out of your lungs.'

But no, she has to be back in London because an important ambassador called Andrei Gromyko will be expecting star treatment at the Savoy Hotel before taking up his post at the Russian Embassy in London. At least Connie agrees when I tell her that the world has gone stark raving mad.

While eating steak washed down with Beaujolais we chat about St Martha's School for Girls. *We shall now sing Psalm fifty-one.* Seated at the organ and looking like a breaking storm, Sister Agnes would always know when Connie sang out of tune. *Behold I was shapen in iniquity and in sin did my mother conceive me.* We clink glasses and giggle like children. *Create in me a clean heart, O God, and renew a right spirit within me.*

Sister Agnes told us about the safe period but I can't have been listening. When Jamie was just a lump in my tummy he embarrassed me but now I love him to bits. I hope to marry his father one of these days – it's my constant prayer, one that even Sister Agnes might approve of.

Connie has also brought freshly ground coffee from London. We have no milk so we drink it black.

Now at last I feel able to tell my best friend everything that happened to me in France, from the beginning with nothing left out. Before I've finished Connie is in tears but I feel as if a great burden has been lifted off my shoulders.

In the morning, while Connie tidies the house, I am outside loading our suitcases into the car.

A man leans over the wall and raises his cap. 'Didn't recognise the car. Wondered if everything was okay. Roger Wilding's the name. Come *here*, Rufus, *heel*.' He takes a leash from his pocket and clips it to the dog's collar. 'This is Connie Erret's house. I don't think I know you.'

We shake hands over the wall. 'Hello, I'm Blanche Longhurst. Connie's in the house. Do you want to speak to her?'

'Not if she's busy. I'm just checking. Can't be too careful these days.' he glances admiringly at the car. 'Nice motor, taking her out for a spin are you? Somewhere nice?'

'Connie's catching the London train and

I'm driving on to Ringmore.'

His smile widens. 'I know it well. Sea fishing's what I remember best from my childhood days. Wish I were coming with you and no mistake. I expect old Rufus does too. There's nothing like a good splash in salty water to keep the fleas off him. Oh yes, dear old Ringmore. Been there before have you?'

I find myself hesitating before answering. 'I spent a night there about eleven years ago, that's all.'

'Is that all, one night? Then you won't know about Smugglers' Path leading to the beach. Take my advice and take a walk down it. If the tide's out you'll find thousands of prawns in the rock pools of Ayrmer Cove.' He bends down to fondle the dog's ear. 'Oh yes, and there's also a grand little pub but only the Lord knows why they call it Journey's End – for me it was more like a beginning really. Now then that's enough from me. Enjoy your holiday and take good care of yourself.' He lifts his hat and continues up the lane with Rufus at his heels.

Connie comes out of the house. 'You got off lightly. Mr Wilding usually keeps me talking for a good twenty minutes.' She looks up at the cloudless sky. 'Lucky bitch, wish I was coming with you.' We lower the hood and stow it behind the back seat.

After dropping Connie off at the station

I'm on my way. The old car pulls up the hills with ease, the steering is positive, the gearbox is behaving. I should be ridiculously happy because I'm hoping to meet the man who saved my life, surprise him, shake his hand and say thank you. But during the first hundred miles of the journey I think about Otto – the man I love, an enemy pilot who survived the war even though his country was defeated and left in ruins. After I've seen Samiah Cable, Otto will be next but how will he react when he sees my face?

I cross the border into Somerset, head west across the Levels and drive through the winding streets of Buckfastleigh under a blackening sky. When the rain starts I stop the car and struggle to erect the hood while the rain wrecks my hair.

Nets of lightning etch across an inky sky as I continue and it's so dark I almost miss the signpost. *Ringmore 1 Mile*. Soon I'm in a leafy tunnel formed by leaning trees on either side of a narrow road. An ancient church is on my right and opposite the church I see a petrol station where I park the MG next to a dilapidated van.

I wait for the rain to stop and get out of the car. I haven't booked a place to stay so I grab my suitcase, walk to the nearest house and knock. A small man with a pipe clenched between his teeth tells me to try the pub. Following his directions I walk down a narrow path until an obliging flash of lighting illuminates the words *Journey's End,* written in black lettering on a white-washed gable.

I push through a spring-loaded door and enter the pub. Glass net-buoys hang from blackened beams. A stag's head above the fireplace reminds me of Madame Cazalet's chateau in spite of a smoker's pipe jutting incongruously from its jaws.

Mercifully the publican has a vacant room and I speak to his back as we climb the stairs. 'Does Samiah Cable ever use this pub?'

He puts down my suitcase on the landing. 'The captain will be in shortly, never fails – friend of yours?'

'We met briefly eleven years ago.'

'Eleven years, that's a long time ago.'

He leaves me and I throw myself on the bed, close my eyes, stretch my legs and press my back into the luxury of a soft mattress. But I can't rest. Guilt has surfaced like a hungry shark – guilt because when I met Madame Cazalet and Dadan my courage failed me. They will never know what happened to me after the Officers' Ball. I am guilty because the men I killed will never make love, never feel the sun on their backs and never grow old like Samiah Cable.

I'm still thinking about him when I go down to the bar – and he's there, sitting at a small table by the fireplace, lighting his pipe. I watch him hunch his shoulders as he cups the flame. The beard has gone. Will he recognise me? I go over to his table and he looks up at me with vacant eyes and breathing out smoke so thick and sweet with fruity undertones that I nearly choke on it. 'Hello, Samiah, do you remember me?'

At least he's not afraid to look me in the face, but he doesn't answer. After a pause he takes a long swallow of beer and says, 'You'd best be warned before we start because believe me the weather in these parts is as fickle as lady luck herself – and the wind's shifting.'

A large cat jumps onto a nearby chair and licks its paws. Samiah continues, 'I know what you're after but I'm bound to say that only one solitary pair of women's feet has ever trod my deck. But never you mind. I've no objection provided you're not a spitter. Can't abide folks who go green when boating fish.'

I'm about to tell him that I don't want to boat fish but stop myself. 'I'm free tomorrow – and I never spit.'

Samiah looks at me more closely and still there's no trace of recognition, not even revulsion in his pale eyes. 'No guarantees, mind. You pay me five pounds whether the fish are inclined to take your bait or not. In return for that I give you a day at sea aboard

324

the *Dartmouth Mermaid*. No guarantees. That's the way we do it.'

That night I think about the sea before I fall asleep and, when I do I dream of Peter, which is something I've grown to hate. I see him flying a Spitfire. I heard gunfire – *bang, bang, bang* – and then I'm awake, securing a window that's swinging in the wind.

In bed again I pull back from the brink of sleep and imagine Samiah on the deck of his trawler – and tell myself that I'm glad that he didn't recognise me.

CHAPTER TWENTY-THREE

A Day at Sea,
Wednesday 3rd of June 1953

I'm finishing my scrambled egg in the deserted bar of the Journey's End Inn when yesterday's cat jumps into my lap and I hear the outside door bang followed by footsteps on the flagstones.

Samiah enters, looks at me, smiles and rubs his hands together. 'The storm has blown itself out but you'd best be warned, the sea will still be rough.' He turns away from me, reaches into his pocket and hands a small parcel to the publican who has entered silently and is standing behind the bar.

When the men have finished their business I leave the pub with Samiah and walk with him up the slope. When we reach the petrol pumps he unlocks his van but when he opens the passenger door the van smells so strongly of stale fish that it reminds me of Dadan. 'What have you got in here?'

'Rubby-dubby.' He falls into the driver's seat, sits back and starts the engine. 'Minced fish, rotten for preference, and a quantity of pilchard oil mixed with bran.'

I ask him what it's for and he tells me to wait and see. After driving for about a mile we descend a wooded track that's barely wide enough to take the van and, at the bottom, the path widens onto a broad estuary with working boats of all shapes and sizes moored in the river. The last breath of last night's storm shakes the reeds growing out of a muddy bank at the water's edge.

Samiah climbs out of the van and goes round to the back while I get out and breathe smells of seaweed and stagnant mud. Wading birds dab for food in the ripples and a family of swans sails past in line astern. Samiah unloads two stinking buckets from the van and hands me a small basket covered with a linen cloth. We pick our way across slippery mud to where a dinghy is beached and I help him push the boat into the water and sit in the stern while he rows away from the bank. Glancing over his shoulder he says. 'There she lies.'

I recognise the vessel immediately in spite of rust patches erupting through the paint-work. I remember the wheelhouse with its square windows and the row of portholes above the waterline. The mast moves like a wandering finger against the tree-lined bank on the far side of the river and, as we get closer, I see that the trawler has a new name painted on her side. But this vessel will always be *Seawitch* to me. We come alongside and I climb the rope ladder.

He follows me up. 'Welcome aboard the *Dartmouth Mermaid*. She won't be here next year. River's silting up, less water every year. What use will a twenty-ton trawler be when she can't clear the sand bar? As it is she can only make it at the top of the tide. A year from now this river will be no place for fifty-foot vessels like this one.'

Samiah goes below to start the engine leaving me on deck to look around. Suddenly my body and face go numb like they did on that fateful day in June 1942. I'm shivering and shaking, almost falling over until the engine, rumbling under my feet, shakes me out of it. Before this trip is over I aim to tell Samiah what I told Connie – he of all people deserves to know the truth.

We steer between tree-clad banks while

Samiah points out the channel and the buoys that mark it. 'See that small beach by the old boathouse with a cottage next to it? Daniel Defoe lived there in 1720 and that little beach is where he saw a human footprint. That's what inspired him to write about Man Friday and Robinson Crusoe. That was the very first book I ever read.'

I'm calmer now as I listen to Samiah and I wonder if he's telling the truth as I watch the river curve and widen to meet the sea. We steer close to a vertical cliff of rock forming the right-hand claw of the estuary's mouth and Samiah explains that this is the only place where it's deep enough to cross the sandbar.

We cruise out past an island dominated by a large building that dazzles white in the morning sun. 'That's the Burgh Island Hotel. I've unloaded many a lobster into that kitchen over the years.'

As we head out to sea I try to work out what I want to say to him and how to broach the subject. Looking around for inspiration I notice a rectangular brass plate screwed to the deck. It looks like a new patch on an old coat.

'What's that for?'

'It covers the spot where the Lewis was mounted.'

'A gun? Did you ever use it?'

'Maybe I'll tell you about it when we've

caught some fish, and maybe I won't.' He lights his pipe with cupped hands and I breathe in the same sweet smell that I remember from yesterday as *Dartmouth Mermaid* runs parallel with the shoreline.

The sea is rougher now. Long waves heave up and splinter to foam as they hit the side of the trawler. I look out to sea, narrow my eyes and lick the salt off my lips.

Taking a hand off the wheel he points forward to where the waves are breaking against the base of a cliff. 'That's Toby's Point. If you'd been standing there seven years ago you would have seen the death of a fine ship. Oh yes, the eighth of February 1945 is a date I have no trouble remembering. We'll soon be over the spot. Five thousand tons of her lying under fifteen fathoms of water, there's not a fisherman in these parts who hasn't snagged his gear on the steamship *Persier*. Bound for Antwerp she was with a cargo of food for the starving devils in Belgium after they'd been liberated from Nazi occupation. But the war wasn't yet over and Jerry's U-boats were still at work. I was coxswain of the Hope Cove lifeboat at that time, volunteer, unpaid. Our coastguard picked up a distress call and I brought the lifeboat alongside the sinking ship in a force seven gale and we took off five of her crew before she sank. I had to leave more than a dozen poor souls struggling in the water. Not a good day for me but at last the fish were happy with an unexpected feed of powdered egg, frozen beef and dried milk. Yes, a sad loss to suffer so close to the shore and barely three-and-a-half days out of Cardiff. But the old ship still has her uses even though she is on the seabed. See that cottage, the white one with the chimney?'

I move closer to Samiah and our shoulders touch as I look along his extended arm. 'Yes, I see it.'

'That's where the coastguard used to live. Now if we sail due west until that cottage is in line with that other one a little higher up the slope, then steer away a bit and look back at Burgh Island until that solitary tree is in line with the top of the hill, we'll be right over the wreck of the *Persier*.' I watch him scanning the land, moving the wheel and adjusting the engine. 'Here we are that'll just about do it.'

The engines quieten to a low rumble. Samiah crosses the heaving deck, catches the toe of his boot on the brass plate and has to grab the rail to break his fall. I offer to help but he shakes his head. 'This job is best done single-handed.'

Picking up a boathook he clings to the rail with one hand and reaches out to stab at a floating bottle. After several attempts he lands it on deck, severs the line attached to

330

it and examines the bottle carefully before stowing it away.

'What was all that about?'

'Nothing that will spoil a day's fishing.'

'Were you a fisherman during the war?'

'When I wasn't coxing the lifeboat.' And now he avoids my eye as he continues. 'Try as I might I can't forget those times. Night was the worst. Lighthouses dimmed till they were barely visible and no leading lights on the houses thanks to blackout regulations. No life for a fisherman and there's a truth. After the war I went long-lining and drift-netting. Fished pilchard for nine months of the year until South Africa killed the market for us. Back to trawling after that. Some folk say that fishing is the worst life a man can have, hard and dangerous, out seven days on the stretch, venturing over a hundred miles from land, gutting fish on deck after every haul. Hard it is right enough but I never found it disagreeable, apart from the poverty that comes when fish stocks dwindle. Now it's the city folk who throw me a lifeline, men who make their living in towns. Yes, that's what keeps me alive today, boating fish for the city boys.'

Pushing his cap to the back of his head Samiah steers for the open sea. 'The Royal Navy requisitioned nearly all the Devonshire trawlers during the war and converted them into minesweepers, but I was luckier than some. This trawler stayed a trawler. Oh yes the *Dartmouth Mermaid* gave a good living throughout the war years.'

I want to ask him why he changed the name but that would give me away. He doesn't know who I am and I want it to stay that way until I'm ready. He seems ready to talk about the war but little does he realise that it was the war that brought us together eleven years ago.

'If you were fishing, out in the Channel in those days you must have a story or two to tell, apart from the *Persier* I mean.'

He pushes back his cap and scratches his forehead. 'Maybe I have and maybe I haven't.'

'Maybe you don't want to tell me.'

He looks at me with watery eyes. 'One fine day I fished a swimmer out of the sea. It was only after he'd swigged half my brandy that I realised he was a Jerry pilot. And there's another day that sticks in my mind. We were ten miles out, heading for the richest mackerel grounds in these parts with no orders over the wireless from the Royal Navy to take sick matelots ashore. No orders from the RAF to search for downed pilots. All was well and all was quiet and I was watching the seabirds because my grandfather taught me that creatures that rely on fish for a living can show us humans a thing or two. I was waiting and I was watching and I was smoking my pipe and my mind was wandering. I'm a fisherman, and fishermen are used to waiting. During those long intervals I sometimes imagined that I was a fish myself, one they would never catch, keeping clear of nets, swimming down to the darkest depths to be with God's most beautiful creature, she that has hair like bootlace-weed and breasts smoother than sand-gaper shells.'

Whatever it is that Samiah is smoking seems to be impairing his grasp on reality but before I can say anything he continues. 'My grandfather saw one, large as life she was, sitting on the Eddystone Lighthouse rock and leaning back and combing her hair with her long scaly tail drying in the sun.'

I try to disguise my smile. 'People say that strange things happen at sea, but I find that one hard to believe.'

'Whether you believe it or not you should never laugh at the legend.'

'What legend?'

'The legend says that when the human instincts of a mermaid urge her to come ashore to find a man, she'll dive to the sea-bed, pluck clothing from the wreck of a sunken ship. Then she'll take on human form and she'll swim to the nearest land. That's the legend. Now where was I?'

'We were talking about the war. I said you must have a story or two to tell and you told me you rescued a German pilot, what else happened?'

He watches the horizon with narrowed eyes. 'You're right, we're not here to talk of legends and fantasies. Nobler purposes beckon. There are fish waiting to taste our bait and I'd be obliged if you don't ask so many questions. It's a veritable shame to waste good rubby-dubby.'

He takes a string bag from the stinking bucket, attaches its line to the rail and lowers it over the side. Back in the wheelhouse he says, 'Have you ever seen the Eddystone?'

I try to stop him changing the subject again. 'Go on, what else happened to you during the war?'

'Take the wheel a minute and I'll start the trail. Watch the compass. Keep her on two-sixty degrees.'

I watch the needle wobbling under salt-encrusted glass. 'Go on, tell me.'

'A lot of things happened.'

'Did you rescue anyone else from the sea?'

'Only a woman in a white dress while we were heading for the mackerel grounds.'

'Tell me about her.'

'Miles from shore she was and just for a moment, seeing her there like that, I believed that mermaids might be part of God's hidden creation after all.'

'A woman? You rescued a woman from the sea? Are you sure?'

'Never you mind about my stories. We came here to fish.'

'I don't mind if we don't fish. I'm happy just hearing what you have to say. Please tell me about the woman.'

'Maybe I will later. Now if you're in no mood for fishing I'll take you right round the lighthouse and we'll be back in time to catch the tide.'

A black finger on the horizon grows steadily as Samiah tells me stories that have nothing to do with the war, the foundering of the *Mary Ellen* on a lee-shore, putting a line on the *Prince Leopold* when she dragged her anchor in St Mary's Sound and how he sealed hatches over a cargo of Cardiff coal that caught fire and smouldered for three thousand miles during the long haul to Buenos Aires.

Soon the Eddystone Lighthouse is so close that I could swim to it and I watch the man who saved my life point at the tapering structure and tell me all about it. I nod my head and pretend to listen. I don't care if the lighthouse is one hundred and fifty feet tall. I don't want to know that its light can be seen thirty miles away. But I believe him when he says we are riding over the graves of fathers and sons and lovers, hundreds of them, all shipwrecked and drowned near this place before there was a warning light to mark the rocks.

'You may have no notion to catch fish but some of us are obliged to. Look at that.' He waves at a man who appears to be launching a kite from the highest window, just below the light itself.

'What's he doing?'

'That's how Ben gets his line to drop into deeper water beyond the rocks. He and his woman will be eating fish tonight, which is more than we'll be doing.'

We drift silently for several minutes, watching hundreds of large seabirds gather in a flying whirlpool high above the mast. 'Gannets know where easy mackerel can be found and a rubby-dubby trail is the surest way of attracting them.' As if to prove it a flurry of silver fish fly out of the sea and splash back like a handful of small change. Samiah nods knowingly. 'We won't have long to wait if my judgement serves.'

Another shoal clears the water less than thirty yards from the boat while the birds continue to fall, one after the other, plummeting out of the sky and folding their black-tipped wings at the moment of impact. 'Where small fish feed, bigger fish will often follow.'

I'm about to tell him that he saved my life and that I wouldn't be here today unless … but something distracts me.

I shout, 'Shark!'

A black triangle cuts the water and below

it I see a monstrous streamlined shape. A small eye is watching me and five slanting gill-slits pulse behind a pointed snout. The shark swims in a half-circle around the stern of the boat and disappears.

Samiah takes out his pipe and fiddles with his tobacco pouch. 'That's the biggest I've seen this year. Two hundred pounds I'll wager, maybe a touch over. The mackerel can smell our rubby-dubby and that shark is after the mackerel. Did you see that white patch at the base of his dorsal? That means he's a Porbeagle. I've seen them a-plenty off the coast of Norway and Iceland but he's a rare sight in these waters.'

I imagine I'm also in the water, sinking and wanting to die. Trying to sound calm I say, 'This woman, the one you rescued, when are you going to tell me about her? When did it happen?'

'It was the mate's birthday. I came on deck with a bottle of Plymouth gin and we were swigging it in turn when the trawl snagged. I started the winch and wound in slow till the warps were tighter than harp wire. I pulled and I lowered and jerked but it wouldn't budge. I've snagged rocks and wrecks and God knows what else in my time but nothing half as stubborn as on that day. Then glory-be the trawl began to lift and I knew we had something big. Inch by inch she came with the boat heeling over and the lift wires making music in the wind.'

'But the woman, tell me about the woman.'

'I *am* telling you about her but I've got half a German aeroplane sticking out of the water and my nets are in a hell of a state.' His eyes are wide. 'Is that all you want to know about, the woman? All right I'll tell you about her. My deck hand came running across to me, jabbering away in his Polish accent and at first I didn't believe the lad when he told me there was a lady swimming in the sea. I left the winch to come for'ard. Fornication and bless me it was just like he said. Peeled naked she was and hair like seaweed, half dead and a white dress floating all round her. I kicked off my boots and dived over the side while the deckie and the mate and the cook stood gawping at me like crows. I shouted at them to put down the climbing net and throw me a line. She wasn't a large woman, about your size if my memory serves, small enough to carry under one arm so I had one hand free to grab the line. Maybe it wasn't the time nor the place but I had a joke with the lads. I told them we'd chanced on a mermaid and the mate believed me because he wasn't thinking straight after swigging half the gin. Then he took a closer look. That's no mermaid, Mr Cable, he said, that's a regular woman if ever I saw one and look at her face, it's all burnt up.'

'When did this happen? You said it was the mate's birthday. What was the date?'

'Twenty-second of June 1942, a Monday if my memory serves.'

'And the aeroplane, German you said, do you know what kind it was?'

'I'd recognise a Butcher Bird with my eyes shut. I'd had the pleasure of shooting one down with the Lewis three months before.'

'What happened to the woman?'

'Carried her below and laid her in my bunk. The deckie thought she was dying. He stood beside her spouting foreign prayers but I reckon she was too far gone to hear him.'

Samiah looks to the horizon as if trying to focus on something far beyond the glass window of the wheelhouse. 'I can remember it like yesterday. Once we got her aboard we set course for land and a great wind growled up and a heaving sea ran at our stern. A following sea is a devil when it comes at you like that. Now when I was seventeen I sailed as apprentice in a four-mast clipper. We were three days out from Perth with a cargo of Australian wool when...'

'What happened to the woman?'

'Questions, questions, you give me no peace and there's a truth. We came up the river, I carried her ashore and took her to my house. Tired as a dog and chilled to the marrow she was, and in precious need of human warmth.'

'Did she say anything to you?'

'Not a word.'

'Where is she now?'

'To them that believe in mermaids she's down there where she belongs. But the truth of it is she was taken away from me and I never saw her again.'

'Who took her away?'

'An ambulance. Her face was in a terrible state.' He exhales a lungful of smoke. 'There's an end to it. I've told you too much already. Some things are best left undisturbed.'

Does Samiah realise who I am? I'm still wondering how to handle this as we cross the sandbar, row ashore and finally drive up a sloping road between the thatched roofs of Ringmore.

'This is where I live now, a seaside bungalow in a friendly village, just the place for an old bachelor. Nice pub five minutes walk away but that doesn't mean I spend all my time down there. It's been a long day. Fancy a nip?'

I follow him across an overgrown lawn to the back door of his house, trying to step on paving stones that are set too far apart for my short stride.

'Come aboard.'

The room is crammed with furniture. Every flat surface is cluttered with relics from

Samiah's long life at sea. He finds a bottle and two tumblers and we sip rum together while he steers me round the room pointing at his treasures in turn, a walrus tusk carved by Eskimos, a three-master squeezed into a wine bottle, a London chronometer that's still ticking, the snout of a swordfish hanging on the wall, telescopes and a sextant in a mahogany case. He picks up a large brass cartridge case. 'This is the one that brought down the Jerry aeroplane.'

And now we're standing in front of a glass-fronted cabinet. 'This cupboard is made of teak salvaged from the *Atholl Princess*.' He opens it and I see strings of beads, cowry shells, a pocket sundial, buttons and rings, a miniature elephant carved in ivory – *and diamonds*.

I take a step forward and look down at a star-shaped medal with swastikas and swords that sparkle like they sparkled when I was held so tightly in Otto's arms that I could hardly breathe, whirling and waltzing and breathless and blushing and falling in love at the Officers' Ball.

Samiah picks up the medal and places it on the flat of my palm and one-by-one he closes my fingers around it.

'I threw away the white dress, all tattered and burnt it was, but I kept this little number. Now you don't have to tell me why you were wearing a Nazi medal if you don't

341

want to.'

The points feel sharp in my hand, and the swords and the eagles and the diamonds surrounding the central swastika – and the pin on the back, I can feel that too as I close my fist tighter and tighter because this is something that will always be mine.

Samiah smiles. 'It is yours. I was wondering when you'd come to claim it.'

CHAPTER TWENTY-FOUR

Finding Otto, Thursday 4th of June 1953

The sun is climbing over Stonehenge. It reminds me of happier times before the war, bumping over the grass right up to the big stones. I can hear the sound of Connie's hand slapping the massive uprights, and her voice. How did they do it? How did primitive men build this temple or whatever it is? How was it done five thousand years ago without cranes and bulldozers?

I carry on across Salisbury Plain and when I see the sign to East Meon it reminds me of Connie again so I follow the road into the village. Standing on the brick-and-flint bridge I ask myself why I'm looking down at this river while time ticks by. Is it because I'm nervous of Otto rejecting me when he sees my burnt face?

Connie caught a trout from this bridge, probably descended from the one Izaak Walton caught over two hundred years ago from this exact spot.

After a long drive I'm negotiating the final bends of the A272 leading into Billings-hurst. Halfway down the town's main street I find the garage, drive onto the forecourt and park close to a sports car with a price tag attached to its windscreen.

My knees are like jelly as I walk past two more used cars and peer into a large work-shop. A man is standing in an inspection pit welding the exhaust pipe of a car. When he sees me he extinguishes the flame but keeps his goggles down.

'Can I help you?'

'I'm looking for Mr Stoeckl.'

The man's mouth is level with my shoes. 'He's in the office. It's round the back.'

Standing outside a small hut behind the garage I wonder if the proprietor of this place will bear any resemblance to the man who, in one short night, showed me an act of love that until then I'd only dreamed about. My face is hot. I bang on the glass. I open the door and… Can it be? Is that Otto sitting behind the desk?

He gets up. 'I'm Otto Stoeckl, can I help

you?' He's looking at me with that quizzical expression that I remember so well from our first meeting in the Café de Paris all those years ago. This is the moment I've been longing for, Otto, standing in front of me, a little older, probably wiser but alive.

I can hardly get the words out. 'I've come about an MG.'

I expect his eyes to flick away from mine but instead he looks at me steadily. 'I'm afraid you've come at a bad time. We have no MGs in stock at the moment but we do get them in from time to time.' He opens a ledger and picks up a pen. 'If you give me your details I'll let you know as soon as something comes up.'

Otto is speaking English to me for the very first time in a heavy German accent that seems out of place in a peaceful world.

'Name?'

'Blanche Longhurst.'

'Miss or mrs?'

'Miss.'

'Address?'

I give him Connie's address in Wiltshire and tell him that I don't want to buy a car. 'I'm worried about my gearbox, that's why I'm here.' *I want to fling myself at him and kiss him, but I'll never tell him that he is my last lifeline to sanity.*

'How did you hear about us?'

I hesitate.

'Perhaps you saw our advertisement in *Classic Car Magazine*.'

I'm staring Otto in the face and willing him to recognise me and talk to me about old times and declare his love for the desperate soul who lives behind my disfigured face. Instead he tells me that he can make spare parts for my car on the premises and I nod my head and try to think of a way to change the subject.

A photograph hanging behind his desk comes to my rescue. 'Is that an Auster?'

He turns to look at it. 'Army surplus, bought it three years ago. Aerial crop spraying is what we did before I opened this garage. I was the pilot and my business partner kept it airworthy.'

'Did you fly during the war?'

He shrugs his shoulders. 'I was on the wrong side. You may have already guessed my nationality by my appalling accent. I hope you won't take your business elsewhere when you discover that this garage is run by a former member of the Luftwaffe.'

He goes on to explain that after his release from a prisoner of war camp he opted to stay in England and got an interest-free loan from the Ministry of Agriculture to set up in business. While crop spraying he crashed, damaged his knee and had to give up flying.

When he asks about my car I have the lie

ready. 'I'd like a second opinion about its gearbox.'

We go outside. He sits behind the wheel, starts the engine and selects the gears in turn.

'It seems all right to me but I'd like to make sure.'

He drives me round the town. He hasn't recognised me, which is hardly surprising.

Five minutes later we're back on the forecourt. 'This car may be fifteen years old but there's absolutely nothing wrong with it. Bring it here after another fifteen years and I'll have another look.'

He suggests we have lunch together so we walk to a pub called Ye Old Six Bells, half-timbered, low ceilings and no customers. Sitting together on a high-backed seat by the empty fireplace I decline Otto's offer of a cigarette but, when he pats his pockets in search of a match to light his, I take Madame Cazalet's lighter out of my handbag without thinking.

'That's a Zippo. Mind if I take a look?' He takes it from me, turns it over in his hand and the cigarette falls from his mouth. 'Where did you get this?'

'A friend gave it to me.'

'This used to be mine, I can hardly believe it. I took this lighter from the dead body of an American pilot. Red Indian headdress and a British crown, that's the emblem of

346

the RAF's American Eagle Squadron. How on earth did...?'

'Madame Cazalet gave it to me. And you gave it to her because in those days you didn't smoke.'

At last it's there, the dawn of recognition and a smile at the corners of his mouth, but it is not the ecstatic welcome that I was hoping for.

'What happened to Seddy?'

'Never mind about the dog what happened to you? I didn't recognise you. Your face...?'

'I got caught in a fire. Please don't ask me about it. Let's talk about you instead. I see you got what you wanted, your own business. You always said it would be either cars or motorbikes.'

He looks away. 'I also wanted Lucette. Unfortunately she left my bed without saying goodbye. I was convinced I'd never see you again and I've had to live with that for the past eleven years.'

I want to tell him everything, about my fear and my guilt, why I pretended to be somebody else and why I never married my English fiancé. I want to tell him how I got myself back to England, and tell him that I'm a mother and how I hope and pray that he's the father of my child. I have so much to say but lack the courage to tell him anything.

'You are German. Why did you choose to live in England?'

He gets up from the desk and walks to the windows. 'Different people, that's what we are now. Nothing can change that, nothing can unwind the clock. We met in a French café and here we are again in an English pub. No piano this time, no rowdy airmen, no Helmut to play the harmonica.'

Helmut, may God forgive me. I look away. I can't talk about Helmut so I tell him about other things instead, the lost Spitfire and about Dadan and how I was taken to the chateau. I tell him how I watched a cabinet-maker amputate the arm of a man who came to Maupertus to steal a Butcher Bird and how I escorted that same man to a beach and nearly got myself killed.

Otto listens without saying anything but I'm watching his look of astonishment turning to hatred. What does he think of me? Will we ever be able to move on from here and make a future together?

But Otto wants to tell me a story. Perhaps he has demons too. He orders a second bottle of wine and...

Hotel de Fleuve, Monday 22nd of June 1942

Otto was lying in bed. His eyes were closed

and a familiar smell of perfume brought back the passion of an unforgettable night with the most beautiful woman in the world. She'd be tired now. Let her sleep. It would be unkind to wake her.

He'd been dreaming of a wedding, his wedding, Lucette's wedding, *their* wedding. She was real, she was warm, she had shown her love for him like no other girl ever had and he was going to need her again, frequently. He would need her after attacking a British convoy shortly after first light, and he would need her again and again for the rest of his life.

He lay still. He could see her at the ball, blushing and smiling like an excited child but he also remembered that she had seemed strangely preoccupied. Was it her frown that had made him stop in the middle of a waltz to give her the Spanish Cross?

He turned over carefully so as not to wake her. When is Hitler's war going to end? I've had enough of it. When it's over I'm going to ask Lucette to marry me and settle down, perhaps it will be here in France. Maybe we won't have long to wait now that America has entered the equation. Stay alive. Marry the nurse from Lille. *Stay alive,* that's easy enough to say while you're lying in bed with your head half-buried in a pillow.

He was reaching out to feel the touch of her hair when he heard two sharp cracks

349

that sounded like pistol shots.

He sat up.

The girl had gone.

The sound of waves boomed inside his skull as he staggered naked to the window. Am I dreaming? Out on the airfield he could see a Butcher Bird spluttering and banging to life on a cold engine.

He stumbled against a chair, pulled on his breeches, stabbed inaccurately at the sleeves of his jacket, found his shoes, crashed down the staircase, swung out through the revolving doors and started to run.

One of the Gruppenstab aircraft was airborne, flying low and fast towards the Channel. He sprinted towards the two remaining Butcher Birds and, as he got closer, saw the slumped figure of a dead man lying under the wing of Oberst Schieder's aircraft. It was Helmut, lying face up, looking at him with dead eyes, mouth open, tongue protruding, a river of blood oozing from the socket of his left eye like cooling lava. A small pistol lay beside him in the turf.

Heinrich came running across the airfield from the direction of the hangars and dropped to his knees by the body. 'My God – it's my brother – he's been shot Herr Major!'

Otto pocketed the pistol and grabbed Heinrich by the lapels. 'Listen to me. Who is flying that aeroplane? *Who is flying it?*'

'I can't tell you, Herr Major. I don't know. I heard it start that's all, that's why I...'

'Tell me the truth.'

'I swear it, Herr Major.'

'Have the Gruppenstab aircraft been refuelled?'

'None have been refuelled but all guns are loaded. Batteries are fully charged. The flight was not scheduled until...' He broke off, dropped to his knees again and put his face against Helmut's bloody face. 'I can't believe it, my twin brother, what have they done to you?'

Otto vaulted into the cockpit and Heinrich climbed up beside him. 'Did you hear what I said, Herr Major? You have no fuel. You have no microphone, no earphones and no parachute.' Tears were streaming down his face.

Otto engaged the starter and shouted at Heinrich above the roar. 'Pull those chocks away and tell the duty officer I'm in pursuit of a stolen aircraft.'

'*Jawohl*, Herr Major.'

Otto opened the throttle to full power and took off cross-wind on a cold engine. *Where is Lucette? Why did she leave me? Who shot Helmut?* He cleared the boundary fence, lifted over the stand of trees and headed north with his right wing pointing at a glimmer of dawn sunlight.

The smell of her sex mingled with

351

perfume was on his body and, in his mind he could see a dented pillow on her side of the bed. Was Helmut right to hesitate before telling her about the Kommandgerat? Was it possible that this woman could have done such a thing? Was Lucette a pilot and a nurse and a murderess and a spy? No, it was impossible – what did she know about flying?

Straining his eyes to penetrate the haze his thumbnail was under the trigger guard, lifting it and dropping it while the engine screamed at full power.

Seventeen minutes later and almost at the point of no return judging by the fuel gauge, Otto was trying to decide whether to turn back while there was still time. Go back and tell Schieder that Madame Cazalet and her girls might be spies and killers, saboteurs and enemies of the Fatherland – but why? Perhaps they were innocent. The coast of England would soon be etching a line on the horizon. *Why not give myself up to the British?*

A glance at the fuel gauge three minutes later told him that there *was* no way back. Now the decision was clear. *Hand over Goering's secret weapon to the Allies and shorten the war.*

He throttled back and switched to the reserve tank. The haze was lifting. Coastal cliffs were dead ahead and Goering's directive came to him almost word for word. *The Focke-Wulf 190 is the Luftwaffe's most guarded secret. No pilot will fly it over enemy territory without my permission.* Otto knew that if he were to land in England his comrades would condemn him as a traitor, but he had already made his decision.

He flew over tangles of barbed wire coiled along a beach above the tide line. A ruined castle enlarged in front of him. Green woods were below him. A herd of startled ponies tried to outrun his speeding shadow. More sand, an island in a broad river, a row of houses bordering a road and finally there it was – a black triangle of tarmac, a windsock, an RAF flag and a control tower. Otto knew that if the enemy recognised the markings on his aircraft they would open fire and the valuable prize would be lost.

Close the throttle – sideslip – canopy back – don't show a side view. While settling into the approach he rehearsed his story. Surely they would know how easy it is to become disoriented during a dogfight and if he talked to them in French they might be easier on him.

Lose height – bounce – burst of throttle – settle – stick back. Safely down, and a smiling airman was already waving his arms to marshal him towards the refuelling area. As Otto reduced his taxiing speed to walking pace, another man ran towards him and climbed onto the wing.

Otto saw the pistol, cut the engine and raised both hands. *'Bonjour.'*

'You are my prisoner.'

'Porquoi.'

'I'll give you poor-bloody-choir if you're not careful!'

Forty-five minutes later a steel door banged shut behind him and Otto was left alone in a cell with a bench and a bed with folded sheets and blankets and an open doorway leading to an adjoining washroom. He sat on the bench and leaned back against white-painted brickwork. There had been no abuse, no strip search.

After a few minutes he got up and walked to the window. The flag hung limply against its English pole. He thought about Oxford University and Magdalen College and lazy days on the river Cherwell with Maggie Ellis. But now his England was a small room with no smell of oiled cricket bats and no friends. 'This England', saying it aloud reminded him of the quotation. *This England never did nor never shall lie at the proud foot of a conqueror.*

Supper came on a tin plate and the airman who brought it made a show of airing his schoolboy German. Afterwards Otto sat alone, thinking about an old Luftwaffe friend. Maybe the world would already be a totally different place if Ludwig Hartmann had succeeded...

But Lucette was also haunting him. He lay on the bed and pulled scratchy blankets to his chin, closed his eyes and remembered standing under the trees in front of Hotel de Fleuve with his mouth dry with anticipation and Schieder coming out of the hotel saying, 'Is that you Otto? Are we mad to organise a glittering ball in the middle of a war?' The Commanding Officer kicked gravel and blew out smoke like an impatient bull. 'I'll never understand the French, especially the women. Henriette says she's going to arrive here in her own automobile but God knows where she finds the gasoline.' He didn't have long to wait. The big car skidded to a stop on the gravel and there she was, with Lucette sitting in the front seat next to her. Otto stepped forward and the brass handle felt cold in his sweating palm. Lucette looked like a virgin bride, white dress, blushing cheeks. He took her hand as she stepped off the running board. Would she ever know the hunger he had felt for her ever since that rain-soaked day when she promised to make love to him after the ball? Hangars were out of bounds to civilians but she had pleaded with him – *I'd do anything to be allowed in there* – and the start of that anything would soon be ticking down to what was going to happen shortly after the end of the last

355

waltz. Madame Cazalet, normally a jaunty woman, had appeared pensive behind her layers of make up. Schieder was crazy about his mature lover but on that night it seemed as though the Mistress of Chateau Chatelain was hiding a secret. Something was up – or was it? Otto put his arm around Lucette and together they pushed in through the revolving doors and soon her cheek was against his as they spun together on the dance floor. He had wanted to give her a ring – but instead he gave her the Spanish Cross, awarded to him by the Fuhrer for an unspeakable act of treachery on a defenceless village in the mountains of Spain. What a night it was. Schieder carried off on a stretcher and the party going on into the small hours and then the rustle of Lucette's dress as she climbed the stairs with her dark curls contrasting with the smooth skin of her shoulders. In a strange way he'd been dreading this moment, dreading it and longing for it, sweating with anticipation and praying that the tide of passion might go on long after this, and on and on during a long life with the girl he loved. Three hours later Otto was awake but his eyes were closed. Satisfaction washed over him as he listened to the wind, hoping it would become a hurricane because he wanted to stay in bed and forget about the war and lie with her for the rest of that day and for ever.

But things were very different now. Lucette was in France and Flight Lieutenant Bellshaw had entered the cell and was standing in front of him, easily recognisable as the man who had jumped onto the wing to threaten him with a flare pistol. An armed guard stood next to Bellshaw and a civilian was there too with a metal hook protruding from the sleeve of his jacket.

Bellshaw said, 'This is Mr Blakeny. He wants to talk to you.'

Otto shook the man's good hand. 'Major Otto Stoeckl at your service.' And just for devilment he raised his arm and shouted, 'Heil Hitler.'

Blakeny asked Bellshaw to leave them alone and they stood facing each other. Otto wondered if he should mention that this was his second attempt to shorten the war but would this man believe it? He reached down and pulled the pistol from the top of his boot.

Blakeny backed away with his arm half raised but Otto held the weapon between finger and thumb, barrel pointing downwards and handed it over. 'They forgot to search me but be careful. Only two shots have been fired. There are four live rounds still in the grip.'

A lengthy cross-examination about the technicalities of the Butcher Bird was followed by the question, 'So why are you here?'

'That is a question I prefer not to answer.'

'Where were you based?'

'Maupertus-sur-Mer near Cherbourg. I belong to Jadgeschwader II, Gruppe III.'

Blakeny shook his head in disbelief. 'If I'd known you were going to fly to England in a Butcher Bird I wouldn't have bothered.'

'What do you mean?'

'I went to Maupertus to steal one three months ago. As a result I was wounded and somebody took me to the local chateau to recover. My companion wasn't so lucky. Never made it back to England and was officially reported as missing.'

Otto walked over to the bench and sat down. So here was the proof of something he'd suspected all along. Madame Cazalet had been working for the Resistance and who could blame her? He said, 'Does the name Philip O'Leary mean anything to you?'

'How the...?'

'If he was the companion you are talking about, his body lies in a French churchyard. My commandant insisted that two of his officers should be present at the funeral and persuaded our padre to officiate.'

'How do you know his name?'

'He was carrying a military identity card. You can visit his grave when it's all over.'

After a pause Otto continued, 'What about Lucette Moreaux, does that name mean anything to you? If you were taken to the chateau you must have met her.'

The one-armed man smiled at last, pulled a hip flask from his pocket and handed it to Otto. 'Go on, have a drink. I expect you could do with one. Yes, I knew her. That woman saved my life. I'm no doctor but from what she told me I would have died from septicaemia if it hadn't been for the care I received in the chateau. That's how I lost my arm but I'm learning to live with that. What else do you know about Lucette?'

'I slept with her last night.'

Blakeny took a step forward. 'I don't believe you.'

'It's hardly surprising. I love her and she loves me even though I am, or rather was, part of the army that occupies her country. As soon as this war is over I'm going over there again because I want to marry her.'

After Blakeny had left Otto sat on the bench and leaned back. He thought about Operation Whirlwind hardly daring to think about his own involvement in it, let alone the outcome. It had been his own idea, one that had come to him during a drinking session at the Café de Paris. *The viper will bite if you tread on his tail. But crush his head and he will die.* That's what he had said at the

359

time and nobody knew what he was talking about until he explained his idea to a chosen group of like-minded collaborators.

It didn't take long to hatch the plan, but on reflection it had been too far-fetched and dangerous. Flying low over mountainous terrain during Franco's war in search of a village was difficult enough, but locating Hitler's favourite tea room at the foot of Mooslahnerk Hill near Obersalzberg in the Bavarian Alps was something entirely different. While residing at his mountain retreat the Fuhrer would, rather obligingly, take a daily walk to arrive at the tearoom at exactly four o'clock accompanied by his personal bodyguard chosen from the Leibstandarte branch of the SS billeted at the Berghoff whenever the Fuhrer was in residence. That cone-shaped roof was to be the bulls-eye with its terra cotta tile showing up against the green of the forest, but the slaughter of innocent customers in the teahouse would have been the unacceptable consequence whatever the prize. The criminal would have to be killed while pausing to admire the Berchtesgaden valley, something he always did at exactly twenty minutes before arriving at the teahouse. Three benches at the observation point would have been easy to spot from the air and the valley was open at both ends for a low-level escape. The Fuhrer would be blown apart by the captured de Havilland Mosquito's gunfire and everybody would think that the RAF had pulled off their most daring attack of the war.

Hartmann had been carefully selected, an experienced pilot who could easily pass himself off as a British citizen in the event of capture. He was an amateur magician, bon viveur and an old comrade from the Spanish war. He was also convinced that Hitler's path was leading to the destruction of Germany. He had volunteered. He was exactly right, educated at Saint Andrews University in Scotland before the war and in every way qualified to masquerade as the fictitious Flight Lieutenant Summerfield. But Hitler didn't die and Hartmann was never heard of again. Did the captured Mosquito crash in the Bavarian Alps?

Otto opened his eyes to the distant shouts of a drill sergeant on a British parade ground and suddenly the reality of the present emphasised the reckless nature of his carefully prepared plan.

CHAPTER TWENTY-FIVE

Billingshurst,
Thursday 4th of June 1953

Summerfield! I can't believe what Otto has just told me. I killed Ludwig Hartmann. I blew my nose and Dadan stabbed the man who had risked his life to bring about the downfall of Adolf Hitler. The death of the man who called himself Summerfield has been with me ever since that day and now it will be a million times worse. If Hartmann had tried again, and succeeded, how many lives would have been saved? But he was never allowed to try again because he didn't know that the town of Sherborne was in the county of Dorset. That was the question, my question, the one he failed to answer, the question that killed him.

But when I close my eyes I'm Lucette again. I see diamonds flashing from Otto's chest and I see the silk handkerchief I gave him, tucked under his chin while he adjusts his music. And I remember how he used to smile at me, the French girl who never told him that she was an active member of the Resistance. It was not Lucette who killed

Mr Summerfield, it was Blanche.

I'm sitting opposite Otto Stoeckl in an English pub and I can see from the expression on his face that although he might not love me any more, which is devastating, he has more to tell.

'We had a cinema and a concert hall, a library with German books, a workshop and classrooms. Those were the things that made life tolerable in captivity, quiet places where prisoners could escape from BBC propaganda blaring out from every radio in the camp. One day I realised I'd spent twenty-four months in that rotting place, two whole years wondering how much longer Hitler's Germany could hold out under constant onslaught. I have to say I was surprised when the Allies took our forces by surprise by deciding to cross the Channel at the widest part.'

'What was it like in prison camp? Where was it?'

'Northumberland. It was called Camp 18, a vast complex of new buildings in a place called Featherstone Park. The low hills and the trees beyond the fence reminded me of summer holidays on my Uncle Erhard's farm in Bavaria. In the summer drying hay lay in the fields and the long stretches of open ground sometimes tempted me to make a run for it. But I was in no mood to risk my life. Our guards had orders to shoot any prisoner who touched the wire.'

Trying to hold on to our last glimmer of friendship I say, 'My father went to Featherstone Preparatory School in Haltwhistle, that's only three miles from the park.'

But Otto doesn't stop there. He goes on to describe something quite terrible that happened to him while he was in captivity...

POW Camp 18, Featherstone Park, Friday 23rd of June 1944

Somebody switched on the wireless and Alvar Lidell of the BBC was reading news about the Fuhrer's new weapon. Pilot-less planes, hundreds of them were falling on London day-after-day and night-after-night and the camp's Nazi-supporters were jubilant.

The news that followed made Otto get off his chair and move closer to the radio. *We have just received news that an important Luftwaffe aerodrome near Cherbourg was captured by three battalions of American infantry...*

Two weeks later a huge intake of German personnel arrived at Featherstone. They climbed out of army trucks, bandaged, limping, demoralised and some on stretchers. Very soon every bed in the sickbay was full and civilian doctors were brought in from outside. Heinrich Voss was amongst them

364

but his wounds were slight and he quickly emerged from the chaos. Three years of his life on the losing side of the war had aged him almost beyond recognition. Physically unscathed he might be but anyone with half an eye could see that something deep inside him was broken.

After a few walks around the compound, Heinrich confessed to a burning desire to avenge the death of his brother. It had become an obsession and it had been dominating his thinking ever since Monday the twenty-second of June 1942.

'Come on Heinrich. You must learn to ignore problems that can't be solved. What happened can't be changed. Nobody will ever know for certain who killed your brother. Think about something else. Tell me what happened to you. Tell me what happened to our airfield.'

'On the sixth of June, shortly after dawn, we received warning that thousands of American troops were landing on the long beach that stretches from Saint Laurent to Quineville. While pushing our aircraft out of the hangars and setting fire to them, all I could think about was Helmut, how he had died, how I would track down his killer and one day take my revenge. We had a new commandant by this time, Oberst Gerhard who is now a prisoner in this camp. He issued every man with a rifle and told us to defend the airfield and if necessary die in the attempt. We expected an immediate attack but nothing happened until eleven o'clock on the morning of the twenty-sixth. American infantry and tanks surrounded the airfield. All we had were anti-aircraft guns so we lowered their barrels to horizontal and the Americans died by the hundred. During the night they brought up heavy artillery and when dawn broke they shelled us without mercy until Gerhard surrendered. The Americans took over and ordered us to dig up our own land mines. We found six hundred of them but lost five of our men in the process. There I was working for the enemy. My God, what was I doing? When the American 834th Aviation Engineers arrived I helped them to lay steel planks over the grass to take their heavy aircraft. We were all very busy, so busy that nobody had time to remove the remains of three dead Americans that were left to rot in the wreckage of their Sherman tank.'

'You've been through a lot. I wish I had been there when the end came instead of cooped up in this place.'

Heinrich looked away. 'There's something I need to tell you.'

'What's that?'

'Gerhard has plans for you. I've heard rumours.'

'What's the trouble?'

366

'After the ball, when you flew away in one of the Gruppenstab aircraft and didn't return, I was expecting it would be Schieder who would make me write a report about everything I'd seen and heard. But Schieder was dead. Evidence of Chloral Hydrate was found in his body after the Officers' Ball and it was thought that he must have committed suicide. So it was Gerhard who called me into his office. He kept asking me how much fuel was in your aircraft and I had to tell him that I had warned you that you had very little fuel. Gerhard believes that your flight to England was a deliberate plan to deliver an undamaged Butcher Bird into the hands of the enemy, and he also suspects that Madame Cazalet was mixed up in it in some way. When he organised a search of the chateau they found the cellars full of Allied airmen. Madame Cazalet and her traitors were sent by train to Ravensbruck but according to rumour the French Resistance sabotaged the train.

'After you had gone all contact with civilians ended abruptly, no more concerts, no more dances, no more sing-songs in the Café de Paris. Things were never the same.'

Otto said, 'Perhaps that's why I have no friends in this place since the Maupertus people arrived, apart from you.'

It took nine months for the festering boil of

367

hatred to finally burst. Two hours before dawn on May the sixth more than four hundred German prisoners of war crammed themselves into Number Three Dormitory. They sat together on a hundred double-decker beds and filled every centimetre of space in the central corridor. Obserst Gerhard sat at a card table at the far end of the building and the accused stood opposite with a noose pulled tight around his neck and thumbs tied together behind his back.

Gerhard spoke with sneering sarcasm. 'We are faced with a painful duty, gentlemen. Treason is a despicable crime at the best of times but when an officer betrays the cause he fights for the gravity of the crime defies description. Who would ever have imagined that the heroic Major Otto Stoeckl would be capable of such a thing? You all know the details of the case against him but the only fact we are concerned with now is that on the twenty-second of June two years ago this man betrayed our Fuhrer. He betrayed the Luftwaffe, he betrayed himself and he betrayed the cause we fight for.'

Gerhard picked up some papers from the card table and studied them briefly. 'Otto Stoeckl you stand before us accused of treason. How do you plead, guilty or not guilty?'

Koenig jerked the rope and the noose

tightened so much that Otto could barely get the words out. 'Hitler is the traitor. He is the...'

'The accused will be strangled and his body will be found hanging in the ablutions block. A suicide note in his own handwriting will be placed on the floor beneath his feet.' Gerhard picked up pencil and paper from the table.

Somebody shouted, 'As a doctor I must inform the court that the suggested method of execution will cause trouble. British pathologists will examine Stoeckl's body and when they fail to find the characteristic V-shaped bruise on the side of his neck, we will be accused of murder. They will know that he was already dead before he was strung up.'

Gerhard said, 'In that case Otto Stoeckl will commit suicide. Those who wish to witness the event will gather in the ablutions block. There won't be room for everybody.'

The rope was tearing the skin on Otto's neck. He fell to his knees and was dragged stumbling and staggering to the ablutions block. Lying on his back in a suffocating atmosphere of disinfectant he saw Koenig throw one end of the rope over a beam. Willing hands took up the slack and somebody came forward to place an upturned bucket under each of his feet.

Gerhard pushed the pencil and the paper

369

under Otto's nose and shouted at him. 'Write these words and be quick about it. I betrayed the Fuhrer.'

Otto wanted to say, *Germany will stand accused long after our generation is dead and forgotten.* But when he opened his mouth to say it one of the buckets was kicked away and he was left to pirouette on one life-saving toe.

'Proceed.'

'STOP.'

Somebody pushed to the front and grabbed Gerhard by the collar. 'Killing a comrade when we've lost the war is madness.'

Gerhard broke the man's grip. 'German soldiers fight to the death. Who the hell are you? How dare you lay hands on me?'

'My name is Heinrich Voss. I wish to explain that the Major was in pursuit of a stolen aircraft. He intended to shoot it down. How was he to know that it would outrun him and land in England? I made a full report at the time in case you have forgotten. The Major had very little fuel and no parachute. After chasing the stolen aircraft halfway to England his only chance of survival was to land there. Think of what he has already done for our beloved Fuhrer. He has destroyed twelve enemy aircraft. He has pressed home low level attacks on English shipping. Are these the acts of a traitor?'

Gerhard pushed Heinrich away. 'The condemned man will die. Proceed at once.'

Nothing happened.

From somewhere behind Otto heard men arguing. The mob became rowdy. Gerhard screamed for order. Men were taking sides and fighting.

Suddenly the noose went slack and Otto fell to the ground. He got up, tripped over the buckets and staggered unaided through the throng with Heinrich close behind him.

That evening Otto pressed his face into the open weave of a British pillow. Although a bruise was throbbing under his right ear he could hear the BBC. *General Jacques Leclerc has entered Paris to reclaim the capital.*

The war in Europe was over but what had happened to Aunt Traudl and her house on Allee Bellevue with its lawns and walnut trees and the broad Unter den Linden, three kilometres of it, and Königgratzerstrasse and Friedrichstrasse, Oranienstrasse and Count Raezynski's Picture Gallery and all the other wonderful places in Berlin. What was the capital like after the RAF's massive raids? The city had been pounded to dust. Dear God has my sister lived through it?

CHAPTER TWENTY-SIX

Billingshurst, Thursday 4th June 1953

Otto lit another cigarette with the Zippo. 'So that is how I was reunited with Heinrich, the brother of Helmut who taught you how to fly a Butcher Bird and how to operate the Kommandgerat.'

'I remember him, he was given extra guard duty because of his hair.'

'What a memory.' Refilling my glass Otto says, 'The fact remains that I found Helmut lying on his back with a bullet hole in his face.'

Trying to sound innocent makes me feel ashamed. 'Who would want to kill a wonderful man like that?'

Otto shrugs. 'Brutal things happen when you're losing a war.'

I take a sip of wine 'What happened to Heinrich where is he now?'

'He's in excellent health and will remain so if he cuts down on the booze. We work together. I live over the shop and he has lodgings across the street. I'm surprised you didn't see him when you arrived at the garage. Heinrich will be the one who fixes your gearbox if it gives you any further trouble.'

I can't face this. I want to leave the pub and crawl away and live alone with my guilt.

Otto seems to have finished his story but so far he hasn't said what he thinks of me – the girl who played a duet with him in the concert, the girl he took to his bed after the ball. Does he know that I would rather die than live without him? But Miss Longhurst is at a disadvantage, she has secrets hidden behind her hideous face and she must live with the everlasting truth that it was Lucette Moreaux, not Blanche, who was Otto's special girl.

I sit opposite him, knowing I'll go mad if I don't tell him what it felt like to find myself on the wrong side of the Channel, that I believed I was in love with Peter and how I remembered Helmut making a fuss of Seddy and reminding me that a cold engine will not fire unless it is primed– *Try that yellow knob by your left elbow, Mademoiselle, and the Bosch magnetos, switch them on...*

And now at last it is time to tell Otto why I left his bed and what I did after the Officers' Ball.

Hotel de Fleuve, Monday 22nd of June 1942

Lucette Moreaux lifted her head from the

373

pillow. The bedroom curtains were billowing inwards and the luminous clock on Otto's side of the bed showed seven minutes past five in the morning. Her man was still asleep.

She inched her left leg sideways, bent her knee, felt cold floorboards under her foot. Her other foot followed, a bedspring twanged as she stood up but her lover's rhythmic breathing never wavered. Shivering in a draught from the window and naked but for suspenders and stockings she picked up Madame Cazalet's dress, stepped into it and struggled to join what was left of the fasteners. Retrieving her handbag from under the bed she opened it, tucked Dadan's pistol into the top of her stocking and pushed it down until it hurt her thigh. Visions of love, war, death, sex, loyalty and duty flickered together in a confused jumble inside her head as she stooped to pick up her shoes.

Turning to look at Otto for the last time she whispered, 'Please God keep him safe until we meet again. Please God give me the courage not to fail.' Was she seeing Otto for the last time, eyes closed, tangled hair?

The handle of the bedroom door turned easily. The corridor was silent. Leaving the door ajar she crept across the landing in her stocking feet, paused at the bottom of the staircase and peered into shadowy areas behind the reception desk before tip-toeing across the foyer.

The revolving doors moved silently. Morning air smelled fresh and clean. She put on her shoes, tiptoed across the gravel, crossed the lawn and, at the fence bordering the airfield, there it was – the gap with cut wires neatly folded back exactly as Dadan had promised. She climbed through, ripping her skirt.

Just visible through the morning mist she could make out three aircraft parked close together on the far side of the field, the *Gruppenstab* trio, waiting for Schieder and Otto and somebody whose name she'd forgotten to fly them against an Allied convoy.

She kicked off her shoes and ran towards them with Madame Cazalet's dress clinging to her legs, ankles twisting, bare feet sliding.

Oh no! Seddy was running towards her from the direction of the hangars, wagging his tail, jumping up and trying to lick her hand as she ran.

The entry step of the nearest aircraft was already down. God help me now.

It was Blanche Longhurst who reached for the handhold while she tried to remember the drill. Ten degrees of flap. Elevator trim neutral. Thumb on the Kommandgerat. 2700 revolutions per minute. One-point-six atmospheres of pressure. And it was Blanche Longhurst who gave Seddy a vicious kick to the ribs and sent him flying.

'What are you doing here, Mademoiselle Lucette? Seddy come here. Let go of the lady's dress.'

'Is that you, Helmut? Don't you ever stop?'

'Why are you...? Where are your shoes, Mademoiselle? Where is Major Stoeckl?'

'Asleep in the hotel.'

Helmut vaulted out of the cockpit. 'Please, Mademoiselle, civilians are not allowed on the airfield.'

'Aren't they?' The wing felt cold under her palm. 'Is this one of the new A4 Butcher Birds?'

He nodded.

She lifted her skirt. 'Will you teach me how to fly it?'

'Don't play with me, Mademoiselle.'

'Let me sit in the cockpit, please Helmut.'

'If we are seen together out here there will be...'

She slid her right hand into the top of her left stocking.

'Please, Mademoiselle, civilians are not allowed to... No, Fräulein Lucette, no, please God no!' But her finger was tightening on the trigger, she pulled it – nothing. She pulled again, the gun went off, the shot missed, she fired again and blew out Helmut's left eyeball.

He hunched forward, shifted a foot, his lips moved on an unspoken word and he fell against her.

Blanche dropped the pistol and scrambled into the cockpit. Fuel tanks, fuel pumps, engine ventilator, fuel primer, starter switch. The flywheel whined, her bare foot pushed own the clutch pedal, the propeller jerked, the engine fired. Oh God what have I done?

Close to the boundary she applied left-hand brake and swung the aircraft to face the wind. Overwhelming guilt was slowing her movements and blurring her judgement as she set the controls for take off. Trying to ignore waves of nausea rising in her throat she pressed the Kommandgerat and opened the throttle. Guilty, guilty of murder.

The engine back-fired and faltered but through her tears the needles were moving on their dials and she was gathering speed across the grass. Easing back on the controls she roared over the steep roofs of Hotel de Fleuve and tilted into a turn for England.

The cliff-edge gave way to the sea. The air-speed needle was touching five hundred kilometres per hour as she skimmed low over the foam with the controls unexpectedly heavy, narrow cockpit, unfamiliar instruments, no time to do up her harness and the dark shape of Alderney appearing through a spray-lashed windscreen. Keep low. Stay under radar. Pray for forgiveness. Twenty minutes to the coast of England.

RAF Bolt Head was difficult at the best of times, half a mile of metal mesh on a grassy cliff top in Devon and no fence to keep the sheep off the runway.

The compass needle was steady on 290 but Blanche was shaking with emotion. Was it tears or sweat blurring her vision? She wiped her eyes with the back of her hand and flakes of congealing blood fell like black confetti into the lap of Madame's Cazalet's wedding dress. She could see the grotesque smile on Helmut's face as he fell against her, a vision that would come to haunt her dreams and beckon her to the brink of insanity in the coming years.

Billinghurst, Thursday 4th June 1953

Otto is staring at me in disbelief. He hates me, I'm sure of it. I can see in his eyes that my confession has thrown petrol onto the fire of his hatred. 'Be honest with me, Otto. Say that you hate me.'

He leans forward. 'Helmut Voss was your enemy. He was also a good man. Why did you have to kill him like that, in cold blood?'

I've had enough. 'For God's sake, Otto, don't you realise? I've already asked myself that question a million times? I've had enough. It's getting late. I'm too tired to drive home tonight.'

'Maybe you could stay here if they have a spare room.' He pays the bill, has a word

378

with the bartender and leaves me sitting alone.

The bed is comfortable but I barely sleep in spite of the tiredness. In the morning, when I go to find my car, will I be able to drive it away without confronting Otto?

And, in the morning he isn't there. I find my car and head for Rock Cottage. Maybe I'll stay there for a day or two, draw breath and ask myself if these adventures have done me any good.

At the end of a long journey I get out of the car and flex my shoulders. Bats are flitting across the lawn in the dying light. Rock Cottage, my refuge where the smell of night-scented stocks always reminds me of holidays long ago. I find the key where Connie left it, under the flower pot.

Once inside I open my suitcase on the kitchen table, find the bottle and pour myself a stiff whisky but for some reason I have no appetite for supper. Upstairs in the bedroom I watch a full moon creeping into the sky. My eyelids droop. Tonight I'll have no trouble sleeping. I go to bed and pull the sheet to my chin, close my eyes and see Peter at Cramlington allowing me to go solo for the first time and in my dream I turn crosswind with the altimeter steady on one thousand feet and I come in to land, bounce three times – *thump, thump, thump* – but it's only a motorbike on the road outside.

Again I'm awake, a creaking floorboard, a footstep. A stranger is in my bedroom. I run for the door, fling myself down the staircase, dash across the kitchen, find something to protect myself, the light clicks on – fuse box– *Phut...*

Hands on my throat are tightening. I can't breathe but I hear squealing brakes and a falling chair.

CHAPTER TWENTY-SEVEN

Trowbridge Hospital, Sunday 7th of June 1953

I hear the hum of machinery, and I hear voices. There's a feeling of broken glass in my throat every time I swallow. I hear music and I'm spinning, yes spinning to the *Trish Trash Polka* and the *Blue Danube* and *Roses from the South,* tunes from the past all jumbled together. My favourite is *Perpetual Motion* because it makes me feel dizzy and mad and makes me see points of light flashing from a diamond-studded medal on Otto's chest. We are together now. We are turning and turning, faster and faster under the chandeliers. Hotter and hotter it gets and suddenly I can't breathe. I'm under water, looking down into the darkness. I feel a touch of canvas on my outstretched finger and when I open my eyes the water on my skin is nothing more than my own sweat.

Will somebody tell me why I'm unable to move? My lips are moving but no sound comes when I try to speak to a man in a white coat who tells me that my thyroid cartilage is fractured.

The distant sound of an aircraft makes me shake. I want to scream in spite of my crushed thyroid cartilage. Who did this to me? I have an idea who it was but I can't be sure. There was something familiar about him.

I lie there trying to blank my mind against memories of the war, my war and the promise I had to break. Thou shalt not kill, but I killed. I killed Schieder with Chloral Hydrate, I shot Helmut the following morning and, later that day I killed another man. God protect me from their ghosts...

Maupertus Airfield,
Monday 22nd of June 1942

Blanche gripped the control column with white-knuckle force. The serrated surfaces of the rudder pedals had destroyed her stockings and were cutting the soles of her feet. As the Butcher Bird flew low over the

381

sea towards England, Blanche looked ahead, straining her eyes in the direction of a well-known cliff top airfield.

This was more than freedom – this was getting away from the enemy with a prize that could change the course of the war, but at what price?

She stayed low. The English coast was coming towards her at the rate of six miles every minute but she wanted to go faster, she willed the aircraft to go faster. A fishing boat loomed ahead and she had to climb to clear its mast. And then...

What was that?

Streaks of light flew over her head and sped away in a curving procession.

Hell. She pushed the stick sideways and kicked the rudder. Pulling into a tight turn another burst of tracer streamed past – and in the mirror above her head she saw it – a Spitfire, trying to match her turn.

Fly for your life. Keep turning, tighter, tighter, keep out of the enemy's gun sight – *the enemy*, a British Spitfire. The ghost of a German mechanic was speaking to her: *You won't need guns when you fly around the world.* Oh Christ. But she had guns. Kill or be killed. Dear God not even a Spitfire was going to stop her now. She flicked into the opposite turn, cheeks drooping with the G-force and vision fading, flipped out of the turn and saw the Spitfire coming at her head on.

Lift the trigger guard, Machine gun and cannon – *kill, kill, kill.*

Whoomph – flames in the cockpit; hair on fire, clothes on fire, face melting. *Yellow lever, blast off the lid.* Something resembling concrete slammed into the Butcher Bird and Blanche was sinking into the seat inside a four-ton metal coffin.

She looked up and saw green light above her. Kicking herself free of the cockpit she swam upwards with lungs bursting and the dress wrapping around her legs. She surfaced on the slope of a wave gasping for air and another wave pushed her under.

Days have passed, they must have. I'm sure of it. I'm half asleep in a bed listening to the buzz of an electric ventilator and out of the corner of my eye I see a rubber pipe looped down to a needle embedded in my right arm. My throat aches. I try to get my voice but every attempted word is agony.

Shoes click on linoleum, a door opens and I hear Matron talking to somebody.

'I'm happy to say that Miss Longhurst has made a remarkable recovery considering the seriousness of her injury. Unfortunately her speaking voice is still little more than a whisper.' Raising her voice Matron says to me, 'You have a visitor Miss Longhurst,' and then a quieter, 'thirty minutes only Mr Stoeckl.'

Matron leaves and Otto dumps a large bunch of flowers on a table by the window. When I try to ask him why he's wearing a black armband he touches my shoulder. 'Let me do the talking.'

He pulls up a chair and sits beside my bed. 'Don't try to speak, just listen. After you left my garage in Billingshurst, Heinrich told me that he recognised you by the ring on your finger. You wore that ring in the Café de Paris when we first met, and you were wearing it when he stopped you at the gate on the day you persuaded me to let you sit in the cockpit of a Luftwaffe aircraft.'

I stare at him. I know what's coming.

'When we were having lunch at the pub in Billingshurst, Heinrich showed me a letter that he had found in the glove compartment of your car, it explained how to find a house called Rock Cottage in Wiltshire. I told him to put the letter back and thought nothing more about it but that night, after I had gone to bed, I heard movement on the fore-court and went to the window. Heinrich was trying to start his motorbike.

'I dressed hurriedly and ran downstairs and opened the door just in time to see him riding off the forecourt and turning right onto the main road.

'I ran for the pick-up and tried to follow him but he was taking the racing line through the bends and I couldn't keep him in sight. I

384

knew where he was going and luckily I could remember the instructions in that letter of yours.

'When I got to Rock Cottage it was dark. In the beam of my headlights I saw Heinrich's bike propped against the garden wall. I ran in through the open door and found the two of you struggling in the kitchen. When he saw me he dashed out of the house without word and rode away. I used the telephone in the cottage to call an ambulance.'

POSTSCRIPT

All Hallows Church, Ringmore
Saturday 28th of November 1953

Jamie is here. He looks great in his new suit and he's over the moon to have a father at last.

It would, I suspect, have been the proudest moment in my rather aloof father's life if he had been able to give his daughter away. I'm still very sad about his recent death but I'll not let clouds gather over this great day.

Samiah Cable has volunteered to take Dad's place after very little persuasion and he seems pleased about it, not having a daughter of his own. I wanted my wedding dress to be an exact copy of the dress I wore at the Officers' Ball and it almost is, at least close enough to surprise my husband to be.

When Alice Mason – she's the organist – asked if we'd like to hear something other than Handel's Wedding March before the Reverent Alexander Cummings tied our knot, Otto suggested the Mozart piece, the one we played together during the war. Alice is playing it now and it brings memories – fear, love and that strange state of not knowing who the hell I was during my time in France. But now I'm Blanche and Connie is my bridesmaid and I'll never be Lucette again, who did things I'd never dream of doing if I'd stayed in England to fly those never ending planes from places called A to other places marked B on my dog-eared map.

'We are gathered together here in the sight of God, and in the face of this Congregation, to join together this man and this woman in holy Matrimony, which is an honourable estate instituted of God in the time of man's innocency, signifying unto us the mystical union...'

That's what this is, a mystical union between two lovers – something that first happened eleven years ago and the thought of it and the thrill of it now is making me shake on the altar steps.

'And therefore is not by any to be enterprised not taken in hand unadvisedly, lightly, or wan-

*tonly to satisfy men's carnal lusts and appetites,
like brute beasts that have no understanding...'*

Maybe it was carnal and lustful, and we certainly didn't do it reverently, discreetly, advisedly or soberly – not in the fear of God.

Otto is looking at me and the vicar is saying, *'Marriage was ordained for a remedy against sin, and to avoid fornication that such persons as have not the gift of continency might marry and keep themselves undefiled...'*

Lucette didn't have the gift of continency.

'Therefore if any man can show any just cause why they may not lawfully be joined together let him now speak or else hereafter forever hold his peace.'

In my imagination the silence is shattered by the familiar voice of a man shouting from the back of the church – and I love this man and yet in the bloody conflict of war I killed him. Somehow, in a shadow on the wall behind the altar, I see a smudge of yellow that looks like his shredded life jacket floating in the sea. I'm in the water and Madame Cazalet's dress is wrapped around my legs. A wave lifts me and from the top of it I glimpse the floating shape of a dying man. I swim closer and grab his arm. I shout his name and he tries to reply but all I hear above the howling wind is a spluttering groan that is snatched away in the wind. I put my arms around him. I press my burnt cheek against what is left of his face. I shout

387

his name as loud as I can. 'Peter, I can see the coast, Peter, stay afloat. Peter, try to swim. Peter...' His lips are moving but no sound comes. He is heavy and slippery. My hands grab his armpits but he's sliding from my grasp, sinking. 'Think of the wedding, Peter. The first of July, remember? Don't leave me.' But my hands are burnt and my skin is shredding and he's slipping from my grasp and sinking under blood stained foam. I take a deep breath and follow him into the darkness. A silvery gulp of breath wobbles up past my face but deeper I go, and deeper, groping, reaching out, deeper and deeper against the short span of my bursting lungs. He is there, yes, in the darkness he is there but the briefest touch of a canvas flying suit on the exposed bone of my burnt fingertip is our last contact. With lungs bursting I break surface – and thank God for the bubble of buoyancy trapped in the tightly woven silk of Madame Cazalet's wedding dress. A wave hits me. I can see my lower lip jutting out, grotesque and swollen – but I press Peter's ring to it and I try to kiss each of its stones in turn. I want to die. I push my face into the water but dare not take the lethal breath.

'*Otto Ludwig, wilt thou have this woman to thy wedded wife to live together after God's ordinance in the holy estate of Matrimony? Wilt thou love her...*'

'I will.'

I will, I will, of course I will, but standing next to Otto outside in the sunshine I can't help thinking what he must have felt when he found Henrich's dead body spread-eagled in the road, close to the remains of his crashed motorbike.

AUTHOR'S NOTE

In August 1993 my hyper-observant wife spotted an advertisement in the *Wiltshire Times* announcing the Great Warbirds Air Display to be held at the former RAF aerodrome at Wroughton near Swindon. Jane is a war baby like me. We both like to revive old memories so we went to the air show where flying relics from our past were sure to revive some of them. After craning our necks at some of the types I have flown myself, a Tiger Moth, a noisy Harvard and a literally screaming Vampire, we walked down long lines of trade stalls – where I pounced on a second-hand book that inspired me to write this novel.

Jane drove the car home after the show while I started on *The Forgotten Pilots* by Lettice Curtis, first published in 1971 by Nelson & Saunders Ltd. In the foreword by Lord Balfour of Inchrye I read: 'ATA pilots were combat pilots in the full sense. They did not fight the enemy with guns but they fought and beat an enemy which can kill just as effectively as the bullet. Snow, ice and storm were faced daily and only triumphed over through skill and courage.' I turned to the index of the book looking for Margie Fairweather, my father's cousin. I had a vague idea that she had been a ferry pilot during WW2 and sure enough her name was mentioned on eleven different pages. I discovered that she and her husband Douglas were both killed in 1944 while piloting aircraft for the Air Transport Auxiliary. Although I never met Margie, I kept her constantly in mind while trying to create my principal character in *Fly the Storm*. The female contribution to the ATA was massive. 164 female pilots were involved including 26 American women who came over from the United States to join.

The subject of local resistance in enemy occupied countries has intrigued me ever since I met a young Danish resistance worker while I was attached to the Royal Canadian Air Force in 1953. He was involved in undercover sabotage operations in Copenhagen during the Second World War and, as the war had ended a mere seven years before, he was able to describe his experiences in vivid detail. I have also read many biographies of men and women engaged in wartime undercover work. Dadan, who I have also met, was real French Resistance operative but he ver described to me what he had done. My dan' therefore can only share his name.

War is sometimes seen as futile, but desperate times call for desperate actions from those who might be otherwise pacifists at heart. Unfortunately many of those who survive are mentally scarred by the traumas they suffered and are usually reluctant to recall their experiences. Shell shock, Post Traumatic Stress, call it what you like.

The character of Madame Cazalet has been largely inspired by true-life heroines such as Andrée Peel who died on March the 5th 2010 aged 105. Known as 'Agent Rose' during WW2, Andrée was running a beauty salon in Brest at the outbreak of war. After her town had been invaded by German troops she made contact with workers in Brest docks and was able to send important information to the Allies about German naval activity and troop movements. She also helped shot-down allied airmen return to England by guiding aircraft to secret landing strips and arranging other night-time pickups by French fishermen or boats sent from England to secluded beaches in France. When caught by the Gestapo, Andrée was stripped naked, interrogated and tortured. She survived the war and was decorated for bravery by France, Great Britain and America. The English version of her book *Miracles D Happen* was published by Loeberias in 19⁻

My character Otto Stoeckl is also base⁻ a real person. On June 23rd 1942, Obe⁻

nant Armin Faber became disorientated after a dogfight over the English Channel. Believing himself to be over France he came in to land only to discover he was at RAF Pembrey in South Wales. Heinz J Nowarra, in his book *The Focke-Wulf 190 A Famous German Fighter*, published by Harleyford Publications Ltd in 1965, describes how Armin Faber as a prisoner of war successfully deceived the British authorities into believing that he suffered from epilepsy. He was repatriated in 1944 and rejoined the war as a fighter pilot. A subsequent examination of the captured Focke-Wulf 190 (Butcher Bird) resulted in technical improvements to the design of the Spitfire.

The character Eric Blakeny is based on the famous test pilot Jeffrey Quill who was persuaded to become involved in Operation Airthief in June 1942. An elaborate plan was hatched along the lines described in this novel, but the 'theft' never took place because Oberleutnant Faber obligingly pre-empted the task by landing on British soil. The late Jeffrey Quill's book, *Spitfire A Test Pilot's Story*, published by John Murray (Publishers) Ltd describes Mr Quill's feelings of relief when the operation was called ff.

While writing this book my friends Rich and Stephanie Grey kindly offered to me on a boat trip round the Eddystone lighthouse. We set off from the river described in this book for the ten-hour round trip motored out and sailed home. The Eddystone lighthouse has had no human keeper since 1982 and now has a flat roof where a helicopter can land technicians to maintain its automatic systems. It is set on a lonely rock so far out that it is barely visible from the nearest land.

The Journey's End Inn goes from strength to strength. It has excellent food, a wide variety of drinks including a selection of real ales and makes an ideal diversion for anyone walking the Coastal Path with Seddy, Rufus or any other dog.

Although *Fly the Storm* never actually happened, I like to think that it might have.

James Stevenson

The publishers hope that this book has given you enjoyable reading. Large Print Books are especially designed to be as easy to see and hold as possible. If you wish a complete list of our books please ask at your local library or write directly to:

Magna Large Print Books
Magna House, Long Preston,
Skipton, North Yorkshire.
BD23 4ND